CW00343744

# NINA IN UTOPIA

# NINA IN UTOPIA

## MIRANDA MILLER

**PETER OWEN**
**London and Chicago**

PETER OWEN PUBLISHERS
73 Kenway Road, London SW5 0RE

Peter Owen books are distributed in the USA and Canada by
Independent Publishers Group/Trafalgar Square
814 North Franklin Street, Chicago, IL 60610, USA

First published in Great Britain 2010 by
Peter Owen Publishers

© Miranda Miller 2010

Excerpt from 'Theses on the Philosophy of History'
from *Illuminations* by Walter Benjamin:
UK and Commonwealth, published by Jonathan Cape, reprinted
by permission of the Random House Group Ltd.
North America, copyright © 1955 by Suhrkamp Verlag, Frankfurt am Main,
English translation by Hary Zohn copyright © 1968 and renewed 1996 by
Houghton Mifflin Harcourt Publishing Company, reprinted
by permission of Houghton Mifflin Harcourt Company.

All Rights Reserved.
No part of this publication may be reproduced in any form or by any means
without the written permission of the publishers.

ISBN 978-0-7206-1355-1

A catalogue record for this book is available from the British Library

Printed and bound in the UK by
CPI Bookmarque, Croydon, CR0 4TD

For Gordon

| DEVON LIBRARIES | |
| --- | --- |
| D12186407X0100 | |
| Bertrams | 17/03/2011 |
| | £8.99 |
| HQACQ | |

'A Klee painting named Angelus Novus shows an angel looking as though he is about to move away from something he is fixedly contemplating. His eyes are staring, his mouth is open, his wings are spread. This is how one pictures the angel of history. His face is turned towards the past. Where we perceive a chain of events, he sees one single catastrophe which keeps piling wreckage upon wreckage and hurls it in front of his feet. The angel would like to stay, awaken the dead, and make whole what has been smashed. But a storm is brewing from Paradise; it has got caught in his wings with such violence that the angel can no longer close them. This storm irresistibly propels him into the future to which his back is turned, while the pile of debris in front of him grows skyward. The storm is what we call Progress.'

– Walter Benjamin,
'Theses on the Philosophy of History', from *Illuminations*

# AUTHOR'S NOTE

I should like to thank Colin Gale at the Bethlem Archives and Mike Taylor, who read Jonathan's chapters from an architect's point of view. I am also grateful to Peter and Antonia Owen, who like eccentric novels, and to my editor Simon Smith. I should also acknowledge the influence of a wonderful book called *London As It Might Have Been* by Felix Barker and Ralph Hyde (John Murray, 1982).

I have taken liberties with the character of Dr Hood but have taken some of his words from his own *Suggestions for the Future Provision of Criminal Lunatics* (1854).

'The Sultan's Elephant' was a show created by the French theatre company Royal de Luxe, which featured a huge mechanical elephant, a giant marionette of a girl and other public-art installations. The show was first staged in 2005 in France and has subsequently appeared in a number of cities around the world, including London in 2006.

# THE SULTAN'S ELEPHANT

W HEN I SEE the elephant I know I am safely in a dream and allow myself to enjoy the spectacle. This delightful creature is as big as several houses, and indeed a couple of quaint windows have been incorporated in its belly. Dancing girls sway on balconies, yet despite all this architectural and human freight the elephant looks happy. His ears wave merrily and his trunk blows steam at the crowd. The girls dancing and the watching multitude are all so scantily dressed that I feel abashed until I remember the etiquette of dreamland. I have often dreamed of my own nakedness – although when I told you, dear Charles, you said you would prefer that I should not dream of such things. In this present dream I have obeyed you to the letter, for I am wearing five times as many clothes as all the others.

One or two stare at me curiously but then turn back to the elephant. There is a loud throbbing sound like music but more savage, which comes from a kind of omnibus where goblins leap and shout upon a stage. The hammer blows of sound make my heart beat faster and stir my feet. I feel quite intoxicated as I pursue the elephant. We are in a park, and the elephant is rolling forward towards a juggernaut.

I am swept forward with the rest of the crowd and feel light-hearted and light-footed. The second carnival figure comes into sight. It is an enormous marionette, and footmen in claret velvet suits who attend this second giant shout in French and swarm all over it as the Lilliputians swarmed over Gulliver. Then I come close enough to see that the giant is a giantess – a vast little girl with long black hair, a short green frock and greenish skin. My eyes fill with tears, for I cannot see any little girl, not even a green one fourteen feet high, without being plunged back into grief for my Bella. I try to turn away, but the crowd presses against me, and as I look into the wall of people I see children everywhere. I do not know if they are girls or boys for they are oddly clothed in their undergarments. They sit in skeletal baby carriages or on the shoulders of their nursemaids or mamas or papas who also seem to have neglected their toilette. Each little face carries some fragment of our darling – a clear blue eye or a charming button of a nose or a tangle of curls. At the thought that the whole wide world both behind and in front of my eyes must now be haunted by Bella, I turn and run and do not stop until I come to another park.

Until I saw Bella's ghost I could not accept her death. She stood in the shadowy alcove at the bend in the stairs where your surgery becomes our house. I saw her first through the banisters from the top landing where I had been tidying the horrid mess Tommy had made in the nursery. The polished wood of the banisters fell in prison bars across her lonely little figure. Her dark curls were thick and long as they were before you had to shave her head, and she was wearing her best lawn nightgown with lace at the sleeves and cuffs. Her arms were outstretched to me, and for a moment I paused because I was afraid that the vision would flutter away if I came too close. My heart was so thunderous that I thought it would burst out of my black weeds, and I yearned to embrace my child one last time but was afraid to touch death and open my arms to a phantom.

I turned and fled from Bella. I fled from our house down Harley Street and across Cavendish Square into the chaos of Oxford Street. There was a hackney cab so close that I could smell the horse's yeasty breath and see the face of the driver twisted with rage. My body flung itself forward as if to embrace the black iron wheels and muddy hooves and ordure of the street, and I longed to hug Bella without the shame of a self-willed death.

I do not know what country this is. It may be dreamland or the Garden of Eden. All here are young and free. Some glide past sitting on wheels, and others have wheels attached to their feet. Strangely dressed or half-naked, they run and shout and chatter like birds in a hundred tongues. On the other side of a fence children play in the rigging of a pirate ship marooned in paradise. Beside me on the bench where I am sitting a lady in a veil screeches unintelligibly to a dusky child. Many have dark skins, and I think they must be freed slaves like the one we saw at the Exhibition. Ladies – but I think modesty has no more meaning here than for our first forefathers in their garden. I am as much stared at as staring in my black bombazine and my weepers and gloves.

All my limbs are aching, and I feel a trifle dizzy as I watch these happy creatures eat and drink. I yearn for a glass of cool lemonade. A tiny barefoot girl is licking a lollipop I long to snatch from her. Young half-naked people – men? women? all wear pantaloons – play with a ball on the grass. The philosophy of Amelia Bloomer seems to have triumphed here, and my petticoats feel quite cumbersome. Other folk sit or lie on the grass listening to invisible music, and I expect Puck or Ariel to appear at any moment.

This is a vast picnic – a feast of brown flesh – but I have not been invited. Alone in all this swift purposeful movement I sit quite still. My stays pinch, and sweat trickles down inside my corset.

A lady passes who is even more encased in black than I. Only her eyes are visible – angry black eyes that meet mine. Here is another grief-stricken one or perhaps a sister of Scheherazade on her way to the Sultan's palace.

My limbs are still painful as I rise and walk away down the path. I hope to find Bella playing happily with the other children, and when I do I shall shed my dark carapace and dance with my darling in these gardens for ever. Mama, why do you always dress like a black beetle now? Tommy asked.

As if to help me orientate myself in this faery realm I find a tree that is so delightful I laugh aloud. A grand old hollow oak is encrusted with tiny folk – elves and pixies and gnomes peer at me mischievously from caves and nooks and crannies. Merrily they climb and gambol and chatter to each other and to birds bigger than their tiny selves.

As I walk around the tree I see some scholar fairies in a book-lined cave – a little lost princess with long golden hair descending the tree – elfin aristocrats enjoying a feast. All these enchanted scenes are enclosed by a round cage as if they are exhibits in the zoological gardens captured on a safari into faeryland.

A little boy holding the hand of a papa as indecently dressed as his charge says plaintively, 'I wish I lived here.' He throws a coin into the enclosure to feed magic with filthy lucre as he might feed buns to an elephant.

I come to a sheet of water where swans and pigeons and sparrows fight for bread. Their swarming bird life is comfortingly familiar. Multicoloured angels sit on the grass and on green-and-white striped chairs. Beyond I can see great towers as if we are surrounded by cathedrals – as one would expect in paradise. The birds skimming and swooping over the lake remind me of our excursion to Virginia Water last summer. Do you remember, Charles? The picnic to celebrate Tommy's sixth birthday, although he was so naughty we had almost to leave him at home.

Bella was exquisite in her white broderie anglaise, and her shining dark curls fell to her pink sash. She took my hand with that dear confiding air, and we walked with our parasols while you and Tommy went ahead with the hamper. A rare Sunday when the beastly invalids as the children called them stayed away from our door and you were just Papa. You looked back at us with such a loving expression, and I basked in your delight. I heard you say to Tommy, 'Bella is like her mama; she is beautiful in both her external and her inner self.' Through the trees I saw the love in your face and hugged our darling child closer.

'Am I really just like you, Mama?'

'Oh yes, but you will grow up to be clever.'

'Aren't you clever?'

'Your papa calls me his dear little goose.'

'I can read much better than Tommy. He's a little goose – no, a disgusting white mouse with pink eyes.'

I smiled because Tommy does have a rodenty look, and Bella was so quick and observant.

'You mustn't be unkind to your little brother.'

'Why not? He's unkind to me. He pulled my hair again this morning.'

I stand among glorious fountains. Their spray dances and catches the sunlight as I hold out my hand to touch it. Water, like the sky, is unchanging and links me with the little face I long to see. Between the fountains there are stone urns full of flowers and stone nymphs. I touch one to make sure she is not a little girl, but the cold moss on her nose is all too convincing.

How long before warm rosy flesh turns cold and green slime bites into a charming nose? Such a little coffin. Hardly as big as the trunk they have delivered for Tommy's school things. I walk over to a balustrade overlooking another great expanse of water. Here are more half-naked savages in boats, and on velvety green banks strange creatures lie and stroll and shout. I am a little afraid of their noise and brazen flesh, but I would brave worse terrors than this for my darling and tell myself I will find Bella among them.

So I walk for a long, long time. I search each strange face and look into eyes that stare back and feel that I am the strangest of all in my heavy black mourning. They look at me as if I was a ghost, and I begin to wonder if I am.

I sink down into a deckchair in a state of exhaustion. Perhaps I am dead or dreaming, yet my flesh feels solid. I am the wrong shape and the wrong colour. These others have no waist or bust, and their flaunted flesh is brown instead of white as they walk and eat as carelessly as a herd of antelopes grazing.

In the chair beside mine a man – I think the figure is a masculine one – is speaking to himself. He holds a curious little box to his ear, and I am reminded of Tommy conversing with his invisible friend personified by a cotton-reel. Now here comes a troupe of Brobding-nagian children. Boys and girls alike are dressed in white camisoles and indecently short brown trowsers. Bloomeriana everywhere. I cannot look at their plump forest of limbs without shame. They march and stride and shout in English with the strangest accent. A group behind me on the grass – male? female? – shout out like costermongers.

'Where you from?'

'Hooston Tecksass.'

Their words make no more sense than the honking geese that fly above our heads, and yet I feel less alien now I know that some kind of English is the language of paradise. Thank goodness it isn't Greek or Latin or horrid French. I am so dreadfully hot and hungry and thirsty and have no money to buy refreshments. Do angels use money? The sky at least is familiar. To gauge the time I stare at the sun behind me, which is quite low, and wonder if there is any night here.

I think I sleep – if dreams can be punctuated by more sleep – and dream perhaps of you, my dearest Charles. I wake with a powerful sensation of your arms around me, and my heart beats fast as if we had just been Saying Goodnight. But I am cramped and alone in my deckchair. My mouth is a dry-shrivelled cave and my head is a throbbing wall of pain behind my weepers. I have been in mourning for so long. For Mama and Papa and now for Bella. I am glad of it, for I am tearful and conscious of the advantage of being able to hide my face like many of the other ladies around me. We black beetles relish the protection of our veils, but I peer out of mine to observe that these gardens are not after all timeless. The birds and strange crowds are scattering. They all have nests.

For the first time I feel afraid of the coming darkness. Crows fly angrily across the setting sun, and on the sheet of water ahead of me a toy boat swoops and zooms all by itself with wild insect humming. Are the nights very long in Heaven? Are there footpads among the angels? I wish now I had asked Henrietta, who has an encyclopaedic knowledge of the afterlife.

The gardens are emptying rapidly. The sweet droves of children fade away, and the few people remaining glow in the rosy sunset. I am too tired to move from my deckchair. I think I will spend the night here after all.

'Love the costume.'

No gentleman would accost an unknown lady. No lady would sit alone as night descends on strange gardens. Flustered by rules I thought had been suspended I stand up. A breeze ripples across the water and billows my skirts around me.

'Bin filmin'? Fancy a drink?'

I don't understand the first part of his insolent proposition, and I most certainly do fancy a drink, but I cut him, of course, and walk swiftly away across the path. My heart beats dreadfully as I think I am almost alone with this stranger who wears neither hat nor gloves and whose voice is unrefined. The human tide bears me out of the gardens on a broad path where people stare at me and I stare back. They are young, and many of them are half-naked with strange metal rings and studs embedded in their noses and mouths. Perhaps some primitive tribe half-civilized by missionaries?

I relieve myself in the bushes and dry myself on my shift. I emerge to meet disapproving stares – I have never felt so many eyes upon me – a most disagreeable sensation. I wish I could run as I used to when I was a child, but I have no strength. My black silk slippers are in ribbons, for I have already walked for miles. Through them I feel a hard surface as I leave the gardens and cling to railings.

Dearest Charles, how I wish that you were here to protect me. The river of people is a mere trickle now, and beyond it there is a torrent of monstrous traffic. I would like to hail a hackney cab, but I have no money and there are no carriages. There is not a horse in sight, only racing behemoths with dazzling yellow eyes. The sky is streaked with pink now, and above me are hideous orange lights. Behind me in the gardens I can hear shouting and laughter, and I fear that some drunken rabble is about to descend on me. There is a fearful noise like wailing banshees as yellow centaurs with wheels where their limbs should be flash past.

I am shaking like a fox that has been chased for miles by a pack of baying hounds. Darkness falls, but it is sprinkled with yellow lights like eyes, and I fear there may be garrotters. Now the gardens behind me, which were so enchanting a few hours ago, seethe with strange noises. On the other side of the broad highway I see lights and houses. Some of them are large and must be inhabited by the better class of people, so I decide to knock on one of the doors and entrust myself to some kind stranger. But as I stand waiting to cross the formidable road a gang of wild urchins surrounds me. They laugh and tug at my dress. 'Weird clothes.'

A case of the pot calling the kettle black, for girls and boys alike wear tight bloomers and a kind of ragged bandage, but I am silent for there are seven of them. I suppose they are about eighteen, and one of them – a girl, I think – presses a painted face near to mine. Curious metal rings and studs inserted in her nostrils and lips remind me of a prize pig.

'Wicked veil.'

'You a Muslim or what, mate?'

Hands pull my weepers from my head. They laugh and shriek as they pull my hair most painfully, and I have no choice but to loosen my hairpins and let them run off with my veil. Now that my head is bare my hair falls around me, and I feel more exposed than ever.

There is a gap in the thunderous traffic. I pick up my skirts and try to run across the road, which is very clean although there is no crossing sweeper. But my torn slippers impede me, and one of them falls off in the middle of the road as a monstrous vehicle bears down upon me. There is a terrible bellowing in my ears, and I am unable to move. I sink to my knees in the middle of the road and hear a screeching sound. I see an enraged red face looming over me – a gentleman – although his language is most intemperate.

I limp to the other side of the road. It is so uncomfortable to walk with only one slipper that I jettison it and continue with just a few shreds of silk stocking between myself and the coarse ground. Close up the houses are substantial. I select the grandest and walk up to the front door. I know I must look a sight, for I am barefoot and my hair is in maenad-like tangles. I feel I am indeed a beggar at the gate and hope the servant who opens the door is amiable and will at least offer me a glass of water and a piece of bread. I long to wash my face and hands and comb my hair. Confusion and thirst and exhaustion have conspired to become a wretched headache as I search for a knocker or bell to pull. There is a row of little buttons to the right of the front door and beside each a box and a name. Mahfouz – Cohen – Gentilleschi – Barnes. I choose Barnes as being the least outlandish and press the button next to it. A female voice squawks out of the wall.

'Who is it?'

'Please excuse me, madam. I have lost my way and feel unwell. My name is Mrs Nina Sanderson, and my husband is a most respectable –'

'If you're selling something I'm not interested.'

'Please could you help me?'

'Phukoph.'

The wall is silent. I look around for the owner of the voice, but there is nobody to be seen.

Outside the unwelcoming house I turn left and hobble past brilliantly lit houses, shops and taverns. Everywhere I see people who are half-undressed and jolly and even intoxicated. They all stare at me but do not speak, and I am afraid to approach anybody else. My bleeding feet and throbbing head pull me forward, but I know not where or why. There is another road with gaudy red and yellow and green lights twinkling above it. This time I dare not cross it alone and wait until a gentleman approaches.

'Got any change?'

I seem to have experienced nothing but change all day, but I don't understand what he means.

'For the night shelter. Can you spare fifty pee?'

I think after all he is not a gentleman. As I follow him across the road I observe his pockmarked skin and unkempt appearance.

'Never mind, love. You look worse than me. You sleeping rough, too?'

I pass on through festive streets where men and women sit at chairs and tables on the pavement. They are eating and drinking, and I think they must be celebrating some great victory. Ladies – or at least scantily dressed females – walk alone in the night. I recall your stories of the poor creatures in the Haymarket, but these women are not desperate or unhappy. Their faces are bold and almost masculine in their brazen gaze. Many of them hold little boxes to their ear and chatter to imaginary friends. They stare at me, and I stare back. I feel alone and dowdy, for my dress is like a black curtain in the midst of their bright garments. A second curtain hangs inside my head – a fog of misery and muddle.

With every step I feel smaller and more like the black beetle Tommy compared me with. I come to palatial buildings with dazzling windows full of gaudily dressed waxworks and curious furnishings and treasure troves of jewellery. Vast red houses on wheels rush past with faces staring out at me from brilliantly lit windows, and black patent vehicles and wheeled centaurs swoop after them. I stand in front of an Ali Baba's cave blazing with brilliant white coffins and shiver to find that death has pursued me. Words leap out at me from the feverish blur of impressions. Zanussi – Indesit – John Lewis – Oxford Street.

There is no scrap of my Oxford Street to be seen. No Marshall & Snelgrove or Pantheon or Queen's Bazaar or Oxford Market. Even slums and rookeries would be a comfort just now. I turn down a side-street to rest my eyes and walk past more of these transparent rooms. They are too rich and dazzling and too crowded with more waxwork figures that stare at me and smile cruelly in shameless semi-nudity.

I walk like an automaton and feel afraid to trust the familiar names that are attached to strange walls. Holles Street and Cavendish Square are like old friends who have disguised themselves for a masked ball. The dear mouth of Harley Street smiles at me, but the gate and the nightwatchman are not there. With my last strength I run towards our house.

I hear your manly voice directing our move from Finsbury after Tommy was born. 'We'll take the lease on the houses nearest to Cavendish Square. It's dearer, but I'm more likely to catch fashionable patients there. If Sir Percy can get hold of the duchess and get himself knighted there's no reason why I can't ensnare a consumptive peeress or two. We'll have to engage a better cook, and I shall entrust you with ordering more stylish dinners to help me on my way.'

I am reminded that Mrs Sturges seemed rather to despise the menu I ordered for our twelve guests next Thursday. These humdrummeries are half a comfort and half a terror as I approach our door. Tommy will be in bed, and perhaps you will be sitting up in your study counting the guineas that will come in at the end of the year. I long to bury my face on your broad shoulder and weep as you explain that I suffered from concussion after I fell beneath the hansom cab and must rest. 'Your hot little head is full of fancies,' I hear you say as your deep chuckle reverberates in my ear. Now that I am so near you I seem to feel your strength through the walls. On our doorstep I reach out to pull the bell and do not care if I wake the household with its clamour.

But there is no bell. Our door is green instead of black, and where your plate should be there is a box set in the wall with a list of strange names – Botox Boutique – Beauty Unlimited – Dr Rudi Fleischer. There is a knocker, but it is not our old iron ring that we always meant to replace but never quite had the money to do so. It is a brassy yellow dolphin, and I reflect I would never have chosen it as I fling myself on it and hammer at the door. Silence. I stand back from the door and force myself to look at the house. The fanlight and the blocked windows and the doorstep are all the same, but the railings are quite different. They are black instead of green, and through them I see a strange bare room. It is not your waiting-room, although the Adam fireplace squints at me like a spiteful child in a game of hide-and-seek.

I fall down on the steps. I want only to return to our life. Even to the worst moments we have known – yes, even to Bella's scarlatina, if it is not blasphemy to say so.

'Are you ill?'

I am staring at the face of a young gentleman who bends over me with a puzzled air. His voice is kind and he is well looking, but I find I cannot speak.

'There won't be anybody here until the morning. Do you want a lift to A & E?'

Of course, in normal circumstances I would not accompany an unknown young bachelor to his chambers. But, my dearest Charles, I am sure you will understand that normality had fled and I was quite alone. I'm sure you will agree that I could not spend the night upon a doorstep, and I know you often say that relations between men and women should be more frank and open.

When I understand that he means to take me to St Mary's Hospital I cry out in terror. I remember your stories of insanitary and drunken nurses and of beds infested with lice and bedbugs. How you said you would rather nurse Bella day and night than entrust her to the brutalities of St Mary's.

'Look, you've obviously been through some kind of trauma. I can't just leave you here. When did you last eat?'

My stomach rumbles are so deafening that I fear he can hear. I explain that I have no money to pay for refreshment.

'No problem. Come and keep me company. Are you an actress? Should I have heard of you?'

'I am not at all notorious, I am glad to say. My name is Mrs Nina Sanderson, and I am the wife of Dr Charles Sanderson –'

'Have you had a row?'

'My husband and I live very quietly and harmoniously –'

'Look, love, you don't have to pretend with me. I know what marriage is like. I'm divorced.'

I rise to my feet and stare at him, for I have never seen a divorced person before. But my new friend is not in any way alarming. He has brown wavy hair and staunch blue eyes, and his skin is as soft and pink as a girl's. From the beginning I talk to Jonathan as freely as if he were my brother.

I know my handsome rugged old bear could not suspect his little Nina puss of anything underhand. And that is why I am writing this to you, my darling Charles. When I first opened my eyes last Monday and saw you all gathered around me as if at my deathbed, I confess that just for a moment I regretted the freedom I had known. You caught that thought, and I saw the pain in your eyes. I have had a strange experience, and I defy your Science to explain what happened to me. Dearest, I have tried to tell you about it, but somehow we are not able to speak as frankly now as – before. I know you always said there should be perfect trust between husband and wife, and so I am scribbling these pages. When I finish I shall creep downstairs and push them under the door of your study. Then I shall lie awake and wait for you to come and Say Goodnight. For we are together again now in our own dear house, and all that is in the past – or in the future – you must admit it is confusing.

Jonathan wants to dine in a restaurant, but I am ashamed of the bird's nest on my head and the beggarly feet poking out of my shabby bombazine.

'You look fabulous. Sort of *Tess* meets *Psycho*. Where did you get that amazing dress?'

'At Jay's. It is not far from here if you should ever require any mourning.'

Then I remember that I do not know where Jay's is any more and brush a tear away.

'Oh G—d, please don't start crying again!'

Jonathan persuades me to let him escort me back to his chambers where he says he will warm up a chicken ticker. It does not sound appetizing, but I am too hungry and tired to care, and so I take his arm. Imagine my surprise when we come to the very mews from where we hire our carriages. But there is no sign of any horses or carriages as Jonathan opens a door and we ascend to a garret.

I am astonished by his poverty. A large room with bare floor-boards contains only a green sofa, shelves of books, a table and chairs and a few boxes. It is very clean but pitifully comfortless. There is no fireplace and not a scrap of wallpaper on the stark white walls, nor any curtains to soften the large dark window. I collapse on to the sofa to rest my poor feet and wish I could loosen my stays and take some smelling salts. I feel so weak that I think my poorly time must have arrived and worry how I shall manage in a strange place.

'Can I get you a drink?'

'Thank you. I do not think I was ever more thirsty in my life.'

He opens a spigot and hands me a glass of water, which I look at nervously.

'What's the matter?'

'I wonder – are you not afraid? My husband says that he who drinks a tumbler of London water has in his stomach more animated beings than there are men women and children on the face of the Globe.'

'I think you'll survive. Trust me.'

I sip the water and – oh, Charles – it is the cleanest, sweetest water you can imagine. I feel better at once. Jonathan bustles about. He is a veritable kitchenmaid as he opens drawers and cupboards and bangs plates. I feel I ought to help with these preparations, but I have no idea what to do, and besides I am exhausted. It is very pleasant to lie back and watch him.

'Is it the housekeeper's day off?'

He laughs. 'And the butler's off, too. Tikka masala or vindaloo? I like it hot.'

Conversing with him is like walking in a forest. There are glades of understanding succeeded by thickets of bewilderment, but I do not want to appear stupid, so I smile my way through the darkest undergrowth.

We picnic on the sofa in a very jolly way, and whatever it is that we eat for our impromptu supper is delicious. I think I was never so hungry in my life. We drink a little wine and a great deal of water, for the food is spicy.

Dear Charles, I think I must have fallen asleep for that is all I remember.

I awake in broad daylight to find Jonathan preparing a frugal breakfast, and there is a mouthwatering smell of coffee. I watch him through my eyelashes for a few minutes and feel a strange wave of happiness.

On reading this I am afraid you will think me callous. Of course, I constantly longed to see you and Tommy and to return to my domestic duties. But where were they?

I am touched by the way Jonathan shares his meagre breakfast with me.

'You've been very good to me. I hope you find employment soon.'

'I'm snowed under with work. But it's Saturday, thank G—d. Don't you think you'd better give your husband a ring?'

I glance down at my wedding ring and the mourning ring we had made of our darling's hair.

Jonathan sighs. 'Bathroom's free if you want to freshen up before you go.'

'Where am I going?'

'Don't you think that's up to you?'

Seeing that I have angered him I flee into the bathroom, which is a tiny white-and-silver cubicle about the size of our linen cupboard. There are objects resembling a bath and a basin, but the commode is fiendishly complicated, and I cannot make any sense at all of a strange box like an upright coffin full of gleaming metal instruments like the ones in your surgery.

I have never undressed without a maid before. It is dreadfully hard, and I think my arms will come out of their sockets as I strain and wriggle to undo all the tiny buttons at the back of my bombazine. But I can hardly ask Jonathan to help me. The bathroom is so small and my dress is so big that it fills all the available space when at last I climb out of it. It swells like a great black balloon and floats between me and the door while the petticoats I shed flutter like frothy white clouds.

At last I stand in my corset and sit down on the commode. I know you always say I should be more frank about my bodily functions and that 'Nature driven out through the door comes back through the window'. I establish that my poorly time is not, in fact, upon me. Then I take off my tattered stockings and struggle to unlace my stays. My corset stands alone like a gate I have just walked through, and I am quite naked. Something shimmers behind me, and I whirl around to find a looking-glass Nina. I have never seen myself unclothed before. So very white with red marks where my corset has bitten into me and my hair like a crazy jungle with dark frightened eyes peering out. I stare for a long time.

'Are you all right in there?'

'Yes!' I cry and make haste to perform my ablutions. But I have no idea how the spigots work and soon become extremely wet without becoming any cleaner. Water floods the floor and laps at the black-and-white cliffs of my discarded clothes.

'What the phuk –'

Jonathan bangs on the door, and I hear him shout above the veritable Niagara I have caused. I wrap myself in a threadbare dressing-gown that hangs beside the coffin and allow him to enter. He squeezes past my mountainous debris, then slips on the wet floor and bangs his head on the side of the basin. For a moment I think I have killed him and grow quite hysterical as I imagine that I shall be executed and never return to my proper self.

Then Jonathan springs up and turns off the spigots. He turns to me, and his cross, red face looms over me. I fear that he is going to shout at me or even hit me – you know how I detest scenes. But suddenly he laughs.

'You're hopeless! Anyone would think you'd never seen a bathroom before. Just go into my bedroom and get dressed there. Think you can manage that?'

'No.'

'What do you mean?'

'I cannot dress myself.'

'So you're going home in my bathrobe?'

I draw it more tightly around me and feel it is the last thin wall between us. The room is so very small and his breath is hot on my cheek.

Dearest Charles, how you would have laughed to see how we resolved this crisis. Your foolish little wife became a disciple of Bloomerism. There was nothing for it but to wear the trowsers – Jonathan's – and a tea shirt. This is a tiny short-sleeved garment that had no buttons to befuddle my fingers. It feels very strange to be inside those clothes. As if I am a little girl again running around in my shift. As if I am quite young and carefree and not a faded matron of twenty-eight with an establishment and a son and a dear dead daughter. On my feet I wear cumbersome great shoes more like boats than boots which are exceedingly ugly but very comfortable. My hair is a mass of tangles, and Jonathan's comb breaks as I try to pull it through. I long for Lucy to come and brush it for me – and then to disappear again before she could be pert about my strange new clothes. Jonathan possesses neither a hairbrush nor a hat, so I bundle my hair up and twist it into my back-comb where it sits on top of my head like an angry porcupine.

Jonathan and I laugh as we mop the bathroom floor. The water has seeped out under the door and made puddles all over the bare floorboards of his little garret.

'What are we going to do with this?'

He holds up my black bombazine, which seems to have grown

again so that it swings from the ceiling like a great dark bell. Suddenly it looks quite ridiculous, and I can hardly believe I have lived inside it for so long. I laugh as I pick up one of my petticoats and fling it at him. My undergarments fly around the room like doves.

'Your garret is very bare, and so I have brought some furnishings to fill it.'

I stand my bombazine and corset upon the floor, and there they remain for the rest of my visit.

A voice comes out of a box behind the sofa. I give a little squeal and listen as a man says horrid things in a most reasonable voice with a sweet smile. He speaks of people dead and wounded in far-flung places, and I can see the face of this man talking in the box. He is in the room with us, and yet when I rush around to the back of the box there is no sign of him. Jonathan stares at me and laughs again.

'Nina, what are you on?'

'Is it a riddle?'

'You're a riddle. Haven't you seen a teavea before?'

'I am very fond of riddles. Only I can't remember any just at the present. Shall I tell you a joke?'

'I can't wait.'

'A lady goes to visit her doctor and asks if the galvanic rings will cure depression. The doctor asks her what has caused the complaint, and the lady replies that it was the loss of her husband. And what do you think the doctor says?'

'You've lost me.'

'He says then you had better get a wedding ring. Oh dear. You don't think it's amusing, do you?'

I stare down at my own wedding ring again because, of course, I have lost my husband, and now Jonathan says I have lost him as well, and then I see my mourning ring and remember the loss of Bella, and I cannot prevent the tears from brimming over. Then Jonathan tries to cheer me up by laughing at my joke, but his laugh is too late to convince me, and so he tries to comfort me.

By this time we are quite famished, and somehow it is clear that Jonathan no longer wishes me to leave. We walk out into bright summery streets.

Oh Charles, I do wish you could have seen the bright, merry place our dull and smoky old London has become. The night before I had been alone and frightened, but with Jonathan beside me every moment was a holiday. If you had been there you would have had your microscope out and your stethoscope and telescope and every other kind of scope, and you would have gone around measuring everything and asking questions. I know it makes you cross that I am not more methodical in my thinking, but I love to see new things – and what a banquet there was for my eyes.

Everywhere men and women walk together and drive in shiny kaas and sit and have luncheon on tables and chairs in public. The pavement is very clean, and I long to join this alfresco party, so Jonathan leads me to a delightful restaurant where charming-looking men and women chatter and laugh and listen to invisible music. I hear dozens of foreign languages and see as many exotic and dusky faces as at the Great Exhibition. All London is an exhibition, and there are very few Anglo-Saxons visible, yet most of these foreigners appear to be perfectly decent and respectable folk.

We sit down at a table in the middle of the thoroughfare, and the waiter brings a menu I cannot decipher.

'You look happy.'

'I think I was never so happy in my life. I hope this restaurant is not a very expensive one?'

Jonathan smiles and shows me a gaudy visiting card. 'That's what I'll pay with.'

'Has money been abolished?'

'In your dreams.'

'Perhaps this really is a dream, but if so it is a very pleasant one, and I am fortunate to dream it.'

In fact, I never once saw Jonathan use money apart from a few small coins. Everywhere we went he paid with his visiting card. I saw many others go to a hole in the wall near the restaurant where we sat and take bundles of money from it! So I think there has been some great Chartist revolution and the Old Lady of Threadneedle Street has opened her coffers to all. I never once saw anyone ragged or starving upon the streets. A man came to our table also asking for 'change', and Jonathan gave him a coin, but this man cannot have been a beggar for he was well clothed and shod.

All of them wear the same clothes. Men and women and masters and servants alike are clad in tea shirts and trowsers. The colours vary and some of the ladies wear brightly coloured short shifts. Last night I felt like an ogress in my heavy dark clothes, but now I feel light and slender. Instead of an hour-glass – who would be made of brittle glass and weighed down by a crinoline and six petticoats? – I feel like a grenadier. No, not even that, for I wear no uniform and carry no sword. Like a boy going out with another boy for a lark. The way Jonathan's trowsers have been rolled up to fit me makes me feel that I am at the seaside and about to go paddling.

Jonathan buys a newspaper as big as an encyclopaedia and hands me part of it. I glimpse the date at the top of the page. It is like a dressmaker's bill – there are too many noughts, so I pretend to myself that I haven't seen it. I already know I am in the future, but I have fallen in love with it and do not want to murder my love by scratching and picking at it. Then I start to read the newspaper, and it is horrid. I become very upset, for all the news is of death and war, and there is a beastly picture of a little child covered with burns. But Jonathan explains that in their wisdom they – the denizens of this happy future – only pretend that evil still exists so that they may appreciate their good fortune all the more.

'Shall we go shopping?'

'I should like it of all things.'

I am longing to ride in a kaa or horseless carriage but fear that the violent motion will make me sick as Mama was – all over my red gingham – the first time she went from Paddington to Maidenhead on G—d's Wonderful Railway. Jonathan leads me through the clean, jolly streets until we come to a sort of scarlet perambulator. He opens a door with an enchanted flashing key and invites me to sit on a very low seat. Off comes the roof and off goes your Nina. I scream with delight as I fly away on this magic kaapet.

How to describe the wonders of that afternoon? Oh Charles, I do wish you had been there. The motion was very swift but not unpleasant. We flew like the wind, which took my breath away and made me more of a scarecrow than ever. Soon the half-familiar streets were far behind us, and we were in a brand-new London of broad highways and buildings vast as cathedrals. I think I shall always see that future London now etched behind our filthy old city.

We leave the kaa and enter an emporium. Not so much carriage trade as celestial trade. Imagine the Great Hall at Euston piled high with bananas and peaches and grapes and strawberries and pine-apples and asparagus and tomatoes and lilies and daffodils and roses and lobsters and oysters and crabs and chickens and turkeys – as if every season had become one and all the countries in the world sacked to tickle the jaded appetite of some capricious queen. For every food I recognize there are six I cannot name. Even the potatoes and cabbages and apples are not our common-or-garden type but come in a multitude of guises. They are all cleaner and brighter and larger than ours. I think of what you said about the March of Progress and fall into step with it as I see how even an onion can evolve into a little spherical masterpiece.

I follow Jonathan as he wheels a metal cart and helps himself to this cornucopia. Invisible musicians play softly, and all around us are other carts pushed by other disciples of Bloomerism. Little children who sit upon some of these carts shriek and laugh and take sweet-meats and whatever they fancy from the munificent shelves. I think how Tommy would adore this place and poor Bella, too, and how a child might well believe itself to be in paradise.

As if in tune with this thought I see people floating above my head. You must not laugh when you read this, Charles, and say that all this happened in the reign of Queen Dick, for it is all true. I look up and see a line of heads ascending to the ceiling. A few yards away another group descends towards me. They glide with blithe insouciance as if it were quite an everyday matter to defy gravity. I run towards them and see that the staircase they stand upon is in motion. I feel quite faint to see this marvel and stand at the foot of the staircase gazing up at them.

'What's the matter with you now?'

I hold my tongue, for I understand that my raptures are not welcome to Jonathan. I try to suppress my gasps as we make our way along the bounteous lanes. Sometimes I seem to meet an old friend – a Cheddar cheese or a steak-and-kidney pie – but all are transformed.

When Jonathan has filled his cart to the brim he wheels it to a desk where a beautiful young lady smiles at us and packs it into bags. Jonathan gives her his visiting card, and that is the end of the transaction. Without paying a penny we carry our booty out to the waiting kaa.

Back in his garret I watch as Jonathan stores the food in his arctic larder and prepare a pot of tea. All these household tasks he performs by himself without a single servant to help him. A poor man – but riches are of no use in a world where all is free.

'Sorry to be so boring.'

'I was never less bored in my life.'

'You're very polite. What would you like to do now?'

'May I really choose?'

'I want you to enjoy yourself. I like it when you laugh.'

'Are there still theatres and opera houses and museums?'

'If they've done away with them since last week nobody's told me.'

'I suppose they are very dear.'

He hands me a shiny little magazine that is a kind of guidebook to his London.

'Clubs. Do you belong to a club, Jonathan?'

'I go occasionally. I never used to bother, but since Kate left . . .'

I remember his divorce and blush to think that he must have been involved in some dreadful scandal, although he seems so gentlemanly.

'Do you fancy going clubbing?'

'Are ladies allowed?'

'I'm not gay, you know. Do you like dancing?'

'I adore it. But I have nothing suitable to wear.'

'Just go as you are. Nobody gives a toss what you wear.'

I smile to think of the two of us dancing a quadrille or even a dashing waltz in our hobbledehoy clothes.

'But they will laugh at us.'

'There'll be much weirder-looking guys than us.'

Indeed there were. I don't think it was a bit like your club, Charles, for it wasn't in St James's, and, in fact, I have no idea where we went. That evening is rather a blur. I remember descending steps and looking around for the billiard tables and Pall Mall butterflies and dandies you have described.

We are in a hot cellar, and it is so dark that I can hardly see what others wear. Dazzling lights cut into this darkness and slice into my brain and quite befuddle me. The air is thick with smoke and throbbing with loud music. Half-naked people stand and twitch galvanically, and it is all a little alarming – more like a cannibals' feast than a ball – but I know that Jonathan will not let anyone eat me. He is very attentive and brings me a plate of sandwiches with a glass of iced lemonade.

We sit at a little table and try to talk, but the music swallows our words and the whirling lights make me feel quite giddy. Jonathan offers me a few puffs of a fragrant object like a pencil wrapped in paper, which he calls a joint, and I accept although it makes me splutter. Of course, I have never smoked before and don't suppose I ever shall again, but I have invented a little motto for myself: 'When in

35

Utopia do as the Utopians do.' So I sit there valiantly pretending this is a delightful party, for it would have been discourteous to complain. I drink a great deal of lemonade as the cellar is stifling hot, and I think perhaps the lemons are not fresh for I began to feel quite sick. A sign above our heads says 'Reality is a delusion caused by alcohol deficiency.' I wonder if this is a joke and if I ought to laugh.

'Shall I tell you a joke?' I shout above the noise. I cannot even hear Jonathan's reply, but I continue regardless. 'What did the corpulent lady say to the crusty old bachelor?' I have to repeat it several times before he can hear what I am saying.

'No idea.'

'She said, "Am I not a little pale?" And what do you think he replied?'

'Haven't a clue.'

'He replied' – and I cannot refrain from laughing at my own joke – '"You look more like a big tub."'

I have to repeat this and explain it by which time my merriment is exhausted and so is our conversation. I cannot help wondering why gentlemen would wish to go to such clubs.

At last we leave, and I feel a little like Persephone rising from the underworld, but Jonathan is more like Demeter my mother than nasty Pluto. He supports me and says he is too pist to drive, and so we walk back to his garret, and after that my mind is quite a blank.

The next morning I feel seedy. I have the most ferocious head-ache and so does Jonathan.

'Why, it's Sunday! But there are no bells.'

'When you start hearing bells it's time for therapy.'

'Don't you go to church?'

'Do you?'

'Naturally I go with my son, and I used to take my daughter. Bella. She died.'

'Oh I'm so sorry! When?'

'Three months ago. A hundred and fifty years ago. I am confused.'

'So am I.'

We stare at each other. I think that perhaps our dear old Church of England has been replaced by elephants and marionettes and remember that it is impolite to speak of religion.

The day passes very quietly. We do not go out but eat tranquilly at home, for this simple garret is beginning to feel like my home. Of course, I still yearn for our home and for you and dear Tommy, but . . . I'm sure you will understand, for you are so clever. It has all been too much for my poor little brain.

Jonathan speaks of his eckswife Kate. This lady, or rather hyena in petticoats, divorced him and stole a great deal of money from him as well as a house. When I ask if married women are allowed to hold property in their own names he laughs bitterly and tells me a lady has even held the post of Prime Minister! However, it was not a great success, and I am not surprised. I wonder she had the effrontery. She was not a crabbed old maid but a married lady. Yet this is not the greatest of the marvels he recounts. Ladies are able to practise any profession, including law and medicine. If a young unmarried lady is seduced and gives birth the child is not called a b—st—rd and abandoned as a foundling but lives with its mama. Young ladies who do not find a husband are not despised but are able to support themselves, as they have received an education equal to their brothers'. I cannot help envying these Amazons who will be born long after Tommy is dead.

The rest is soon told. Jonathan prepares a delicious supper, and we watch the teavea. This is something like the Panorama in the Egyptian Hall or a kind of magic lantern projecting wonders – whether imaginary or actual I do not venture to ask. Jonathan finds my questions foolish, and I feel a little like that family of bumpkins we overheard at the Exhibition. Do you remember? A man in a smock and a woman smelling of the piggery who was oohing and aahing at the sight of a water closet and saying she wouldn't give sixpence for the Koh-i-Noor diamond.

Dearest Charles, I know your love of the theatre and wish you could have sat with me to watch this drama that took place in our very own room as if a vast troupe of actors and musicians and magicians had, by enchantment, visited Jonathan's tiny garret.

I stare at machines that fly and excavate mountains and explore beneath the ocean and at towers that kiss the clouds. I see trains rumbling through tunnels beneath a great city and young girls cavorting shamelessly in their undergarments (perhaps as a cautionary tale). There is a kind of play about a young lady whose husband has abandoned her with three children – a tale so sad that I cannot help but weep – which Jonathan thinks a very foolish thing to do.

'What will you do tomorrow when I'm at work?'

'Must you leave me?'

'Well, I can't very well take you to work with me.'

'What is your work?'

'I'm an architect.'

'A noble profession!'

'Is it? I spend most of my time haggling over planning permission for shopping molls.'

I do not like to ask what or who a shopping moll is. My lip trembles to think of the desert of solitude that lies ahead. For since our darling Bella died I have come to fear the phantoms – hers and others – that rush to fill an empty room. I hear Papa's voice telling me that time is precious and must never be wasted, and his kind eyes watch me as I do waste it. I hear Mama's voice singing an Italian lullaby and then sinking into what she called her Finsbury Gloom. Sometimes, too, I see the two dead little babies who came between Bella and Tommy. They have no names or voices but stare at me reproachfully for carrying them beneath my heart and then failing to give them life. So when I am at home I take care to have a servant or even Tommy (if he is good, which he never is) in the room with me at all times.

I lie awake in dread of the moment when Jonathan will abandon me. At breakfast the next morning he looks at me over the coffee pot, and I see he is too busy to be bothered with neurasthenic females. Like you, Charles, dear, after Bella . . . left me.

'Here are some spare keys in case you want to go out.'

'You are very kind.'

'Don't get lost'.

'I am lost.'

'If you do go out you'd better not go far. And don't get the tube or you'll never find your way back.'

'The tube?'

'The underground. Oh G—d, Nina – the railway that goes under London.'

'How very dangerous. Do you mean there are tunnels beneath our feet? Are you not afraid the Russians will invade?'

'You sound like McCarthy.'

'Do you mean Josiah McCarthy of Finsbury Square? He was a great friend of my father's. Such a dear old –'

'Oh for G—d's sake!'

I see that I have annoyed Jonathan again and do not understand why. He is wearing a grey jacket and trowsers and carries a thin, sharp suitcase. I think it must be full of knives. He looks clever and power-ful, and I see that he is not a poor man at all. He has been happy to play at being a pauper for a few days, but now he is a prince again rushing off to his palace. And I the pumpkin untransformed.

I hear his footsteps descending and run to the window to watch him stride over the cobblestones to his awaiting kingdom. He does not look back at me, and I weep to think I might never see him again.

My dress is still hanging from the low ceiling. When I first tried it on in Jay's its blackness left dark stains all over my arms and shoulders. It has been dyed with the night sky and carries its darkness deep within. I want to wear it again and put my arms around it as if it were my partner in a waltz. I bury my face in its sour black folds. Jonathan complained of the smell and wanted to send it to the dry cleaners, but death cannot be cleaned.

I look around for my corset but cannot see it anywhere. I am glad, for my body has grown soft and free, and I do not think I would be able to lace my own stays. Without my corset's strict government my black bombazine cannot master my rebellious body. The tiny buttons attack my fingers, and my flesh peeps slyly through the gaps.

In the long mirror in the bathroom I stare at myself for the last time. My hair falls wildly to my waist, and my eyes stare back at me boldly. I have lost my gloves and my feet are bare, but in between are respectable acres of rusty black. I twist my head over my shoulder to see if the holes between the buttons are unseemly but decide it does not matter as I have such a short distance to walk.

You know the rest.

Dear Charles

I have seen the future and I wish I could show it to you. If we could hold hands and run together over that shining bridge I know you would be filled with hope and would understand why I have returned somewhat changed. Whatever the force that stole me away for those days, rest assured that it was more good than evil and that the message I bring you is one of hope and freedom. You are right about the March of Progress, and when I am stronger we will march there together.

With so much love – you cannot know how much – from

Your dear little Nina

P.S. Please do not show this to Henrietta. She is inclined to be censorious, and I know she thinks me frivolous and worldly.

# CHARLES

TODAY MY DARLING girl looks almost herself. I think the three days of her disappearance were the worst of my life. When Emma knocked on the door of my surgery on Monday morning and told me that madam had just returned I dropped my stethoscope, brusquely ushered out Lady Clarissa, who was lying on my consultation couch after yet another of her nervous fits, and rushed up the stairs two at a time to the drawing-room.

My angel lay on the sofa beneath a tartan rug. Her eyes were shut and her wonderful dark hair spread all over the cushions. Tommy was already beside her, sitting on the floor with his arms around her neck. In the darkened room he looked so like Bella that for a moment I was afraid, as if I found myself watching a *tableau vivant* of the dead; then, of course, Reason came to my aid and I saw that my darling was breathing evenly, and Tommy turned to me with an expression of malice his sister's sweet face would never have worn.

So it was that when she opened those enchanting blue eyes Nina saw us gathered around her. All the servants had come to watch, for the household had been in a state of upheaval for three days. A paragraph had even appeared in that morning's newspaper about the mysterious vanishing of a married lady from H— Street.

Before she spoke I saw unease and sadness in those eyes I know so well. Almost as if she expected to look on other faces and scenes. I dismissed the servants and sent Tommy back to the nursery, where he went with a very bad grace, screaming and shouting.

Alone with Nina, I locked the drawing-room door and kneeled at her dear little feet, which were bare and somewhat grubby. Her eyes were shut again, and her silky hair smelled of flowers. I caressed her, discovering that her t—s were quite bare beneath her rumpled dress. Despite her illness she seemed exceedingly, one might say excessively, pleased to see me. I was quite transported and forgot the waiting-room downstairs full of patients.

'My own little wife.'

'Dearest Charles.'

'You must tell me where you have been.'

She opened her lovely eyes, and tears came brimming out.

'My poor little girl! Did I hurt you just now?'

'I'm so tired.'

'You haven't slept?'

'I don't remember.'

'You don't remember where you have been these last three days?'

Her only reply was more tears, and I felt like a brute. I was lying beside her on the sofa, stroking her brow. At moments the ten years between us seem an age. I was remembering the little maid I first saw in her father's house, in that wholesome atmosphere so different from the one in which I grew up. I attached myself to her family, happy to assist her excellent father, and as the years passed I began to hope that some day my dear little Nina might become my wife. I could scarcely believe my happiness on our wedding day, and the following year Bella arrived as the sweet little outward sign of our union. Now that Nina's parents and poor little Bella are dead Nina is my own property, and I feel my responsibility to cherish her. She is as fresh and pure as she was then – I have taken pains to keep her so – I know that she could walk through the vilest rookery and remain unsullied.

'Perhaps some kind lady took you in?'

'Yes,' she sobbed.

'When you are better we will go and thank her.'

'No!'

'Now you mustn't distress yourself. You must rest. Do you think you'll be strong enough for the dinner on Thursday?'

She groaned and shut her eyes, and I tiptoed out.

As soon as I shut the door and stood on the landing my duties besieged me. Upstairs in the nursery I could hear Tommy howling, while downstairs impatient patients waited. I worried that I had offended Lady Clarissa and that some of these others would not return if I made them wait too long.

By the time I had seen them all (gout and nerves, as usual; if it is true that medical men die of the diseases they have studied most, I have not much to look forward to), luncheon was cold. As I ate I wrote out notes to the twelve guests – all owed – I had invited for Thursday, apologizing that my wife is still prostrated with grief and so we will not be able to receive them. I sent for James to deliver the notes, and he was sulky, for his wages have not been paid this month. James is my medical assistant-cum-butler-cum-footman. As he has so many functions I generally refer to him as 'the boy', although in truth he is a somewhat senile boy, being at least sixty and found in the workhouse. I puzzled over his livery – two crossed shovels with a hook rampant. In the end I borrowed the coat of arms of some very respectable Sandersons, yeoman farmers in Norfolk. When James is delivering medicine to my patients he wears a natty pot-hat and a smart shell-jacket with silver buttons – at least it was smart three years ago. I cannot really afford him or indeed expensive dinners, but without them how am I to attract patients of family?

I had to speak to James, Lucy and Emma to remind them not to gossip. The paragraph in the newspaper must have come from somewhere.

'Mrs Sanderson has been visiting a friend.'

James snorted and looked at Emma, who pursed her lips and sniffed. She was my wife's nurse and knows rather too much about us all. As a baby, Tommy howled day and night and consumed as many nursemaids as he now consumes sugarplums, so Nina said, 'We will have to send for Emmie, because the baby never has been born that Emma cannot manage.'

So we did, and she has stayed, and indeed she does manage

Tommy and all of us, but she is a great grumbletonian, and I fear she has no very high opinion of me. I often feel she has hired us as her family and finds Nina and Tommy quite satisfactory but would like to dismiss me. As for Lucy, our parlourmaid, she is a fat, red-faced girl who always looks untidy in her uniform, and her silence was pert. Henrietta passed her on when she reduced her household, and I would be happy to pass her back again, only Nina is fond of her. Together with Mrs Sturges the cook, who is more often than not drunk as a wheelbarrow on the cooking sherry, that is my household. It would be hard to find four more imperfect servants, but until I am able to pay them their back wages I must make do with them.

When I am in my consulting-room I am another man. I know these West End patients (particularly the ladies) require genial conversation, and I supply it liberally. I must see at least three patients an hour, but I have trained myself not to look at my watch. I have built up quite a distinguished practice, and I know I have the ability to become a 'bedside baronet' like Sir Percy.

I put up my brass plate here just after Tommy was born. I bought this practice from an old fellow who assured me it was worth a thousand a year, but I have yet to extract more than six hundred from it. We doctors are still considered parvenus by the other residents of Harley Street – retired ambassadors, admirals and generals. Of those few who deign to sample my professional services many have turned out to be neverpay villains. Each Christmas I send out the bills, and slow, dribbling payments come from patients who must not be offended. However, with hard work and foresight and a smoothly run household I have every confidence I can double my income. Even three hundred more would pay for the servants, the tradesmen, Tommy's school, poor little Bella's tombstone, our mourning clothes and a convalescent holiday for darling Nina.

Mr Gladstone has just raised income tax to one shilling and fourpence in the pound – as if sevenpence were not extortionate enough – to pay for the Russian war. In The Thunderer I also read, with more pleasure, that Bunhill Fields is to be closed next year. I know too well that the London burial grounds are consecrated cesspools. They say we doctors bury our mistakes, but what about those we have dug up? The sooner they close it, close them all, the better.

This house at least was a bargain. No one else wanted to take it, as it is full of leaks with bad drains. I have said nothing to Nina but fear that the miasma that spreads the filth beneath our houses and emanates from the rookery may have been the cause of darling Bella's death. I know that poisoned air causes cholera and see no reason why it should not also produce scarlet fever. Odours of food and gas and worse pollute the waiting-room and surgery, for all my efforts to keep the rooms well aired.

Enough complaints. My little helpmate has brought the spring back into my life, and in her gentle presence I can shelter from the cares of the world. My bright household fairy presides again over the pure values and sweet delights of our home.

Damnation! James has just shown in the Hypochondriac. I never saw a healthier man in my life, but he is so convinced that he shall one day or another die suddenly (as we all must) that he has his name and residence written inside the crown of his hat so that people may know where to carry his body. I think he has studied as many medical texts as I have, and he loves to spend an hour a week merrily discussing his possible diseases. I will have to go down and give him his guinea's worth.

Fashionable couples, I am told, sleep in separate rooms as if their home were a hotel and they but travellers meeting in the corridor. I would not give up my hymeneal altar, not even for a knighthood. Last night as my Nina slept she cried out in distress, and trouble clouded her girlish brow. I held her tight and felt so happy that we were together again. Our little family is an empire of love, with myself as emperor and Nina as empress, the chief ornament of the fireside with her adorable dimples and cherry cheeks. I know she is incapable of trickery or falsehood. She has been everything to me: my virgin

45

princess, plaything, companion, devoted mother of my children and domestic manager (although in the last she is somewhat wanting).

Tomorrow I will soothe my little frightened dove and discover the truth of her mysterious disappearance. I am confident there will be some harmless explanation, for she is a delightfully simple girl. I remember when we were first married she made me some shirts – they were all crooked, but I have kept them out of love. My little girl is foolish but never vicious. I attribute her unhappy state to natural grief. Sorrow for our darling Bella has sapped her vitality and all but broken her spirit. Only time can heal that, but I can correct my child wife's other weaknesses – her taste for tight stays, tea drinking and reading. Her father encouraged her enthusiasm for three-decker novels and sentimental poetry, but I won't let her get any more books from Mudie's. I have put her on a lowering diet with total abstinence from stimulants.

This morning my little maiden woke in a gale of sobs and woe. I held her close and told her all was well, but she wailed of strange adventures and said I would not understand. I understand that she is weaving a little web of romance for herself and wish she could be satisfied with fireside virtues. I begged her to rest and tiptoed down here to my study where I study nothing more congenial than our household accounts.

In two years I will be forty, at which age they say a man is either a fool or a physician. I am not a fool, but I haven't achieved half of what I once aspired to. Compared with Sir Astley Cooper, my child-hood hero and my father's employer, if one can use such a genteel word to describe Pa's fishing trips in the London cemeteries, I am a failure. Once, Pa told me, Sir Astley performed an operation on a West Indian millionaire who rewarded his physicians with three hundred guineas each. Sir Astley waited. The millionaire said, 'But you, sir, shall have something better', and flung his nightcap at Sir Astley, who, mightily offended, went home, where he found in the nightcap a draft for a thousand guineas!

But where is my West Indian millionaire? And if he doesn't appear soon, how am I to stay out of the debtors' prison? We should save a great deal of money if we were to leave London, leave England altogether and go and live at Calais where I'm sure they have need of a good English doctor. I could sell this house and the lease and contents and my practice here. But London is my city, and I love it with all its expensive warts.

A letter has just been pushed under the door. I recognize my angel's handwriting, and my heart leaps as I remember the love notes we used to exchange when we were courting. I rush eagerly to the door and open it, hoping to embrace my little nymph. But there is only the rustle of her skirts disappearing up the stairs.

# NINA AT HOME

I NEITHER KNOW nor care what day this is. Time is no longer to be trusted. I suppose Charles must have read my letter by now. I told him the truth, the whole truth. Almost. My head feels like a ton-weight, but I need to write this other truth which I will hide in my workbasket. C. says I must rest and must not take any exercise or read or write. How jog-trotty and humdrum my life seems now. Back in the deadly hush of Harley Street where nothing ever happens I remember those days when so much did happen.

From my window I can see the little girls flocking to the door of the Queen's College. I hear they are to be quite scandalously well edu-cated. They study mathematics and natural science and even Latin. I doubt if C. would have sent Bella to such a den of bluestockings, for he detests strong-minded women and says that higher education would make it difficult for a woman to conceive and bear a child. I suppose he must be right – yet Jonathan told me that in his London women may do any job that a man does. Lady lawyers and lady politi-cians and doctresses and even lady cabbies! I smile, yet my head is whirling for Jonathan and Charles cannot both be right. Somehow I must live with the conflicting truths of these two Londons.

Back to the window where the world I must accept is framed. Many of these little girls are also the daughters of physicians, but how different their schooldays are from mine at the little dame-school around the corner from our house in Finsbury Square.

A shabby schoolroom where fifty girls sat on forms and Miss Amelia lay on a couch with a work-table beside her. She was strict and very terrifying to a little girl of five who had only known a mother who petted her. I was expected to learn long lists of words and to do endless needlework. On my first day at school I rebelled and tried to run away home to Mama, who reluctantly returned me. I think she cried as much as I did, for my mother had a light and tender heart and hated to see a suffering creature – especially me.

I spent a great deal of my education standing in a corner wearing a dunce's cap made of brown paper. When my samplers still failed to please, Miss Amelia locked me in a dark closet. My boxed ears were a swollen wall that kept lessons out and my dreams and fancies sealed deep inside my head. It made matters worse that Henrietta, who loomed five vast years ahead of me, was a pattern girl. Her fingers flew over her needlework, and she led the school in prayers. Miss Amelia and Miss Jemima were great evangelists – all good works and bad temper.

Henrietta's acceptance of their dreary paradise seemed to me a great disloyalty to Mama, whom I would accompany on her furtive visits to St Peter's Saffron Hill. There I would hold her hand and kneel in the fragrant darkness to cross myself before I lit a candle for Nonno Giuseppe. My grandfather was a political refugee from Naples who came to London during the Napoleonic Wars and set up as a plaster-image maker in Saffron Hill. I enjoyed these secret games that pleased my mama and shocked my sister.

The only lessons I enjoyed were the extras – French and pianoforte and drawing. French reminded me of home and Mama's cheerful babble of Italian. Music was always a joy, but drawing was my passion, although I managed to get bad marks even for that because I wanted to draw the stories I told myself, and Miss Amelia said that only flowers were a proper subject. At the beginning of each lesson she propped up a rose that gradually wilted beneath the gaze of fifty girls and the harsh criticism of Miss Amelia as she crept behind us to count each thorn and belittle our efforts. Smudged with tears and a dozen rubbings out, even a dewy rose soon looked like a battered lamp-post to be held up to the class as another example of my stupidity.

I left my dame-school with a smattering of everything. Enough French to read novels and enough history to adore Joan of Arc and Mary Stuart and enough music to flaunt myself at evening parties. I finished my education in the Finsbury circulating library and in Papa's study where I learned to draw from his great book of anatomy, which was bound in green leather and heavy as a tombstone. It revealed to me the mysterious world that Papa said was hidden inside us all. And do I have a skull like this? I would ask in wonder as I turned the musty pages. Henrietta said it was blasphemous to open up a body and look inside it as if it was a grandfather clock, but Papa said Heaven had no use for ignoramuses.

When I wasn't drawing I devoured novels. I made friends with the Dombeys and Jane and Rochester and Becky Sharp and Rawdon and admired Diana Vernon in *Rob Roy* because (like her) I never could sew a tucker nor work cross-stitch nor make a pudding. The only novel my sister approved of was *Coelebs in Search of a Wife*, which I read – and cordially loathed that monstrous prig of a Lucilla.

My parents would take me to Shakespeare at Sadler's Wells and to the Drury Lane pantomimes. The theatre was my greatest joy, and Henrietta said that was the final proof if proof were needed that I was worldly and frivolous. By the time I was sixteen and started to wear stays Henrietta seemed older and certainly more solemn than Mama, and there were very few matters we could agree on. When we were at school she was Mount Olympus and I was a muddy foothill, but now we were both young ladies living at home she seemed less formidable.

Papa used to take us to visit patients because he said girls should see life and death as well as drawing-rooms, and if Henrietta must be so good she could at least be useful. I adored babies and loved to be in a house where a new little miracle had just arrived. Most visits were not so exciting – to the homes of what my father called languishing females with too much time on their hands. C. and I used to laugh at the beastly invalids later and imitate their voices. Henrietta took great pleasure in visiting the dying. Like Henry V rousing his troops before Agincourt she prepared them for the spiritual battle ahead. Once I said I wouldn't want her at my deathbed, and C. laughed and Henrietta sulked for days. She seemed to like C. even less than she liked me and often refused to look at him. When I opened my eyes the other day to see C. and Tommy and all the servants gathered around me waiting for a beautiful deathbed scene I was very glad indeed of my sister's absence and even gladder to disappoint the assembled handkerchiefs.

C. was very jolly in those days, and he and I were great friends. His father was my father's apothecary, and I can hardly remember a time when C. was not at our house. Later he lived with us as Papa's assistant, and my gentle giant was always full of larks. We were play-mates long before he became spoony, and when he did it seemed the most natural progression in the world.

For just as he noticed I was no longer a little girl I began to feel my pulse and heart dance a fandango whenever C. was in the room. I could not tear my eyes away from his face, from the way his skin glowed as if the sun rose behind it and his blue eyes full of humour and tenderness. Henrietta said it was improper to gaze at him like a slave girl at a sultan.

That was more than ten years ago. Now I can hear him coming upstairs, and I'm afraid he will prose again. When I first returned he was most affectionate, but since he read my letter he has grown cold. Yet what was I to do but tell the truth as I have always done?

Before C. came in I hid my journal in my work-basket and rearranged myself to look as delicate as possible. When he opened the door of my darkened room daylight from the landing fell on him, and I saw what ten years have done to that face I have just been remembering. It is shrivelled now and stretched and sprinkled with flour, and his eyes are cold and grey as the sea at Ramsgate.

He did not smile at me or caress my hair. I might have been a patient as he asked me how I was feeling. He sounded like an animated corpse, which reminded me of Bella and brought tears to my eyes.

'More hysterics,' he muttered impatiently. 'Now sit up.' The cold spoon hit my teeth and Mother Bailey's Quieting Syrup flowed down my throat in a sugary torrent. 'I am giving you a stronger dose to help you sleep. Lie back again, Nina, for you must rest. You have been through – a great ordeal.'

'You have read my letter?' I sat up again, and he pushed me back down ungently as if I were a cork and he a chilly wave. 'We must talk about it.'

His face was still and pale as marble in my dark room as he stared down at me. I have known him all my life, yet I could not tell what he was thinking or feeling. 'Charles? Are you angry with your little Nina?'

He winced. 'Little no longer.'

'But always your Nina? Dearest?'

'You are my wife. Marriage is for always,' he said joylessly. 'We will discuss your letter another day. First you must recover your strength and not upset yourself in any way. No reading or writing or drawing . . .' He followed my guilty gaze to my work-basket. He has always known when I was fibbing, and, in fact, I have hardly ever deceived him in anything, great or small. But I was relieved when he continued, 'And no sewing either. I did not know you were so keen a needlewoman.'

My lack of prowess as a domestic goddess has always been one of our jokes. But there was no laughter in his voice as he said, 'Let Mother Bailey do her work. As soon as you are stronger you must see Tommy who is becoming a little monster. The sooner he goes away to school the better. He cries for you night and day and screams that he has murdered you.'

'He has always been melodramatic. I will see him as soon as I am better.' The thought of Tommy's tricks and tantrums wearied me, and I was glad to postpone his visit. Tommy in a sickroom is like a baboon at a tea table.

'We must also discuss the dinner.'

'But you said you had cancelled it.' There are advantages in being ill.

'I have only postponed it. Somehow the story of your disappearance has leaked out. I suspect Emma, but she protests her devotion and discretion. Naturally I have told everybody that you have been visiting friends for a few days.'

'And who is everybody?'

'The servants. My patients. Henrietta. It is most unfortunate how swiftly bad news spreads. So, of course, we must give a dinner as soon as possible to establish that all is as it should be. I have sent out invitations for the 18th.'

I did not ask the 18th of what. I had no wish to re-enter time. 'What did you tell my sister? Has she been here?'

'Now, you must not upset yourself.'

'You know Henrietta always upsets me. It's her vocation.'

'No, her vocation is sainthood. A calling she follows with too much zeal as we have always agreed. But on this occasion she has behaved well. She called on Monday while you were – away – and I told her you were visiting friends.'

'What friends? She knows all my friends.'

'She did not interrogate me. She sent a note yesterday to ask after you, and I replied that you had returned exhausted and were resting. She only enquired out of kindness.'

'Henrietta? Kind? She hates me and has always hated me –'

'Now you sound like Tommy. I do not like to hear that passion in your voice. You must be calm.'

He had his wish, for at that moment Mother Bailey pulled me down into her cauldron of opium dreams.

When I awoke Tommy was sitting on my bed. He looked so much like Bella naughtily dressed in boy's clothes (my little angel was never naughty) that I could not bear to look at him. He stared at me out of those deep-blue eyes with dark lashes reflected in them like reeds.

Charles's eyes are grey and smooth as pebbles, but Tommy's were like whirlpools as he clutched me and smothered me with kisses and sobs and hot tears until my mouth was full of his hair and I had to push him away.

'I'm so glad I didn't kill you.'

'What morbid nonsense is this?'

'I thought I had. I thought it was all my fault. Where did you go?'

'If you will sit quietly on that chair I will tell you.' Suddenly I wanted to talk about the wonderful civilization I had seen, and goodness knows Tommy needs civilizing. 'Your mama has been to another London.'

'Is it in Australia? Did you see kangaroos?'

'It is not in any atlas. I did not travel by sea or land. I saw many wonderful things and heard invisible music and walked in beautiful gardens. But there were no kangaroos.'

'Oh, you mean boring old Heaven that Aunt Henrietta's always talking about. But you have to die to get there.'

'As you see I am very much alive.'

'Not so very much. You look pale and droopy and lie in this dark smelly room all the time.'

'I am ill. Little gentlemen are considerate to ladies' indispositions.'

'Now you're cross and won't tell about the wonderfulness.'

'How am I to tell you anything when you constantly interrupt me?'

Tommy sat with Sunday stillness and covered his mouth with his hand to keep the words in.

My words had to be forced out. It was the first time I had spoken of my experience, and I told it all in a rush of elephants and pantaloons and kaas and flying staircases. I told him solemnly that these things will happen as surely as Julius Caesar once happened. 'And you, Tommy, are a bridge between our world and that other one. Perhaps your grandchildren will see this wonderful city and will live there without sickness or poverty. Instead of fighting or killing, those people of the future will watch moving pictures of war.'

He got down from his chair and came to sit beside me on the bed where he stared at me. 'Really truly, Mama? I hate it in the storybooks when the little girl wakes up and it was all a dream. There isn't a beastly moral?'

'If there is I don't know what it is.' I hugged him and took comfort from his warm little body. For once he didn't wriggle or flee but lay peacefully in my arms.

Then Charles came back and said Tommy was tiring me, and I said he wasn't, and Tommy said, 'Go away! I want to stay here for ever and ever. We were talking about the wonderful things Mama has seen –'

'Why is a talkative young man like a great pig, Tommy?'

'Don't know and don't care.'

'Because if he lives he is likely to become a great bore.'

Then Tommy yelled and screamed, and Charles had to take him out. Where he had lain in my arms there was a child-shaped hole that filled with Bella. I still see her in every corner of these rooms. Her dark curls fall over the shoulders of her white nightgown, and she clutches her dolly that fell sick with her. Seeing her in the alcove above C.'s surgery that morning was not so much a haunting as a note I had heard many times before which was suddenly played with unbearable intensity. Bella will not and cannot go away.

If only we had not been a medical family we would not have realized so swiftly what her symptoms meant and there would have been a few days when we could hope. I ran to Charles in panic as soon as Bella complained of her aching head and sore throat and her nausea at the smell of food. She was standing on the stairs that April morning dressed in her little blue velvet coat and hat to go out to the Regent's Park with Tommy and Emmie. Charles and I ignored the waiting patients and desperately questioned Bella. Then she crumpled and would have fallen downstairs if Charles had not caught her as she fainted.

He carried her to the night nursery to examine her and sadly confirmed her scarlet rash. I sponged her forehead and tried to sing her favourite lullaby, but she was too ill to speak or move, and her silent paralysis spread to me. Words died in my throat, and I could not leave her bedside.

Charles came back into the room and said gently, 'You must not stay here, Nina. Scarlet fever is like a plague and carries off whole families.'

I could not answer him or leave my child. Wherever she was carried off to I wanted to be carried with her. They spread straw outside to muffle the sound of traffic, and Charles shaved her beautiful head to prevent infection. I think that was when time began to play tricks on me, for I have no idea how many days and nights I sat beside her bed. My little bald angel could not speak coherently but cried out in terror.

'Mama! Stop them! It hurts! They are boiling me! Make them go away!'

But I could not stop her torments.

Henrietta sniffed the opportunity for martyrdom and knocked on the door. I tried to ignore her bossy voice, but she bustled into the room. 'Nina, you must rest. If you stay here you will catch the fever.'

It was not a fever but a frozen silence that consumed me as I sat holding my darling child's hand.

'Nina, I will nurse Bella. I have no husband or children, and if I die I shall not be missed.' I did not give her the pleasure of contradiction. 'Nina, you must go to your own bed now. Charles is frantic with worry, and Tommy needs you. Your first duty is to them. You must wash your hands and change your clothes.'

I would not move. I had learned to be deaf to Henrietta's talk of duty long ago. She gripped my shoulders and tried to pull me away from my child. I turned to her and whispered my rage for fear that shouting would add to Bella's suffering. 'Leave us alone! I am the only one who can nurse her.'

'But the quarantine –'

'Take Tommy. If you must interfere, take him to your house and keep him safe. I will not leave Bella.'

Henrietta left and Charles came. They were like shadows passing behind the fire of Bella's destruction. Days and nights turned upside down as I slept in the chair in the night nursery or fell asleep on Bella's pillow beside her tossing head. Charles sat beside me, and we kept our sad watch until her pure soul parted from her sweet form.

I would have liked to grieve in silence, but the world does not stop for the broken-hearted. The servants laid out her body, and the night nursery had to be cleaned and whitewashed before Tommy could be allowed in. He returned from Henrietta's house more obstreperous and demanding than ever but very glad to be home.

As she entered the room my sister said with an air of triumph, 'Our bright little Bella is now most certainly among those blessed ones that surround the throne of Our Saviour.'

My eyes filled with tears. I bit my lips and stared at Charles, who said nothing.

'When is she coming back?' practical Tommy asked.

Henrietta patted his head with a radiant smile. 'You must rejoice, for your sister will stay for ever in that wonderful place.'

Although Tommy had done nothing but quarrel with his sister this good news reduced him to sobs and wails, and I joined with him. Charles detests emotional outbursts, so he left the room, and Henrietta enveloped me in a scratchy hug.

'I will stay with you, Nina, and you will find the greatest balm to your sorrowing heart in the bosom of your affectionate family.'

Stay she did and forgave my outbursts of temper most infuriatingly. Charles would not allow me to attend Bella's funeral, as I could not control my feelings. I begged to be allowed to go to the cemetery with the men to say goodbye to my little darling, but he was firm.

'The service would be too long for you, Nina. I'm afraid you are unequal to it in mind and body.'

I tried to be very good and brave as I sat in the drawing-room with Henrietta and Tommy and waited for the men to return. My heart sank in sadness and despondency as Henrietta sat at the piano playing hymns and the lullaby our mother used to sing to us. That lilting ninna-nanna I used to sing to my own children reminded me of happiness gone for ever.

Last month I visited Bella's grave in Kensal Green Cemetery. I took a hackney cab when Charles was working and Tommy was in the Regent's Park with his nurse. All alone in my weeds I stood beside her grave and let my tears flow behind my veil. It was some relief to see that the cemetery in midsummer bloomed and blossomed, and Bella lay in a pretty spot where we may grow flowers over her bed. One day there will be space for Charles and Tommy and I to sleep by her side.

Charles says I must not exert myself. He found me writing this just now and was very cross. This morning I tried to get up but could hear Tommy screaming in the nursery, so I sank back into my delicious bed. I am so well looked after here by Emmie, whose solicitude is quite marvellous. When I was Tommy's age she was a second mother to me, and now I am a matron she still looks after me as if I were the child she never had. She and Lucy bustle about the room tirelessly and rush between Tommy and myself. How fortunate women of that class are not to have any nerves. Meals appear on trays and baths are drawn for me. I heard the doorbell ring just now, but I can ignore the callers. For the time being I am freed from the tyranny of the fifteen-minute visit and the obligatory prittle-prattle over the teacups.

I am reminded of those periods of retirement before the little strangers came when I was too unsightly to pay visits. Now only Tommy remains, and I do not think there will be any more. This morning when I sat on the commode I was relieved to see scarlet proof – the spinster's curse and the married woman's friend. I luxuriate in being alone in the dreamy quiet of my room.

After Bella died I could not bear to be alone even for a moment, but as my thoughts grow darker I need to hide them beneath the cloak of solitude. When I am well I have not a half-hour in the day I can call my own, but now I am quite helpless and need not be fretted I hope I shall not be thought selfish, for I am truly indisposed. I thank Heaven that dear Charles is a doctor and can . . .

Before I could finish writing that sentence he burst into my room. I had no time to hide this journal – my friend, my only friend now – before he started to shout at me in a most terrifying way.

'What is this arrant nonsense you have been filling Tommy's head with?'

'Why, Charles! My heart –'

'I am no longer to be ruled by your heart. A very fickle and untrustworthy organ. If I catch you writing against my wishes again I will confiscate that document. I realize now that I have married a woman with no regard for truth or decency. Whatever corruption you have learned in your days of debauchery I will not have our son contaminated.'

Charles had never spoken to me like that before, and I could only weep with shock.

'More tears! No, Nina, you shall not escape into hysteria. I will have rational discourse even if I cannot have an honest wife. Tommy has been blabbing to the servants. Ridiculous tales of talking boxes and horseless transport and a city where women wear pantaloons and sickness and poverty have been abolished. The servants are laughing at him – at us – at me. How long do you think it will be before their tittle-tattle reaches my patients? Who will want to be cured by a doctor with a mad wife and son? Do you think I have struggled all these years to build up my practice just to have it destroyed by your ravings?'

'But, Charles, it is all quite true. I did see those things. I wanted Tommy to know because some of these wonderful inventions may occur in his lifetime. He is to be a bridge to a glorious future, and I am happy for him –'

'What kind of future have we now? How am I to support you and

Tommy if you make me a figure of fun? You must never speak of these things again – not to me or to anyone else. The Golden Age is now, and we are fortunate to be alive. There is no need to look backwards or forwards. We must embrace the progress and innovations around us, for all of London is a great exhibition, and I intend to flourish here. Not to be exhibited as a great gaby who believes old Mother Shipton's ridiculous phantasies.'

Charles grows very long-winded when he is angry, and he is always angry now. I stopped crying and felt snappish in return. 'I know what I have seen. However much you try to crush me with that moral flat-iron called common sense –'

'They were dreams, my dear Nina.' But I am not his dear any more and do not know what I am. 'The delusions of an uneducated mind.'

'Dreams do not last for three days.'

'Do you taunt me with that? With those days when you were lost to me and lost to yourself in a moral quagmire I cannot bear to think of.'

We stared at each other in silence, and he left the room.

His face and voice were so hard and cold. Charles has always been my friend as well as my husband, and I cannot believe he has changed so much towards me. It is as if I stand in a room where open french windows invite me on to a balcony. I step forward, but instead of feeling safety beneath my feet I fall into darkness where I am alone and unloved.

I disobey Charles and look backwards. I see him as a young man glowing with optimism and idealism as he smiles into my eyes. I think we were sitting in the parlour at my parents' old house in Finsbury. Well, it does not matter where we were, for lovers make their own geography. We were engaged, and I was head over heels in love, for my life was settled and Charles would love me always.

Nowadays there is a fashion for expensive weddings with dozens of guests and presents. My mother sewed a few nightdresses for me and gave me some linen and furniture. We simply read the banns and went to our local parish church one morning. I had a new brown silk dress and bonnet, which remained my best for a few years, and I carried a little bouquet of orange blossom. At home we had a simple breakfast for a few friends and relations – Charles had no relations, so I laughed and told him he could borrow mine.

We had a wedding trip to Ramsgate. I had never stayed in an hotel before and thought it very grand and expensive – ten pounds for the week. But the real luxury was to be all alone with Charles and walk by the sea and stare at his wonderful face. At school the girls whispered about the horrid things men did to you after you married them, but I did not find anything Charles did horrid. Perhaps those books of anatomy had prepared me.

We lived with my parents at first, and I enjoyed being busy around the house with Mama. We used to bake together and make wine, and friends used to come with work of a morning. We would all sit and sew together and chatter. Henrietta was still at home, as no man had appreciated her perfections, and she disapproved of my marriage. Once I tried to explain to her what it was to love, but she grew very chilly and remote, for there is no music in her soul.

I was married and my story was over, and I was extremely happy. I expected Charles to be a doctor as Papa had been with a shabby practice that yielded more friendship than money. Papa's patients were city merchants who were prosperous but not too alarmingly fashionable.

After Bella was born Charles grew impatient with our quiet Finsbury ways. I had hoped that when Papa grew too old to work Charles would simply take his place, but he began to mutter about the West End and repeated his stories of Sir Astley's exploits with more admiration in his voice each time. Papa called Sir Astley Cooper 'Satan's quack', admitting his brilliance but doubting his honesty.

Well, now we have risen. My dear parents died of cholera soon after we left Finsbury, and I feel very much alone here. Bella was my dear little companion, but with her death the joy has gone out of this house, and I cannot transfer my affections to Tommy, for he is such a difficult child. Charles wants me to live this caged-bird life. He says that to bake and bustle as I did in Finsbury would be to poach on the servants' right to earn a living. When I am better he says I can do a little embroidery. Perhaps some watercolours of flowers and a little singing and piano playing. He does not like it when I question him too eagerly about his work. I often asked Papa about the details of his patients' lives and deaths. But as a wife it seems my only duties are to pour out Charles's tea at breakfast and brush his hat and help him put on his overcoat.

I have a new duty. Charles has just sent Emmie with a curt note about the dinner. Perhaps I have tempted providence by gloating on my timeless solitude. Now the calendar looms over me again, and I have only three weeks to send out the invitations and worry about the menu. Oh, and I must see that the best china and glasses are pristine and order the flowers and the fruit.

A hundred decisions jostle in my head. The most important guests must be invited first – but who are they? Charles will know. He has a *Burke's Peerage* in his head. Shall we be old-fashioned and dine at three or fashionably at six? After dinner shall we have music and sandwiches or only tea? Shall we hold one dinner or two? If we have two we can use the leftovers from the first the following day when we can invite the less important guests. I must order enough excess food to fill all the dishes the first night that we shall not be thought mean. Should James pretend to be a butler or a footman? What must I wear? It is vulgar to be vain but unforgivable to look singular. I will have to have a new black silk made up to contrive to stay in mourning without looking a frump. Tomorrow morning Cook is coming to discuss the menu, and I have a pile of household books beside me from which I must concoct a dinner that will not shame us.

I have been to many such dinners without enjoying any of them. The hostess enjoys them least of all, for she has run around for weeks in a state of exhaustion preparing for these shining hours. Her heart is in the kitchen in case her soufflé should not rise.

All night I shall be in a state of nervous anxiety for fear that my guests' conversation does not flow or my dress is not chic or my music does not please. Yet I must appear to be calm and enchanted to see these people I hardly know. After dinner we ladies must retire to the drawing-room and talk in low voices about illnesses and servants and children. No rattling gossip and laughter like at Finsbury Square, for in fashionable circles it is polite to complain and ill bred to express any enthusiasm or pleasure.

Oh dear, this journal is becoming quite revolutionary. I shall have to put a padlock on my work-basket and bury it under the floorboards. Am I a very wicked wife? Since this is a secret journal I will confess to the floorboards that I do think of J. a great deal.

Thinking about the terrors of the dinner party put me in a great panic so that I could no longer lie still in my bed. I got up and walked around my darkened room and felt how the walls press in on me. These walls must be my whole life now. I am a housewife. I am married to this house and to a man who no longer loves me. My heart was beating very fast, and my breath came in sharp needles as if the air was poison for me. For I have breathed another air, and my lungs need it now.

And then I saw him. Through the dark walls I saw Jonathan at his desk in his garret above the stables. Just a few paces away as if the years that separate us were only a layer of gauze. I walked towards him – I was quite certain that I could pass through to him again. He looked up and saw me. He stood up and we stared at each other, and I held out my arms to him, and there was a moment when we could have conquered time.

The door opened. The wrong door. Emmie barged in with a tray. 'Miss Nina! Whatever are you doing out of bed, you wicked girl?'

I was not even a sick woman but a sick child. Jonathan's handsome face receded and shrank to the size of a farthing and slid back inside my head. I cannot see him any longer, but how deeply I feel him.

I don't think there was any harm in what we did together. Henrietta always said I was a capricious little simpleton, and I am proving her right. When I was then I longed to return to my life here with Charles, and now I am now I crave the freedom and freshness of Jonathan's utopia.

Now the walls are solid again and the dinner party looms.

I must put aside my illness and my mourning and my . . . accidents with time. I am afraid of making Charles any more angry than he already is. These mechanical forms of good breeding are important, for Charles's career depends on them and I depend on him. So there is nothing for it but to make believe that our dinner on the 18th is a great military campaign I must fight and win.

# CHARLES

I THOUGHT NINA'S thunderbolt had done its worst, that my heart was shrivelled and charred and could feel no more pain. Yet as I passed her door just now tears came to my eyes, and I could not turn the handle and go in. The face that once gave me such joy is repugnant to me now. Where I used to see girlish innocence, coquetry and false-hood leer out at me. Unable to breathe the same air as Nina, I communicate with her by notes I give to Emma, who looks at me with pity. How much does she know? The servants' impudent curiosity wounds me almost more than Nina's . . . what? I have diagnosed so many illnesses yet know not how to label my wife's disease, which is more in her mind than in her body. Mine is at best a science of guesswork.

It is late at night. My patients have gone, and the household sleeps. I sit here alone in my study where I sleep now, alone, unable to join Nina in the bed where once we were so happy. Out of her wild letter and my own knowledge I search for answers to the riddle my wife has become.

I must begin with the death of Bella. This sorrow drew us closer together and, I thought, opened our hearts to one another. When the order of nature is reversed and the parent witnesses the death of his child, who was entwined around my heart – I did not know the final parting would be such a pang. Our treasure seemed to suffer fearfully at the end. I never expected it to be such a life-embittering trial. I was thoroughly broken up, and Nina, who was a most affectionate mother, was half-crazed with grief. In the first days after Bella's death my poor wife looked behind every door and into every corner, expecting to find her darling.

As for her tale of imagining Bella's ghost on the landing above my surgery – I blame myself for allowing Nina to read foolish novels full of ghosts and goblins and gibberish. Nina's mother was a Papist, and it may be that her blood is tainted or, at least, that she is susceptible to unhealthy superstitions. Women, being little capable of reasoning, are feeble and timid and require protection. Somehow, she slipped out of our house and walked the streets alone. Nina has – or rather had – that ignorance of vice which one desires in a lady.

Who knows what really happened to her? London is changing so fast that it seems like enchantment; buildings are torn down and vast new monsters erected; advertising is on every wall and van, and the streets are full of boys distributing advertising bills, some of them no doubt for shady enterprises. Just a few hundred yards from our house are the squalid courts behind Oxford Street where she may have fallen prey to some designing man.

Nina may have become the victim of mesmerism or ether, which destroys the memory. Perhaps an electro-biologist abducted her for some sinister experiment, or perhaps she had a cataleptic dream. But a dream could not have lasted for three days. How those three lost days torture me.

Electro-biologists have the power to banish susceptible females from their own minds. A few years back I was present at a performance at the Egyptian Hall by some Yankee professor. He plucked several young ladies from the audience and, using electric forces, induced the most suggestible to humiliate themselves, much to the amusement of the public. Nina's sensibility, the delicate mind I so adored, would make her very responsive to such manipulations. The imaginative faculties, the nervous sensations and the muscular motions are not always under the control of the will. One young boy, in Northamptonshire, I believe, was driven temporarily insane by such an experience, although I seem to remember that it was mesmerism that restored his wits just as it destroyed them.

Electro-nervous currents and animal magnetism have now been exploded by most respectable scientists, but perhaps this Jonathan was one of these itinerant mountebanks. Such fellows exploit women, somnambules as they are called, pathetic creatures who follow their masters around provincial mechanics' institutes and assembly rooms where they perform like circus horses and obey their masters' cruel whims with the devotion of a priestess. Such careers begin on stage and end in the workhouse.

I am a tolerant man, but I would thrash the scoundrel if I could find him. He must still have some grip over my wife, for she refuses to tell me his full name or address. No doubt he has already exposed her degradations in some tuppenny chapbook that is circulating on the streets of London. What did he make her do? What secret experiments and obscenities have been performed upon my darling while she was in a trance? The magnetizer has unlimited power over the magnetized and may do anything, anything at all, with her . . . I cannot bear to think of those three days. Yet I cannot look at Nina without a thousand diabolical images – better that she had never awoken from her mesmeric state! I had rather be a widower than the husband of a debauched and degraded woman

Out of the maze of Nina's imagination I have extracted a few facts about this future where she claims to have been, where poverty and money and illness have been abolished, men and women dress alike in tatterdemalion attire, a talking box produces daguerreotypes, mechanical slaves perform all practical tasks and ascending carriages float up to the ceiling. My interrogation made her weep, made me feel a brute, and still I am none the wiser about what really happened. Her fancies have a whiff of the fairy-tale about them. If that were all I think I could ignore her as I ignore Tommy when he prattles of hob-goblins and sprites.

But I cannot ignore or forget her depraved and unchaste behaviour with me. When first she returned it was very clear that she had coarsened, had been degraded below her rank. She transgressed the bounds of decency, and in my delight at seeing her again I did not at first suspect her.

My upbringing was not a sheltered one. There was a girlery in the next house, and as a student I attended routs and balls where filthy harlots lured me on. I adored Nina, above all, for her very innocence, which separated her from the trumpery minxes I knew as a boy. Who is this Jonathan? When I demand where I can find him, to give him a thrashing, she points to the wall and says he is on the other side of it but has not yet been born.

Criminal conversation may have taken place between them. I can hardly bear to think of it, but a woman can be taken by storm. This man must be a consummate coward and blackguard. He must have mesmerized her! It is as clear as any proposition in Euclid: she has been a false wife to a simple-hearted and trusting husband. He must have dragged her to his poisoned habitation and have stimulated her venereal appetite with alcohol or narcotics – my little Nina. I am sick and sorry. Like a wounded beast I long to creep into a hole quite alone.

But I must be sociable to succeed. I need a wife beside me and cannot afford to divorce the one I have, however unsatisfactory she may be. Gentlemen are different; our peccadilloes are natural and harmless. When I was young I whored and caroused with the best of them, and if I were to disappear for a night or two even now it would be no great matter. But a lady who has been defiled must stink for ever of moral corruption. I must take care that no other nostrils but my own are assaulted.

Remembering those wild parties when we were medical students, before we were let loose upon the public, reminds me of William Porter, the most debauched of us all when we were young and now the most successful. He has married a cousin of Lord Cavendish and flourishes just this side of quackery. It is many years since we have spoken, but I have invited them to dinner on the 18th, before the season ends and anybody who is anybody leaves London. I am tempted to confide in William, who was never fastidious about women and, to judge by the advertisements I see in the less exclusive newspapers, is even less so now. Porter's Electrical Belt and Balm of

Elysium, indeed – yet he has a house in Hanover Square and sends his sons to Eton, I hear.

I hope Nina may call on his wife, become intimate with her and learn a little polish and ease. Such women are exquisitely poised, always elegant, hardly stirring a muscle except to embroider or attend a musical soirée or indulge in a little philanthropy. Or so I imagine Mrs Porter to be. Women like her run the social world from their morning-rooms, and their support is invaluable. I look forward to meeting her and hope she will be a calming influence on Nina. Her vivacity was all very well as a young girl, but now she is a matron I would like her to devote herself more to her domestic pursuits.

No man ever prospered without the cooperation of his wife, and our household leaves much to be desired. As soon as Nina has recovered I will insist that she takes her housewifery seriously. Lucy and James treat her as if she were Tommy, and when I asked Cook if Mrs Sanderson had given her clear orders for the 18th she replied that she couldn't understand the menu. Neither could I when she showed it to me. It consisted of an illegible scrawl with a caricature of a lady in evening dress emptying a soup tureen over the head of a gentleman. I sent Nina a very sharp note, reminding her that puerile humour belongs to the nursery, not the kitchen.

My anxiety about our dinner is mounting. We have had acceptances from ten of the guests, and I have invited Arthur Meredith, a briefless barrister of my acquaintance, and his wife to make up our missing numbers. I worry that the extra flap in our mahogany dining-table will not be strong enough, that our crystal and cutlery will not shine, that our best dinner plates may have cracks in them from being carelessly washed. What is the correct precedence for us to go down to dinner? As a cousin of Lord Cavendish, does Mrs Porter go before or after Sir Percy, who is only a 'bedside baronet'. Such a dinner requires weeks of preparation by perfect servants and a devoted wife, and I possess neither. Whole books are written to explain all this etiquette, but I have not time to read them.

Really, it is monstrous that I should have to concern myself with such trivial yet vital details. Nina is . . .

What Nina is may have become clear in my dreams as I slept fitfully in my armchair by the dying fire in my study. I awoke hardly knowing who I myself was, with a very stiff neck, to yells that pierced the grey shroud of the dawn. I was tempted to feign deafness and shrink back into my sanctuary, but Tommy's lungs would galvanize a corpse. I ran upstairs before his uproar woke all the neighbours and caused more gossip. A tortured child as well as a mad wife.

Old Emma stood helpless in the door of the night nursery where Tommy writhed on the floor, an eel in a nightgown.

'I want Mama, not you. Go away, Papa.'

'Your mama must rest.'

'Go away!'

'You must learn to govern your temper.'

'Is that why you're called the guv'nor? I hate you.'

'You are a very spoiled little boy. Too much petticoat government has enfeebled you. You must go away to school and learn to be a man, then you and I will be able to have civilized conversations together.'

'Don't want them. Don't want to be a man. I want to be a little girl. Like . . .'

He didn't name her, but Bella was in the room with us. I saw her in his face and his long dark curls. She can't come back, a ton of stone and three coffins weigh her safely down, and yet . . . A tear fell down my nose, and I was glad of the darkness and more than ever determined that Tommy will enjoy the privileges I was denied. Dinner parties will hold no terrors for him. At school he will make aristocratic connections, will learn to construe Greek and play cricket and a thousand other mysteries.

'This fashion for making girls out of boys is detestable. Frocks and drawers and long curls are effeminate. No wonder you cry all the time.'

'Let go of my hair! You're pulling.'

70

'When I was a boy I would have been thrashed for speaking to my father as you have spoken to me.' Not true, for Pa was always kind to me, but he is dead now and may serve as a caution. 'Be thankful it is only your hair I hurt.'

I told Emma to bring a candle and scissors. By the flickering light I saw her disapproval and Tommy's fear, as if I were some great bully and not a decent man trying to prepare his son for life. While I sheared him Tommy wriggled and yelled and bit me and did his best to make me harm him. The scissors twisted in my hands and nicked him, but I didn't really hurt him. He just likes to make a commotion.

'You look much better now. The other boys will see you are a little man and not a little girl to be teased and tormented.'

He did look better. His hair stopped at his collar, and his face had lost that sickening prettiness. Pa was a barber as well as an apothecary, and I have the knack, even by candlelight. There were bloodstains on the pillow, and Tommy's dark fleece covered the bed and floor.

'I want Mama.'

'She will not come to naughty children. You should be among other boys to give you a more manly bearing and spirit. If you live to grow up you will appreciate what your papa has done for you tonight.'

The sooner he starts the better. I told Emma to buy him some knickerbockers and a jacket on account at Marshall and Snelgrove and to be sure he mixes with other boys in the park. Emma glared back at me and muttered under her breath, 'I am not to be frightened by fee-faw-fum.' Why the devil is it that other men have obedient servants and wives and children and well-run households?

If Tommy's sister had lived and his mother had been strong we might have waited a few years, but next January Tommy will be seven, quite old enough to be sent away. By the time I was seven years old I had seen more of the seamy side of life than my son, I hope, will see in his entire lifetime.

Our shop was on Bunhill Row and backed, most conveniently,

on to the graveyard. I was very proud of the sign outside Pa's shop, with its serpent S like a stick of delectable red-and-white barley sugar, and learned my letters on it:

SS APOTHECARY AND BARBER.

PRESCRIPTIONS AND FAMILY MEDICINE ACCURATELY COMPOUNDED.

TEETH EXTRACTED AT 1s. EACH.

WOMEN ATTENDED IN LABOUR 2s. 6d. EACH.

PATENT MEDICINES AND PERFUMERY. HAIR CUT.

BEST LONDON PICKLES.

BEAR'S GREASE. GINGER BEER.

No mention of his other services. The little bedroom I shared with poor Sam overlooked the graves and the shed where lived the vat that still haunts my dreams. After Pa had removed the women's hair for wigs and their grinders to sell for dentures, the bodies were immersed in near boiling water to flay them and make them unrecognizable. Of course, Sir Astley was too much of a gentleman to raise his own bodies, and Pa was very faithful in his interests.

I was five years old when my father first suggested that I should go with him on a fishing trip, and I was very proud to be woken up in the middle of the night to go to work. Pa was over six foot tall and heavy set, so my littleness and nimbleness were handy when it came to squeezing through railings and clambering over walls in the dark. He always took pride in leaving a grave as he found it, and on many a night my fingers would be raw with cold after carefully replacing flowers.

Once we were chased by a rival gang of Resurrection men who fired a blunderbuss at us. It was when we were at work in the old St Mary's churchyard that got closed down a few years later when the authorities found the bodies stacked twenty deep in the charnel-house and under the chapel. The stench was so bad that the windows in the surrounding houses had to be kept shut all year round for fear of body bugs. Anyway, it was a bright moonlit night, and I remember how exciting and terrifying it was to run with my pa, the body in its sack bumping between us. He hailed a cab – the cabbies charged twice the going rate when they saw the sack – and we escaped to Sir Astley's. Pa handed the subject to the porter, who gave him nine flashing sovereigns and a pot of ale from which I was allowed to sip .

In those days magistrates turned a blind eye to mysterious sacks and hampers, for they didn't want to obstruct the progress of medical education. Legally, fishing in graveyards was only a misdemeanour, but the mob hated the Resurrection men, and before I was Tommy's age I knew I had to keep quiet about our nocturnal excursions. I never sold any body that had not died a natural death, neither did Pa, I am quite certain. I was well acquainted with skeletons long before I met them in the dissecting-room. How like the Gothic tales that Nina used to love, that I used to prevent her reading, my childhood was. Little does she know she has married Varney the Vampire. Well, and whom have I married?

Dr Phipps, Nina's father, used to come to our shop to pick up parcels of drugs. Sometimes I would deliver them to his house in Finsbury Square, where the two exquisitely dressed little girls lived their celestial life with a mama angel who sang to them. My own mama had died when I was born, or so I was told. Perhaps she had a squeamish nature and bolted. If she did die, I hope she was allowed to rest in peace and not sold on to Sir Astley's dissection-room. Our mothering was done by Betty, a kind old woman who stank of gin and snuff. She was our nurse and housekeeper and cook, and she also helped Pa to boil up the horrors in the vat in the shed. Pa never married again, for Betty took care of all his practical needs and his others were taken care of by the brothel next door.

My father, Joshua, was as lively as his sign, with a social range that extended from cockney cant to drawing-room manners. Having been left with two sons, or a vegetable and a monkey as he sometimes said, he didn't allow fatherhood to cramp his style. On the evenings when we were not out fishing, the warm stone-flagged kitchen behind our shop was a club for prostitutes, surgeons, tradesmen and their wives and soldiers from the nearby barracks who had agreed not to see Pa's nocturnal activities. They all drank and played cards and gossiped together, discussing religion and politics with a passion that was very attractive to a listening monkey. Pa was a Freethinker, even an atheist, and I grew up with radical ideas.

That was back in the twenties, when London was more horizontal than it is now. The People's Charter and memories of the French Revolution quivered in the air, and there were many who hoped to abolish our own *ancien régime*. Old men still had powder on their heads, ruffles on their shirts and great silver buckles on their shoes. Our kitchen glowed with candlelit faces and throbbed with argument. I was the only child present, for poor Sam lay upstairs, drugged with Godfrey's Cordial lest he had one of his fits in the night and disgraced us before our friends. I remember nothing but hugs and sweetmeats from the women and kindness from the men, many of whom were later transported or hanged for their dangerous ideas.

I soon decided I didn't want to be an apothecary's apprentice with a pestle and mortar but a respectable medical man with a big house and a wife and daughters. Pa was proud of my ambition and delighted when a professor of phrenology, who did some shady business with him involving skulls, examined my bumps and said I had the head of a genius and was destined for greatness. My favourite visitor was Jackie Scraggs, who had left one of his limbs at Waterloo and had a fascinating wooden one to entertain me with. He was nightwatchman at Bart's and was carefully blind when Pa turned up to claim a body. In those days most patients in London hospitals died, so if friends and relations didn't claim the body it was easy pickings and saved the hospital the expense of burying it. Many hospital patients still die, for powder and pills can be as fatal as powder and ball, but operations are not as lethal as they once were since the introduction of the leech, that most singular and valuable reptile, which can be applied before and after operations to reduce swelling.

Sometimes, when the talk in our kitchen grew fiery with republicanism and radicalism, I was sent up to my damp bed and would creep back down again to listen. Sitting on the cold stone stairs, shivering and a little drunk with the porter I had been indulged with, I would hear the excited voices shouting and laughing through the door and think our house a very fine one that so many people came to visit.

After the scandal of the London Burkers blew up, working the graves became dangerous. But I had set my heart on being a doctor. At first I dreamed of becoming a surgeon like Sir Astley, but a good surgeon must have an eagle's eye, a lion's heart and a lady's hand. I was a clumsy-boots, and for all Pa's loyalty to him Sir Astley never offered to help me on my way. Unmentored, the best I could hope for was to be broiled for a pittance in the West Indies. All I needed to become a doctor was the constitution of a rhinoceros and twenty guineas. We had to have three bodies during our sixteen-month training: two for anatomy and one for operations. So Pa and I went back to work for just long enough to let me pocket my profits and put them towards my expensive medical education. My dear old father died of a pox just before I presented myself for my viva voce. I always thought he caught it from one of the Subjects, but perhaps he caught it from the girls next door. I miss him still, for if he was not the most respectable of men he was certainly one of the kindest.

I must be getting old to think fondly on my sordid childhood. Fortunate Tommy, to grow up with servants and a nursery and an education he doesn't have to burke for. Times change, and sensible people change with them. Now I am quite contented with the *ancien régime* and want to be a part of it. I am still sometimes expected to use the tradesman's entrance, but Tommy will be a gentleman. Will he read this one day? I wonder. If not for him, for whom am I writing, here in the early morning as I wait for Lucy to bring breakfast and for my first patients to arrive?

Downstairs I can hear mothers and babies arrive, waiting to be vaccinated with a fine lancet on the top of their arms against small-pox, that hideous, disfiguring disease that used to carry off thousands of children every year. But we are about to conquer it. We must work towards the future, not Nina's ravings but the actual scientific tomorrow. Lucy has just brought a note from Lady B— to say that Clara has had another of those distressing nervous attacks. I will have to call on them later and play a hand of whist with her ladyship to prove my medical acumen.

Somewhere in the crowded day I must find space enough to meet with the servants and make sure that all the arrangements for Wednesday night are in place. Do they give dinners? That is the question they ask about smart young couples at my club. I was so proud when I joined it five years ago, although since Nina's 'illness' I have not been there once and will soon lose my right to attend if I am not able to pay my overdue subscription. The couple that does not give dinners is doomed to suburban life and social extinction. We do. We must. We will.

How happy I was on Monday when I thought a villa in Stockwell was the worst fate that could befall me. All night I have lain awake counting the excruciating degrees of embarrassment I suffered. At a post mortem it is customary for the corpse to be present, but my ambition is already six feet under and my wife and son dance on it, laughing at my discomfort. No, I shall go mad myself if I believe they acted out of malice.

I had been over the guest list with Nina many times to establish the intricacies of precedence and seating.

'Why can't they just go downstairs with whoever they like best and sit next to the person they want to talk to?'

'It is not helpful of you to laugh at such serious matters.'

'But, Charles, you always said you despised snobbery and had no wish to pretend to be richer and grander than you really were.'

'Did I? I must have been extremely young.'

'You were extremely nice.'

'Very well, I shall have to be both host and hostess. All that is required of you is to look elegant and to listen with delight to the conversation of the men on either side of you. Remember not to mention Malta to Sir Archibald – it was there that his wife bolted – or to stare at the Reverend Humphreys's glass eye. Do not give more than fifty per cent of your attention to either gentleman, and after each course you must turn to your other side and direct your conversation to your other neighbour. Not in mid sentence, naturally. And do not remove your gloves until we have all been seated at the table.'

'Perhaps I should carry an etiquette book on a chain around my neck to consult it during dinner?'

'I see you are determined to be facetious.'

The evening began well enough. James looked convincing in his butler costume, with the local greengrocer dressed as a flunky and Lucy in a beautifully starched apron trying to look as if she had an army of servants to supervise. Nina and I inspected the dining-table, which looked charming, with red and white roses to match our best china. There were half a dozen glasses for each person and a battalion of cutlery. The ancestors I bought at auction last year looked very dignified, glaring down at the table with authentic aristocratic disdain. I told Nina they were the Norfolk Sandersons, for how are we to flourish without roots and a tree? Pa would approve. He always said I would rise in the world. Wherever could I have fallen to?

We went down to the kitchen to taste the lobster sauce for the turbot and check that Cook had not cracked or burned the Chantilly basket filled with whipped cream and strawberries. I hoped that Nina's black silk and my own black armband would remind our guests of our bereavement only two months ago and excuse any imperfections in our hospitality. I had persuaded Emma to act as an additional maid and bribed Tommy (another half-crown) to put himself to bed.

'Charles, why do you look so terrified? Are they not our friends?'

'Certainly not. They are patients and potential patients, and it is important to please them.'

'Well, if we poison them they shall need you all the more.'

'I hope you do not intend to make any bizarre remarks during dinner.'

'I shall be too frightened to open my mouth.'

If only both she and Tommy had taken a vow of silence.

All our guests were punctual. The business of introductions and precedence went better than I had feared. William looked quite disgustingly prosperous, and his wife, a rather plain lady several years older than him with a prominent nose, had that enviable air of having been born speaking French and eating oysters. If one could buy such confidence in Marshall and Snelgrove I would go down there this morning and buy several yards for Nina. Perhaps it is not a deficiency of confidence but a surfeit of frankness that is the problem; a quality delightful in a girl of ten but not in a matron nearing thirty. Our dining-table was not long enough to muffle her clear high voice as it trilled singularities above the symphony I was trying to conduct. I sat with William's wife on my right and Mrs Humphreys on my left, their ears as sharp as their mouths were bland. As they boasted of their genealogy, lowering their eyes modestly and blushing as they launched each knight and peer into the contest between them, they were riveted by the other end of the table.

Nina was dissecting the fowl when I saw the abyss into which she was plunging the conversation.

'As you say, Reverend, it's all very dreadful – cholera, poverty, the depravity and ignorance of our rookeries. And yet we can rejoice, for a beautiful dawn is coming soon.'

'I did not know you had become an evangelical, Mrs Sanderson.' The Reverend Humphreys, an Epicurean High Church man, shot me a look of sympathy.

'Oh no, you're thinking of my sister, Henrietta. I do not speak of the next world but of this.'

'Chartism?' The Reverend looked ready to throw his napkin on the floor and flee.

'There is no word for the things I have seen, for they are in the future. We are watched by our ancestors' (she pointed rather melodramatically to my recent acquisitions), 'but how much more inspirational to fix our gaze on our descendants!' Nina's face was flushed with wine, and her voice was alarmingly passionate. She was the prettiest woman at the table – William couldn't take his eyes off her – and certainly the most garrulous.

'My wife has been ill. Our guests are waiting for their fowl, my dear. It will be cold by the time you have finished your little flight of fancy. More sirloin, Mrs Humphreys, or would you prefer the fowl?'

I carved and valiantly talked of the weather as I recommended the new potatoes, but Nina was beyond my control. She waved the carving knife and fork alarmingly as her eyes flashed like a demented diva.

'My husband thinks I should not speak of these things. But why should we speak of vegetables?'

Our guests, although plainly hungry, were not looking at their plates at all but staring at their hostess.

'You are overwrought, my dear,' I said in my best bedside voice. Then I muttered to Lucy, who stood at the sideboard beside me, 'Get your mistress up to her bedroom and lock the door from the outside!'

Lucy obediently sidled down the table but hesitated to disarm Nina of her carving weapons. As she approached Nina gave her a beatific and wholly inappropriate smile. 'Dear Lucy! In this life you are only a servant. But there will come a day when there will be no more servants and masters, no division at all between men and women or rich and poor. All will dress alike and live in perfect freedom and our stuffy old customs and formalities will be buried with us.'

The Reverend Humphreys caught a whiff of religion and asked distastefully, 'Have you been vouchsafed some, ah, vision, Mrs Sanderson?'

Nina turned to him rapturously. 'Yes! It is only now I realize how blessed I have been. When my beloved child was taken from me and I was in the slough of despond I was comforted by a vision of a future London. You don't believe me?' She looked around at their incredulous faces.

William gave a snort of laughter, disguised as a cough. Muscles twitched around the mouths of the ladies on either side of me. The fowl was cold, the atmosphere colder. Lucy had given up trying to restrain her mistress and the guests turned back to their food as I talked about our plans for the summer, trying to imply that it was only grief that prevented us from going yachting in Nice or shooting in Scotland or taking a cure in Baden Baden. My envy seethed as our guests languidly exchanged boasts, as if sitting in a first-class railway carriage were almost too much effort to bear.

William turned to me. 'And what do you think of this Russian war, Charles? I take the view that it's a quarrel between two packs of monks about a key and a star, and we should not have involved ourselves!'

The Reverend Humphreys and Sir Archibald frowned, and I remembered that they are not yet my patients. I heard the death rattle of the last of Pa's liberal sentiments as I said with a straight face, 'Our national honour is at stake, William. If only the Duke were still alive to save us. Let us raise a toast to the great man and ask ourselves how he would have acted.' I looked bellicose and so did our guests, with the exception of William who has married a large private income and can afford controversial opinions.

Nina had fallen ominously silent at the other end of the table, aware that her utopian seed had fallen on sterile ground.

Lucy and Emma removed our plates and brought in a dazzling array of sweets: strawberries in a meringue basket; a raspberry mousse; preserved ginger; a pink ice in the shape of a pear. We drank Moselle with lumps of ice in each glass, and there was a general murmur of appreciation. For ten minutes I was able to believe that my dinner party had survived the dangerous rocks of Nina and was sailing into a safe harbour where happy, well-fed patients waved at me from the quay.

There was a wave of cooing and ahhing, the tribal noises with which ladies greet a child. Looking behind me, I saw Tommy standing in the doorway, very small and fragile in his white nightgown. I gestured to Emma to remove him at once – the child had been well bribed to put himself to bed and stay there – but before she could catch him he ran down the table to Nina.

A sensible woman would have told Emma to carry him firmly off to bed. My wife, however, embraced him and sat him on her knee, making a great deal more fuss of him than she has made of me these last few weeks. Our guests smiled and pretended to be charmed by her maternal affection, but I was bitterly aware that their own brats never see their parents for more than five minutes a day. Tommy, having made himself the centre of attention, ate a few strawberries from his mother's plate and gazed around the table for amusement. Our guests' smiles were stretched to breaking point by the time he turned to Nina, stroked her hair (the soft curls I used to play with every night) and announced, 'My mama can see what's going to happen when we're all dead. My sister's dead. I don't want to die.'

I trust that at his expensive school my son will learn the art of conversation.

'Bedtime!' I approached him with what was intended to be a playful roar. 'Here comes the Bedfordshire bear!'

'No!' he screamed 'I don't like you, Papa. I want to stay with Mama.'

Tommy's eyes and nose were a river of tears and snot. I paused in mid growl, aware that instead of being charmed by my jocularity our guests were embarrassed.

Never have I been so relieved to see the ladies leave the table, carrying Tommy and his tantrum with them. With six men in the room the temperature lowered, port was passed and a civilized atmosphere prevailed. At first William and I sat in silence while the other gentlemen present discussed the Russian war and the Irish famine, which was, they agreed, the result of free trade, sloth and fecklessness. It was also, the Reverend Humphreys insisted, a punishment for Catholicism.

When William came to sit beside me some of our old student intimacy revived, although I was uncomfortably aware of his superior fortunes and told him so.

'I believe, as did Napoleon, in destiny, Charles. An unlucky man has generally only himself to blame.'

'Then I must have sinned greatly if these are my just desserts,' I muttered bitterly into my second glass of port.

'Come now! You have a comfortable house here, a charming wife and son, the seeds of an excellent practice.' My silence encouraged him to be franker. 'Your wife – what a delightful woman, so unspoiled – must have suffered greatly from the loss of your child. Women live so much in their emotions. And I know how hard it is to survive in London on the rather dour principles we learned in our youth. We must meet one day and discuss the alternatives.'

The conversation became general again.

Soon after we joined the ladies for tea and some wobbling Mendelssohn from Mrs Porter, who doubtless learned to sing and play and embroider by the time she was six. But that was a long time ago. As our guests departed at half past ten I was struck by Nina's comparative youth and beauty.

As she turned away from the door after bidding goodnight to the last of our guests Nina made a heartbreaking picture. Seen against the black-and-white tiles in the hall her face and shoulders and arms looked so very white, her dress and hair in its chignon black as the rage I could feel dissolving in me together with the angry words I had been saving up all evening. I tried to caress the lovely curve of her neck, but she turned away from me.

'No more songs, Nina? I should have enjoyed it if you had sung for us. Far more than the mechanical warblings of that accomplished scarecrow William has married. You used to sing so spontaneously, for sheer joy, like a nightingale.'

'No more songs,' she repeated in an unfeeling voice before climbing the stairs to her solitary bed.

And I lie here on mine, the couch in my study that is becoming far too familiar. I feel like an uninvited guest in my own house. With night and loneliness come the sour aftertaste of wine and the painful questions I could not ask that drooping, childlike figure in the hall. Once I could say anything to Nina, but now I need to talk about her, to discuss and judge and strive to understand the stranger I am married to. In all of London there are only two people in whom I can confide: her sister, who for all her limitations is a good woman and has known Nina all her life; and William, who most certainly is not a good man but whose devious and ingenious mind might help me out of my predicament.

# HENRIETTA'S JOURNAL

**SATURDAY**

I have not kept a journal since I was fourteen years old and full of spleen against the world. Since then I have wielded a needle more often than a pen, and I ask myself for whom I am writing this. For GOD sees all our thoughts and has no need of written communication. I must confess at the outset that the impulse behind these words is all too human. I write for you, to you, in the foolish hope that one day you will read these words.

This afternoon I could hardly believe it was really your name, mumbled by Rachel so that it sounded like 'dockersudden', and suddenly there you were. You transformed my tiny sitting-room. How many silent hours I have spent here, working away at my embroidery and longing to see you, to talk to you. Now that you were with me I could only stare.

'Are you unwell, Henrietta?' you asked in your dear voice, that some might think brusque but not I, for I know there is a treasure trove of kindness buried in you.

'Only surprised. You have never been here before. Rachel, it is very hot. Fetch Dr Sanderson some seedcake and lemonade.'

Rachel is a dear girl. When she came to me from the workhouse at twelve she could hardly speak for stammering. She said her name was Rat and her mother and father were Don't Know. But I have made a Christian out of her, and as she poured our lemonade she asked in a terrified whisper if I was very ill.

'No, Rachel, I am quite well. But I am afraid my sister is not – is that right, Charles?'

'How quickly you come to the point,' you said with relief. 'In fact, she is simply not. I mean I have not seen her since yesterday morning.'

'She has abandoned you?'

'It seems she left the house yesterday morning at about midday and did not tell the servants where she was going. I fear for her safety – my Nina is such an innocent – yet I fear more for a scandal if I advertise her disappearance.'

'What kind of scandal?'

'Henrietta, you know as well as I how tongues wag, even though my wife is the purest of creatures.'

'I have always thought you tolerate her caprices wonderfully well.'

'Caprices?'

'Come, we have known one another too long to be reserved. You have always indulged my sister's childish whims, her trivial interests and airs and graces. I remember once, seeing her with poor darling Bella, thinking they were like two little girls playing together instead of a mama with her child.'

'Why, Henrietta, I did not know you had so sharp a tongue. Not having had any sisters myself, I thought you loved one another.'

You lay back on my *chaise-longue*, so handsome in your black suit, a glass of lemonade in your hand. You studied me, as if for the first time. I could not sit. Your presence galvanized me. I walked up and down the tiny room as thoughts and feelings I had strangled fought for life.

'I have tried to love her, have prayed that she might change. But Nina and I are so different, it amazes we that we shared the same parents. As a child she was false, simpering, flirtatious –'

'You seem to forget that I knew you both as children. And Nina was a most enchanting child who has grown into a delightful little woman. I am lost without her.'

The adoration in your voice silenced me. I never was adored.

'You must help me, Henrietta. Where can she be? I know she would never willingly leave our happy nest, and who could want to injure my sweet little bird? Come, you know her, is there anything in her past that could explain this disappearance?'

Before your visit I had been sitting contemplating a dismal future. No sweet little bird but a stringy old hen of thirty-three years, dwindling dividends from my railway shares have left me struggling to maintain my tiny rooms in Newington Green. Last year I had to let Lucy go to your household and make do with Rachel, who is more of a charity case than a servant. Even if I moved further outside London, humiliating economies would be necessary. I have begun to study advertisements for governesses, although I have known too many of that victimized regiment to have any illusions about their fate – at best to grow old in genteel poverty in a stranger's house and, at worst, to be the butt of contemptuous insults. I do not wish to live in idleness, but a lady who turns her talents to any profitable use is degraded.

Yet now you were showing me another path. I could be helpful to you and perhaps make friends with my sister at last. I shivered to think that at last I could play a useful part in your life. I would be able to see you more often, and perhaps, if Nina's spiritual condition were very bad, I might even live beneath the same roof as you.

'I hesitate to speak ill of my own sister . . .'

'I ask only for the truth. If you bear bad news I shall not shoot you.'

You sat on the edge of my *chaise-longue*, your knees almost touching mine in the tiny room. I had never before seen your face so close. I gazed into your grey eyes, bloodshot from lack of sleep, with wrinkles in the corners I had never noticed, and saw railway tracks on your brow. You had promised not to shoot me, but Cupid's arrows targeted me when I was fourteen, and it was sweet torture to be alone with you. My heart danced a tarantella, my hands shook, but my voice was steady, as if this was a speech I had learned long ago.

'Nina was always my parents' pet. A kitten with fluffy fur and adorable purrs and sharp claws she kept for me. Of course you adored her. Everybody did. It was only at our school, where souls and brains were more admired than looks, that Nina's charm failed to work.'

'You must have been very jealous.'

The word stung as if you rubbed lemon juice into my flayed skin. 'Of what? Of sly tricks and coquettery and simpering falsity?'

'Was she a coquette? Did she tell falsehoods?'

I felt my power over you like a gas lamp flaring on a foggy day. 'Nina flirted and fibbed from the moment she could talk until that day when you first saw her. Do you remember? We were gathered around the pianoforte in our old parlour and she was singing with our mother, who had long been her slave.'

'It is among my most sacred memories. She wore a white dress with a blue sash and clung to your beautiful mama so tenderly. But I don't remember that you were there, Henrietta.'

'Of course not. I was in the shadows, unwatched, watching. I watched your enslavement over many years, and until you came today I thought you were still worshipping at her tawdry altar.'

'And now? You are not concerned for her safety?'

'I would pity the villain who tried to abduct my sister.' As soon as I had spoken I was ashamed and wished I could staunch the venom that wells up in me.

You stared at me in silence for a long time. I watched you weigh two Ninas, two Henriettas: your darling plaything sat in the scales of your judgement, as on a seesaw, with her double, duplicitous in every sense, opposite her. Beside your two wives you saw the sister-in-law you had always known, heavy, grim and charmless, weighing down the scales against her new and surprising self. Identical in plainness, alas, but very different in spirit and of interest to you for the first time.

Well, my sister is exceeding light. She sprang out of the scales and floated up to your heart. I watched as she possessed you again, like a fickle lodger who has gone off on holiday but returns at last to her old home.

When you left my house an hour ago it was with a reserved and nervous air. You had no use for scales or four different women, you only longed for the one wife you thought you owned. At the door you gave me a look full of suspicion. I have been weighed and found wanting. Wanting you, Charles.

## SUNDAY

Now my words sprawl across the pages for May. This plain brown leather journal was not bought to record thoughts and feelings, and the pages are almost empty for the first months of 1854: committee meetings, prayer meetings and household accounts. I have run ahead of time, I am already writing in June although the May sun illuminates my shabby upholstery and every line in my face.

Today I placed an advertisement in The Thunderer, since you had refused to do so. Mrs S— of H— Street could only be recognized by a handful of people. Naturally, I don't wish to draw attention to my sister's disappearance but to help to find her. I sent Rachel with a note to enquire if Nina had returned.

## MONDAY

This morning James brought a note to say that my sister has reappeared. It was raining, but I crossed London at once to call on her. Arriving very wet and anxious, I was told by an embarrassed Lucy that Mrs Sanderson was indisposed. I looked up at the drawn blinds on the bedroom window and back at the face of Lucy, whom I have known since she first came to work in my house as a grubby child of twelve.

'I am not some old dowager to be fibbed to.'

'I'm not fibbing, ma'am.' Lucy was near to tears, for I have told her what happened to false witnesses. She spends enough time in the kitchen for hellfire and griddles to be very real to her.

'Where is the child?'

'Master Tommy is in the nursery, ma'am.'

I longed to storm your house, to question Nina and educate Tommy and bring you the spiritual succour of which, I sensed, you were in so much need. Lucy stood there like a guppy, her mouth open as if she were terrified of me. In fact, it was I who felt afraid, of your family fortress that excluded me. I let Lucy close the front door on me and stood for a moment on the pavement, gazing up at the rows of blank windows as I thought how far you have come since you were our father's assistant.

The omnibus was cramped and muddy, and when I returned to my poky rooms they seemed to have shrunk. The *chaise-longue* you sat on a few days ago shines in my dismal parlour.

Nina replied to my notes with unsisterly reserve, and I still do not know what really happened.

TUESDAY

There is a rookery near by where I try to be of use, bringing soup and good advice into the lives of those less fortunate than myself. I do not feel very fortunate just now, so it is a salutary reminder of my relative prosperity to visit families who live ten to a room without any drainage or sanitation.

This morning I spent an hour with Mrs Jenks (a courtesy Mrs, I fear), trying to persuade her that seven children are more than enough and that, having foolishly conceived an eighth, she had much better leave it at the foundling hospital where it will be properly cared for and brought up. The woman was most ungrateful and called me an interfering old c—w and threatened to trample me to pieces if I 'come canting into our court again'. She is not a bad but an ignorant woman. I left her some pamphlets on abstinence and temperance and a copy of the Bible. She and her so-called husband cannot read, but perhaps one of their verminous brood will acquire an education some day.

The Misses Devirill-Prendergasts (a long name for two short dumpy ladies) have organized a Fancy Fair to raise money for the Missionary Society. They hope to raise as much as a thousand pounds, and I am kept busy with their committee meetings. Well, it is better to wear out than to rust. Tonight I am sitting up late, crocheting shawls and working on my patchwork quilt. The one I worked for the Lighten Their Darkness Benevolent Society was sold for three guineas. I am very sensible of my own darkness as I sit alone by my fire. I wonder if I should go to Africa as a missionary instead of to Bath as a governess. Would it not be more rewarding to bring the true faith into the lives of the benighted than to teach creatures of fiddlers and dancing masters how to come into a room and get into a carriage? Whenever I consider leaving London it is the thought of leaving you that I cannot bear. Knowing that you exist in the same city has been a great comfort to me all these long years. Foolishness, of course, but your face etched itself on my heart so long ago that I cannot remove it. Your face, and my heart, grow older.

I know my own face is, if possible, even plainer than it was when I was seventeen and Miss Baker said, 'My dear, if you don't marry you will find that you have on your shoulders half-a-dozen husbands and as many families of children.' There is a freemasonry among plain women. Miss Baker meant, but did not say, that I should get a husband, any husband, no matter how old or ugly or beastly, rather than slave away teaching spiteful girls as she had done all her life. She knew too well that it is the lot of unmarried daughters to perform cheerless duties and watch by thankless sickbeds until they fade into querulous and disappointed old age. Who was it that nursed our parents in their final illnesses? Not my frivolous sister.

### FRIDAY

I knew you would come to me again, my prince, but did not think that it would be so soon. This time you came before breakfast. When I heard the bell I thought you were the baker's boy. When Rachel showed you in I was still in my old grey dressing-gown, but I don't suppose you noticed what I was wearing. Your handsome face was shrouded with anxiety, and your hand was cold despite the warm sun outside. You slumped in the chair opposite mine, usually so empty, and refused all refreshment except black coffee. Then you pushed a package at me across the table with a helpless gesture that made me long to embrace you. I did not, of course. My arms are so unaccustomed to the feel of another human being that they ignored the wild cries of my heart and went on buttering my toast.

'I want you to read this, Henrietta. It's a letter Nina wrote to me after her . . . disappearance. It seems to me quite unbalanced, but I can't separate my medical opinion from my private sentiments.'

Eagerly, I tore open the envelope, but you put out your hand to prevent me. You cannot know, I don't wish you to know, how your touch disturbs me.

'Don't read it until I have gone.'

'Is my sister . . . you think her insane?'

'She is so changed that I hardly know how to describe her. You must see her and judge for yourself.'

'I have called several times and have sent her notes, but she has made it very clear she does not wish to see me.'

'Don't be angry, Henrietta.'

'I always try to forgive, to submit cheerfully to the evils of life. But this is not the first time she has rebuffed me. When poor little Bella died Nina refused to let me near her. I only wanted to ensure the child had a beautiful death.'

'Nina was distraught. Naturally. She objected to being told to rejoice at such a time.'

'Bella had gone to a better world. I felt joy as well as sorrow as her innocent spirit winged its way to Heaven.'

'However, we were so grateful to you for taking Tommy away.'

'Grateful? Were you? But he was not. When I told him his sister was safe with Jesus he howled and shouted that Jesus should give her back and get his own sister. Really, Charles, the child seems to have had no religious instruction whatsoever. Perhaps I should begin my career as a missionary in Harley Street.'

'Are you going to be a missionary? What an extraordinary woman you are! I can just picture you keeping the cannibals in order.'

'"Care to our coffin adds a nail no doubt / While every laugh so many, draws one out,"' I said, hurt by his levity. 'I am glad my misfortune amuses you.'

'Oh dear – I didn't realize – are you short of cash?'

'Uninterrupted prosperity is not the lot of man. Or woman.'

'Not my lot either, unfortunately, otherwise I'd help. What about your railway shares? In the old Worse and Worse, weren't they?'

'I sold them a few years ago. At the wrong time, it seems. Whenever I go to Oxford, Worcester or Wolverhampton I feel quite indignant, as if those cities had robbed me.'

'Poor Henrietta.'

Your sympathy brought shameful tears to my eyes. 'Yes, I must work hard in the Lord's vineyards. A governess in Bath or a missionary in Bulawayo – that, it seems, is to be my fate.'

'We shall miss you.'

'I don't believe Nina will miss me one little bit.'

'She is very ill, Henrietta. Not physically, perhaps, but . . . that is really why I have come today. Last night we had a dinner party and her behaviour was . . . most singular. She has some delusion about the future – that she has been there – you will understand better when you have read this.' You tapped the bulging envelope propped up against my teapot and gazed at me, hurt and puzzled.

'She has always been eccentric, but I had no idea she was actually . . .'

'Her grief over darling Bella's death may have brought on some temporary derangement. In a few months, quite possibly, she will be herself again.'

'How can I help, Charles?' Behind your eyes I glimpsed a desperate man.

'I was going to ask if you would come to stay. Just until Nina is better. Our household is in disorder. Tommy is quite out of control, the servants do as they please, and I'm afraid of driving away the patients I have and discouraging new ones. It will hardly be a holiday for you, but it would make my life so much easier if I knew a woman of sense was under our roof.'

You have never before asked me for a favour. I have always been the beggar at your gate, silently longing for the alms of your attention. Now I held it, and Bath and Bulawayo receded as I tried to restrain my joy.

'Perhaps we might attempt this domestic experiment. For a short period.'

'I should be so grateful. One cannot put a price on such help and, in fact . . . my finances are not . . .'

'I shan't expect any payment, Charles.'

'How wonderfully selfless you are.'

My self roared like a hungry tigress. If my sister has lost her self I think I have found mine for the first time. No, there was a brief period in early childhood when I felt beloved and at peace. I know what paradise is, for I lived there for five years until my serpent sister was born. You were subdued, so I tried to look and sound less jubilant than I felt. 'I am deeply conscious of my deficiencies, but I shall attempt to be of service.'

'How soon can you come to us?'

'Perhaps . . . would Friday morning be convenient?'

'The sooner you come, the longer you stay, the happier I shall be. Now, I must go. I have a patient to visit in Cavendish Square, and I cannot be absent from home for too long or the household will fall into anarchy.'

'Poor Charles. What a trial this year has been for you.' I went to the front door with you. On the doorstep you kissed me. A chaste kiss, on the brow, but still the first kiss you have ever given me.

'I am so grateful to you, Henrietta. You are the only one in whom I can confide.'

I watched you into the hackney cab you had kept waiting, and when I returned to my sitting-room I was shaking so much that I could hardly pour myself a cup of tea.

## SATURDAY

I have read it. My sister's spiritual state is very grave. During those lost days Nina writes of so strangely, what was the extent of her intimacy with this Jonathan? I understand now why you are distraught. Dearest Charles! In my imagination I see such scenes between us – I dare not write of them, even here.

But I must not be fanciful. 'Tis Fancy that has ruined my foolish sister. It was no great shock to hear from you that she is worse than foolish, for I always knew her for a whore, from the first moment she sucked my mother's nipple and seduced her away from me. She stole you, too, but not for ever, for you have come to me at last.

As Miss Amelia used to warn us when we were children, if you want to become weak-headed, nervous and good for nothing, read novels. My sister haunted the circulating library, and when she was fifteen I even caught her reading George Sand. I told our father, but he only laughed and said I was a prig and that Nina should be a free citizen in the world of books.

The only novel I have ever felt able to read with a clear conscience was Hannah More's beautiful offering *Coelebs in Search of a Wife*. I read it first when I was sixteen, when the coincidence that the hero, so full of admirable qualities, is called Charles, seemed most fateful. Eventually he sees through Miss Flams and Miss Rattle, who read only bosh and study only music and whim-whams, and learns to appreciate the intellectual worth of Lucilla. 'How intelligent her silence! How well bred her attention!' Nightingales sing but are of no further use. Women such as Lucilla may not be decorative, but we are practical and sensible and may be entrusted with the spiritual life of a family.

Well, it is only a story. Now at last I have my own story, and it grows more interesting by the moment. In a few hours I shall be beneath your roof, not as a despised poor relation but as a valued confidante. I must discover the truth about my slyboots sister. Can it really be that she had some form of criminal conversation with this fellow? I will draw out Lucy on the matter. Rachel will accompany me, and I shall pump her for the servants' gossip.

My mother used to say, if you want to know the truth about a marriage, ask the servants. She had a dreadfully *louche* way of talking of such things; indeed it was her indelicacy that led me to reject her Catholic faith. From the age of eleven I refused to go to church with her on Sundays. But my sister always went and later made a great fuss about her first communion, looking like a little meringue in her ridiculous white frock and veil. The two of them used to sneak off together for their nasty foreign rites. For all I know Nina goes to confession still, and she would appear to have a great deal to confess to.

# CHARLES

A MOST ILLUMINATING conversation with William. I carved a couple of hours out of my frantic afternoon to visit him in Hanover Square. As soon as I entered his magnificent hallway I felt the contrast between our lives: his flunkeys grovel convincingly; his marble floors and classical busts are genuine, not veneer; and his wife and children are enviably invisible. By the time the butler had shown me up to his library (designed by Adam, first editions of Johnson's *Rasselas* and Byron's *Childe Harold*) I was distinctly green. But William is still a charmer, and my meanness of spirit soon dissolved in his warmth and fine Madeira.

'The boys are away at school, and Emily is in the country,' he explained when I marvelled at his domestic peace. 'And how is your own dear wife, Charles?'

'Sadly reduced. She grieves for our little one, which is natural, and still raves about the future, which is not.'

'Poor lady. Is she being well nursed?'

'My sister-in-law has kindly agreed to stay with us.'

'So you now live with two beautiful ladies!'

'Not at all. Henrietta does not resemble her sister. She is over thirty, faded and worn, but she is extremely practical.'

'That must be a great comfort.'

'To me, most certainly. I naturally have no aptitude for domestic duties, which are the realm of women. Now that Henrietta rules our household my son stays in his nursery and meals arrive on time. But Nina is mightily huffed.'

'The two sisters do not . . . ?'

'Can't bear each other. Henrietta is a spinster, a monstrous prig but a great organizer. She has always been jealous of her younger, prettier sister and lives in fear of the ghastly genteel fate of being a governess. The poor creature fancies herself in love with me, but I take no notice.'

William roared with laughter. 'My dear chap, you have a harem in Harley Street. But why should she be a governess? Are they not from a wealthy family? I thought you would marry some great heiress with your lady-killing looks.'

William stared at me, and I recalled drunken late-night conversations long ago when we both vowed to get on in the world. He did, looking past an unfortunate nose to a great fortune. 'Nina had but three thousand *pour tout potage*. Her papa was a doctor in Finsbury Square, too kind-hearted to prosper much.'

'Three thousand?'

'And that is all gone now.'

'My dear Charles, you should have struck a better bargain than that. I remember Mrs Porter's papa wouldn't come down with more than six thousand, but my governor said it shouldn't be done under eight. I could have had a baronet's daughter, a woman as tall and whiskery as a grenadier with ten thousand, but I felt that Emily's social accomplishments were worth a great deal. Three thousand! You should have come to me sooner.'

'Thank goodness I have come now.'

And, indeed, after a couple of glasses I felt that William was my dearest friend. It was immensely cheering to recall our student days and the scrapes we got into. We chanted together the old ditty:

> Should a body want a body
> Anatomy to teach,
> Should a body snatch a body,
> Need a body peach?

We were soon quite helpless with laughter, recollecting Sir Astley and his unconventional experiments.

'And the elephant!' I gasped. 'Did you ever hear about Sir Astley and the elephant?'

'No, old boy, tell me the one about the elephant.'

'The elephant died in the menagerie at the Tower. Mr Cooper (as he was then, before George IV knighted him for removing a tumour from his scalp) naturally wanted to obtain the beast's body. Pa helped him to hire a cart and covered the dead elephant with a cloth. I think my father would have done anything for him, in the interests of Science. I think he would have dissected the Holy Ghost to please him. Don't tell Henrietta I said that. Well, the elephantine corpse was so heavy that the cart had to be left in front of the great surgeon's house at St Mary Axe. A crowd collected outside the gates, and Mr C— had to dissect the animal in the open air with a carpet thrown over the railings to hide him.

'Didn't his neighbours complain about his activities?'

'Not a bit of it. Everybody was charmed by Sir Astley. I loved to visit his house. You might say my medical education began there. My father brought me up to live by Sir Astley's motto: "Be kind to everyone and most active to oblige".'

'And did he oblige you, when the time to choose a career?'

'Up to a point. I would have liked to become a surgeon, but one had to pay a premium of fifty guineas to become a dresser and Sir Astley preferred to help his godson and his nephews. Well-connected boobies all of them. How I seethed with envy. He told me to try my luck in the army, the navy or the provinces.'

'Never mind. Here you are, twenty years later, a distinguished medical man in the best part of London.'

Not wishing to gloat over achievements that felt distinctly shaky, I returned to the past. 'Yes, what an amazing fellow he was. He was a great friend of the Lord Mayor, you know, who assured him he wouldn't be bothered by constables if he occasionally stored a corpse or two in his attic. Henry, Sir Astley's butler, stole dogs which were kept in the attic for experiments. He paid us boys two shillings and sixpence per dog.'

'You must have had a rather more entertaining childhood than I did, growing up in Tunbridge Wells with a parson for a father.'

'Ah, but your family was respectable. Being motherless, I accompanied my father everywhere. There were no toys at home, but I was allowed to play with the bones in Sir Astley's private museum. He had Napoleon's gut, you know. I adored his museum. All my life I have wanted to assemble my own. As a birthday treat Pa would take me to Don Saltero's Coffee House at Cheyne Walk, near the Chelsea Bun shop. Did you ever see Don Saltero's museum, William? I wonder if it still exists. It was founded by a servant of Sir Hans Sloane. How I loved that place! There one could see Pontius Pilate's wife's chambermaid's straw hat and a largish chunk of manna from Canaan. I longed to eat it. I was sure it would be even more delicious than a Chelsea bun.'

'When we were students I was deeply impressed by your medical knowledge. Now I know how you acquired it. Do you remember the lengths we had to go to to obtain the three cadavers required for our training?'

'Yes, medical students nowadays have too easy a time of it. Do you remember the trick we played on that drunkard in Aldersgate? How we wrapped him up in a sack and left him with the porter outside Bart's, who remarked that there were complaints issuing from the package?'

'Of course I remember. And that evening we had on the razzle after we sold the teeth your father claimed to have procured on the battlefield of Waterloo to that dentist in Berkeley Square! How picturesque London was then in the days of the Resurrection men, not like our quiet, dull old town. Plate-glass windows and gas lights, not to mention the Anatomy Act, have put paid to all the romance.'

I kept quiet about some of my other, less romantic memories and looked admiringly around his library. 'How far you have come, William, since we walked the wards together.'

'All built on feminine weaknesses. Bless the dear little ladies, for they are only fit for love. And when love goes awry, as it generally does, they come to me.'

'What exactly is it that you do to help them?'

'I very soon realized that bodily aches and pains are only manifestations of sicknesses of the soul. And the soul, in women, is always
amorous. Men are less inclined to resort to physic for every passing
ailment, for we have less time and opportunity for doing so, from the
greater vigour of our constitution and a more nourishing diet. Our
nervous system is less excitable and our moral sensibility is less acute.'

'And what do you prescribe for these broken-hearted females
who besiege you?'

William bestowed his warm and cynical smile on me. The smile
that has launched a thousand bank drafts. 'Why, Charles, each case is
different. Thomas Aquinas tells us that woman is a misbegotten male.
Overstimulation of the female brain causes nervousness, hysteria,
difficult childbirth, inflammation of the brain – how they suffer, the
poor little darlings. Sometimes it is enough to recommend Porter's
Balm of Elysium (five shillings and sixpence) and Porter's Electric Belt
(two guineas, old chap!) – as part of my patent cure. Erotomania is so
often the result of disappointment in love. Other ladies, particularly
young unmarried ones, require help disposing of their little mistakes, and such help does not come cheaply. Sponges, pessaries,
douches – the armies of Cupid require an arsenal of weapons. No pun
intended.'

I laughed none the less, torn between disapproval and envy. Two
guineas for a few pieces of elastic and a couple of wires in a fancy
box!

'And does your wife permit these intimacies with other women?'

'My wife has milliner's and dressmaker's bills like any other. She
does not interfere with my work. But this is too much about me. Tell
me about your work, Charles.'

'There's not much to tell. I see patients, attend committee meetings and generally do a great deal for other people for very little pay.'

'And are you satisfied?'

'No!' I shouted with a vehemence that surprised me.

'I am sorry to hear it. I know you are honest and hard-working and married for love, whereas I –'

'You are the happiest man I know.'

'I would like to help you. I wonder, could I put you up for my club? Meeting the right people can make all the difference. The ladies are always eager to talk about their amorous problems, but gentleman also confide after two or three brandies. '

'I scarcely have time to go to a club.' I didn't want to admit that I can't pay this year's subscription to my own shabby little club let alone the exorbitant cost of William's Pall Mall mansion.

'I hesitate to intrude where angels fear to tread, not that I have ever seen myself as an angel. I mean one ought not to ask too many questions about a fellow's marriage . . .'

'Go on. You seem to be an expert on every other marriage in London.'

'Well then, Mrs Sanderson's delusions, are they foolish fancies or something more serious?'

'She has written a long account of the days she claims to have spent in the remote future. You may read it if you wish.'

'I should be fascinated. And how do we get on? The human race, I mean.'

'We flourish, apparently. Money and war are to be abolished, differences between the sexes also. We are all to wear bloomers –'

'Marvellous! The ladies of the future will have no need of me.'

'They are quite Amazonian. They work as doctors and even prime ministers –'

'A female Gladstone! In bloomers and a bonnet, of course. I'm so sorry, Charles, I should not make light of your wife's misfortune. How does she react to her ejection from this utopia?'

'Very badly. She seems to feel quite an aversion to me. Instead of her former modest and respectable demeanour her behaviour has become most odd, as you saw yourself at dinner the other night. She says my face has become a mask, and she will not be polite to callers.

I have told her to rest, but on Monday I found her attempting to escape the house to go on a solitary walk. She displays great irregularities of temper, and, although I have warned her again and again that she must rest her brain and have tried to confiscate her journal and sketchpad and books, she disobeys me and still spends much time in writing and drawing and serious reading. Yesterday I found her with a volume of Kant.'

'Let us hope she has studied him well. Kant warned that a woman who escapes from the natural domination of father and husband might become a dangerous rebel and revolutionary. Or, as Hegel would say, without the family there is only the mob. Women and children must, of course, be totally dependent.'

'Yes, but she has got it into her noddle –'

'Charles, a woman's noddle is no place for philosophy. Nature has made women more like children in order that they might better understand children. You must be firm with her. Home is the appointed scene of women's labour, the shop window for their unselfish love and cheerful industry. Women have neither heart nor head for abstract political or philosophical speculation. Such matters may be safely left to men.'

'I don't know what to do, William.'

'You have come to me with your troubles, and that is the very best thing you could have done. Now tell me more. You say you have known your wife since childhood. Was she restless, excited and stubborn at puberty?'

'It always seemed to me she was the most enchanting and delightful child, and when she was a young girl I was in love with her. I found no fault with her until this event – her disappearance – she was gone for three days.'

'And you really have no idea where she went?'

'No,' I whispered, ashamed to confess my inability to control my wife. 'But in this letter she speaks of a fellow called Jonathan –'

'Aha! So there is another man! Three days! I have come across other cases of seemingly respectable females who escaped from their domestic leash and were ruined. Since her return to the fold, has she suffered from depression or loss of appetite?'

'Yes, both. But it is far worse than that. She seems quite another person, sullen and angry and undutiful.'

'Ah yes! The subterranean fires become active and smoke and flames gush forth.'

'We are discussing my wife, not Mount Etna.'

'It is the same thing, my dear fellow. Is there any hereditary disposition to insanity?'

'Her mother was a very kind lady but somewhat eccentric. Italian by birth, a Catholic –'

'Tainted foreign blood, no doubt. That would make your poor wife more susceptible to evil influences, more easily unbalanced. Her vital powers are depressed. She has been deranged by the death of your little girl and suffers from delusions. A clear case of moral insanity. We must act, Charles.'

'But what action can I take?'

'I assume you don't have enough money to divorce her? Any court would accept her criminal conversation with this man as justified grounds for divorce.'

'How much?'

'At least seven hundred pounds.'

'It is more than I earn in a year!'

'My poor fellow. Then we must find another way. Do you wish her to be cared for at home or in an institution?'

'But – this is so sudden – I do not feel I have the right –'

'You have every right. We physicians are the guardians of women's interests and the custodians of their honour. They are weak, and we are strong.'

I fell silent. I was bewildered by the solution to my domestic chaos he dangled before me (and more than a little drunk). William's voice boomed on, offering me a lifeboat into which I longed to jump.

'It's really quite a simple matter. You remember Bob Jenkins and Richard Temple? We were students together. They've made a great success of the mad business. They'll come to your house and interview your wife – only a formality, of course – and sign a certificate. You could find a keeper to look after her at home, but it would be difficult for your son, not to mention you, and your patients might get to hear of it. Some of the private asylums around Hoxton are good, but they are rather expensive, so if you're strapped for cash you should send her to the Royal Bethlem. I hear that Dr Hood has worked marvels there and has turned it into quite a palace. He will only expect a small premium.'

Thank you, I mouthed, but words failed me as I felt I had failed Nina. I could never have done this to her, but it was being done for me. I had only to allow it to happen. And, after all, the woman it was happening to was not really my Nina at all.

Our mood became more jovial again until William's magnificent Jacobean grandfather clock struck five, and I realized I was due for tea with Lady B— in fifteen minutes.

'Do give her my regards. And ask her how her husband's little problem is. She will know to what I allude.'

I tried to look stern but found myself laughing instead. For all our greying hair and professional gravitas I felt that we were still students and could not resist quoting Thomas Hood's ditty in a shrill falsetto before I left:

> 'The cock it crows – I must be gone;
> My William we must part;
> But I'll be yours in death, altho'
> Sir Astley has my heart.'

I left William's house shaking with laughter. Yet by the time I turned the corner of Hanover Square my mood had changed. I felt a wave of anger against Nina, a cold wave that washed me out of

William's lifeboat and left me floundering again in the treacherous currents of love.

As I stared at the chaotic traffic and blank passing faces of Oxford Street I thought how my wife, my Nina, must have passed here on that summer morning, dressed in her mourning weeds. Some heartless villain with smiling face and genteel clothes must have accosted her. Must have told her some brazen lie or artful subterfuge and lured her to a house or hotel where – tears obscured my outer vision, but my inner eye ruthlessly narrated the scene.

My darling, naïve girl follows him upstairs – perhaps she has been drugged or rendered unconscious with chloroform. In the dark he steals from me the most precious . . . when a woman has lost that inestimable jewel, her virtue, she can never be the same again. Hours later she must have woken in the dark beside him and have concocted her ridiculous tale from fear of what she had done. It was done to her, but she let it happen. Did she feel pleasure or only shame? The man who ruined her should die.

There, on the corner of Oxford Street, I experienced a moment when, as Byron says, the Fates change horses. My jealousy was so violent that I felt dizzy. I vomited there where I stood in the filthy street, stooped in helplessness like some repulsive old drunkard. Out spewed William's Madeira, my boyish adoration of Nina, my bitter grief for Bella and my medical ideals, to mingle with the foul ordure of horse dung, rotting vegetables and rotten humanity. I was no longer standing on the banks of the river of life but floundering in it. My mouth tasted of death, and death was on my mind when I was able stand up straight again.

I wished I could kill this Jonathan. I have asked Nina a thousand times where he lives, but she only weeps and points to the other side of our wall, where the horses are stabled. If I could find him I would gladly challenge him to a duel. However absurd, there would be satisfaction in such a death. Honour is the word that boomed in my head like a gong summoning me to judgement. My wife has been dishonoured and since I cannot find the blackguard I must punish her.

For a second I saw Nina's corpse sprawled on the *chaise-longue* where she spends her days now, still dressed in her mourning clothes. Mourning Bella and our love and her own death. I could see it quite clearly, the useless doll in the long black dress with the necklace of red marks upon its waxen neck. I knew whose fingers had put them there. My murdered wife floated above the sordid street, as vivid as the poster advertising Dr Kahn's Anatomical Museum in Piccadilly.

Then the horrid phantom passed. I reached in my pocket for my little tin of peppermints and sucked one to sweeten my breath and my temper. My pocket-watch warned me that I was already late for tea with Lady B—. I looked around me, suddenly terrified that a patient or servant might have witnessed my vile weakness. With time, reason returned and opened her arms to me again. Reason is a plain, churchy sort of creature, rather like Henrietta. There was not much comfort in her embrace, but I felt safer.

To argue that Nina must die because she has deceived me is the argument of the sultan who sends the erring inmate of his harem on her last sail on the Bosporus. Besides, I am not a sultan and should hang for it. Yet if she is not to die, what is to be done with her? I cannot live with such a wife.

Foul thoughts emanated from the cesspit of Oxford Street. Within minutes I had reached the privacy of Wimpole Street, and my mood became more serene and dignified. I am more and more convinced that our actions are determined as much by our surroundings, health and the weather as by our principles. My conversation with William has made it very clear to me how feeble my principles are.

In Lady B—'s drawing-room beautiful ideas shone like the chandeliers, and the most violent topic was the elopement of Miss Barrett. Here, a scandal titillates for at least a quarter of a century, and I have no wish to become gossip fodder. As I bowed over her ladyship's hand I murmured my apologies and mentioned William's name.

'Ah, the charming Dr Porter.' Her horsey, languid face was as animated as I have ever seen it.

'He sends his respects. And enquires after Lord Bingham's little problem.'

It was as if a secret panel had sprung open in the stolid mahogany of her dark eyes. I glimpsed amusement, even a grotesque flirtatiousness. Her arthritic fingers, encrusted with rings, pumped her fan so vigorously that I felt the draught and more: the engine of her repressed life. 'I did not know that you and Dr Porter work together.'

'We are very old friends.'

'And do you bring me anything from him?'

An electric belt? Porter's Balm of Elysium?

'Next time, your ladyship.'

I'm sure I didn't imagine the change in her manner towards me. We doctors are considered parvenus in these very grand houses, where I am still often shown to the tradesmen's entrance. But this afternoon I progressed from local doctor to initiate into some kind of freemasonry. The other guests, who had ignored me at first, also defrosted, and I was passed around the drawing-room like a muffin. They all complained of their arthritis and their gout. Only people of family can have bona fide gout.

I left the house with the distinct impression that William's name was an 'open sesame' that will unlock many doors formerly slammed in my face. The last of my doubts about treating sexual hypochondria dissolved between Cavendish Square and Harley Street. A man ought not throw away such a chance of extending his practice.

Henrietta's regime has brought many improvements, but I find her insistence on daily family prayers rather a trial. We are commanded to gather before supper so that Tommy can improve his soul, which is apparently in disrepair. Tonight he came into the drawing-room, which now doubles as a chapel, very sulky, tugged by Emma. The servants followed more willingly, no doubt pleased to rest from their duties for an hour (although I would not say that the sound of

Henrietta preaching is exactly restful; her voice is so very scratchy, and she is on such embarrassingly intimate terms with God). Nina was the last to join us, after Lucy had been sent to fetch her from her room.

It was the first time I had seen my wife all day, and I was struck by her mutinous air. In the past, Nina often reminded me of Tennyson's Princess: 'A rosebud set with little wilful thorns, / And sweet as English air could make her.' The thorns are growing like beanstalks, and her sweetness is but a memory now.

Since I showed Henrietta Nina's extraordinary letter to me her disapproval has been very obvious. The little sister seems diminished, disappearing into silence and gloom, while the big sister expands and fills our house. I sometimes feel these prayer meetings are a gladiatorial contest between the two women. My wife cannot win this battle. I watch her nightly punishment and do not intervene.

I am, as Henrietta constantly reminds me, the head of a Christian household. She pushes the Bible under my nose and points to the passage I am to read from St Paul: 'Wives, submit yourselves unto your own husbands, as it is fit in the Lord.' My own upbringing was cheerfully heathen, but I try to read as if the passage were familiar to me. I am learning that religion, like electrical belts, can be a social asset. My voice stumbles over the unfamiliar words, and I really have no idea what I am saying. I try to say it in a suitably Sunday voice.

Henrietta removes the Bible and strides purposefully over to the piano. She does not so much walk with Christ as strut with Him. Her skirts balloon over the piano stool as she indicates that we are to sing:

> Trust no forms of guilty passion –
> Fiends can look like angels bright;
> Trust no custom, school or fashion –
> Trust in God and do the right.

Our singing is ragged, and I am not familiar with the tune. Nina does not sing at all and Tommy, I observe with shame, makes uncouth noises, raspberries as we used to call them when we were urchins. It really is time he was sent away to school. If, as Henrietta claims, our family has become a 'little church', there is no doubt who are the sheep and who the shepherdess. She does not wield her crook lightly.

After the hymns the soul searching begins. Despite Lady B—'s excellent simnel cake I long for supper, and my stomach groans and rumbles as Henrietta's voice improves us. I worry that Cook, who is yawning beside Emma, will not have had time to prepare the food. Henrietta, as if reading my mind, warns us not be too entangled in the world. I long to become entangled with a lamb chop and a jam roly-poly.

'You cannot have two sets of conscience,' Henrietta sternly rebukes us. We all look guilty except Nina, who stares back at her sister with hard blue eyes. I used to compare her eyes to celestial pools, but now they remind me of broken shards of sapphire glass. Arrogantly, Henrietta drones on about submission and obedience. Why do we permit these spiritual insults? I suppose they are the wages of her virtue.

'The self must be denounced and laid in dust.' There would be more dust if she were not in the house. Henrietta's long nose twitches as she prepares to sniff out our faults. Nina grows more pale and looks so beautiful I almost reach out to her across the red-and-green acres of carpet. Once, on this same carpet, we used to read poetry aloud to each other when the children were in bed. I would stand behind Nina while she sat at the piano singing Italian songs about love. Some-where in our old pianoforte those songs lie curled and shrivelled, listening to the hymns that have supplanted them. Nina's hair is very soft, and the curve of her neck at the back, where the fine black wisps curl, always reminds me of a . . . I was going to say, of an alabaster carving of a tree, but, no, it is the human flesh that is so touching.

Henrietta does not care for flesh. She turns on Nina and demands that she unbosom herself, pronouncing the word 'bosom' with distaste. Her own are so very flat. I wonder if she uses a rolling-pin on them.

Suddenly there is a flash in the glooming room. Nina's temper illuminates the fog that has seeped in from the street or out from our brains.

'Yes, Henrietta, I'll open my heart to you. A bleeding heart, like the one Mama had on the wall of her bedroom. Shall I take my dress off so you can see it properly? Or serve it to you on a dish?'

Henrietta blushes and looks away as Nina, to my horror, starts to undo her dress. Tommy cries drearily, the servants exchange glances and titter. I am supposed to do something, to preside over this prayer meeting that has turned into a bear garden, but I cannot bear to touch my wife. I indicate to Lucy that she should remove Nina.

Henrietta sits down to punish the piano, and there is another hymn. I don't know the words, but I open my mouth and look pious. Henrietta is the only person in the room who is actually singing, her husky contralto would be pleasant if it were not for her intonation of dreadful certainty.

'Content to live but not afraid to die . . .' Oh, but I am. And, when I do, a vast stone monument and at least four coffins will pin me down.

Without Nina the ceremony comes smoothly to an end and we are at last allowed to eat. As I rush into the dining-room with undignified haste I overhear an argument between Tommy and Henrietta on the stairs.

'I don't want to say any more prayers. I should think God has heard enough from me today. He wants to listen to a new little boy.'

'Now, Tommy, you cannot go to bed without saying your prayers. You must do all you can to make your little mind-house good and beautiful.'

'Your aunt is quite right, Tommy,' I call out, pouring a glass of Bordeaux to drink with my oxtail soup. 'Your aunt is always right.'

And, indeed, by the time Henrietta sits down at the table the good food – better since she sacked our old cook – has restored my cheerfulness. 'Thank you so much for managing Tommy, my dear. For managing all of us. I never knew the household run so smooth.'

'A man has no business to meddle in the management of his house. You are the nobler sex. You should return from your toil to a quiet, happy home.'

I wipe my mouth with my napkin and try to look noble. 'Nina was not always able to –'

'Ah, Nina! I'm afraid there is another problem –'

I groan. 'Let me eat my pudding before I hear of it, please.'

When I have eaten the last crumb of an excellent apple pie Henrietta hands me a green leather folder. 'I did not want to bother you but felt you should see these very singular drawings your wife – my sister – has made.'

After Lucy has removed our plates I lay out Nina's sketches upon the dining-table.

I see at once that they are the products of a diseased mind. Angular towers loom over a wide road where bizarre carriages move as if by magic. No horses are to be seen. The road is serpentine, winding in and out of the towers in a most improbable fashion. More disturbing is the population of Nina's phantastic metropolis. Females – for I cannot call them ladies – are very scantily attired, like ragged beggarmaids, with brazen faces and hideous coiffure. Gentlemen, or at least the males of this degenerate species, are also semi-naked, exhibiting their limbs like navvies. It is as if the Resurrection men had dug up graves and flung out the still-warm bodies of benighted criminals. Shameless, vicious, godless, they leer and strut, not yet dead but clearly incapable of civilized life. There is in these savage faces a lack of refinement, a want of delicacy, that makes me wince and turn away. I shudder as I remember that these are the very people Nina admired and regarded as the prize at the finishing line of the March of Progress. I force myself to confront this painful evidence of my wife's moral insanity.

'Charles? Are you feeling faint?'

Henrietta pours me a glass of brandy and stands over me anxiously. Close up, she exudes an aroma of camphor and sweat that is most unenticing. Nina used to smell of lavender and hope, and her skin was soft, so soft, perhaps because she had been kept in cotton wool. But for all her personal unattractiveness Henrietta has been a staunch friend in these last terrible weeks.

I must stop being sentimental about Nina, for it does no good. She has murdered our marriage and has almost murdered me.

# JONATHAN

A T THE WEEKEND, when I don't have to go to work, it's so hard to wake up. This morning my dreams flowed into the morning, leaving a tide-mark of fractured memory. Last night Nina stared at me through the wall with huge, sad eyes. When I walked over to reach out my arms to her the wall became opaque again, and she disappeared.

I struggle out of bed, make coffee and stagger over to my desk. There is always work to be done, emails to be sent and answered, and I would rather do it than face the void of another lonely Saturday. I switch on my iMac, cheered by the optimistic chime it greets me with, press 'connect' and wish it would – connect me, I mean, with the world out there, with who I was when I was married to Kate and who I might become when I find someone new with whom I can share my life. I have a virtual social life, of course – twelve new emails, a white twelve dancing on a stamp, proclaim my virtual popularity.

Most of them are about work. I sip my coffee and read about the progress of the shopping mall in Dubai and the right-to-light issues of the clinic in Grimsby. They aren't great monuments, but they will function and stand up. I'm never going to build the romantic follies I once dreamed of, but neither is anyone else. These are commercial products for the global market, and I do at least have work at a time when many architects are unemployed. I earn enough to pay the mortgage on my garret (Nina!) and Ben's school fees. I still don't see why he can't go to the local state primary school, but I don't want to argue with Kate. We've argued enough. I'm just so glad that Ben is going to stay at home instead of being abandoned in a Gulag as I was at seven.

Replying to my colleagues, I use the bland language of professional friendship: 'Hi'; 'Cheers'; 'Best'. This used to be 'best wishes', but that was too specific, so now we just order each other to enjoy the best while having a nice day. We could even see each other on our computer screens, but I wouldn't want anybody to see me this morning. The seediness of solitude is creeping over me like moss; I'm sitting here wearing an ancient blue jersey full of holes, and the purple-and-green striped silk trousers I rashly bought in Dubai last month when I went to inspect the site. I haven't combed my hair or had a shower since yesterday, and when I glimpsed my eyes just now in the bathroom mirror they were bloodshot and disorientated.

I have a message from Dreamgirlocean42. A few weeks ago I registered with an online dating agency, bliss.com. I was sitting here one morning, unlovely and unloved, when a spam message drifted across my screen. Soft-focus images of a couple showering together and floating through a meadow hand in hand hid my plans for a waiting area with disability access.

I despised myself for being seduced by this corn, but it turns out there are twenty million of us. The population of a small country: Desolationland. We are spread across the globe, we will pay ten quid a month and go a long way for that shared shower. The ghost of a village matchmaker falls on my bright white screen with advice for long-distance dates: book your own hotel; get a taxi to and from the airport; don't leave your drink unattended. I'm not looking further afield than London. There are 237 other Jonathans also looking for love, so I have taken Optimistlondon as my *nom d'amour* or *nom de guerre*. I'm a cowardly warrior. I wait for women to contact me and then take pleasure in ignoring them. I have already been rebuked by cyberCupid: What are you waiting for, Optimistlondon?

I open Dreamgirlocean42's message. She is feisty (not another one!), funky, yet sensitive. A surprisingly lovely woman, she claims. I study her unsurprising photo. She suggests meeting for a drink, and I hesitate to reply. There is no scope for hesitation on bliss.com; you are not allowed to draft a reply but have to bang out an instant response. I'll reply before I go to the gym this evening. Annabel might be there. She looks alarmingly rich and glamorous and probably wouldn't be interested in slumming it with me, but she does keep smiling and chatting and doing sexy things with her arms on the adjoining treadmill.

This is a rather long-winded way of reassuring myself that I'm not depressed or mad. I go through this most days now, while staring at Nina's corset in the corner of the room. The cage she opened and stepped out of. It's a formidable structure, metal ribs covered with strips of grubby, coarse linen and a dozen black tapes to squeeze and distort her lovely, slender young body. It smells of sweat and decay and coal dust. Nina's white underwear – layers and layers of it, like a frilly onion – was threaded with black ribbons because she was in mourning for her little girl. I deleted the photos I took of Nina on my mobile phone by mistake, so that corset is the only tangible evidence that she was ever here. I stare at the wall where I saw her in my dream. I think it was a dream.

Shall I tell you a joke, Jonathan? If you must. Why is an infant like a diamond? I don't know, Nina. Because it is a dear little thing. I've tried squirting her corset with Artemis for Men, but it still pongs of her sweat. I shall have to get rid of it, of course, in case Annabel and I ever get it together and she thinks I'm into fetishism. As if we're not both terrified enough of any kind of new commitment. I could probably flog it on eBay – an early Victorian corset, mint condition – but it is the only proof I have. I shall never be able to throw it away. I could hide it in the tiny loft where I have stored Kate's old love letters and Ben's toys and the album of photographs of my parents. A loft is the place where you put away your past.

But Nina wouldn't stay there. Her persistence is quite extraordinary. Her awful puns hover in the air. Why are young ladies like arrows? I don't know, Nina. Because they are all in a quiver when the beaux come.

I went to the Family Records Office at Kew and discovered that there really was a Dr Charles Sanderson living in that house from 1851 to 1865. But whatever was between me and Nina doesn't grow on family trees. I thought of looking for her grave, but even that wouldn't convince me. I don't want to be convinced. There is little enough poetry or magic in my life, so why should I reason her away? That extraordinary laugh, at once childish, refined and depraved. She made everything seem fresh and exciting, even me.

When I first saw her that evening, sitting on the doorstep, I thought of Tenniel's illustrations of Alice. The long tangled hair, huge eyes and complicated clothes that struck my first erotic nerve when I was about six. Nina was a fantasy that had been waiting to happen to me all my life, far more potent than any porn I could download.

A pretty girl complained she had a cold and was sadly plagued by chaps. You should never suffer the chaps to come near your lips. If we hadn't both been very drunk I probably never would have got around to it. But she was so astonishingly passionate. I thought Victorian women were passive – lie back and think of England and all that. Alice was about seven, and Nina must have died years ago, so I suppose that makes me a necrophile and a paedophile. Well, nobody's perfect.

The first night (talking of perfection) I felt like Sir Galahad, which is quite pleasant after your ex-wife has been screaming at you down the phone, calling you a shit and a bastard. I mean Nina so obviously *was* a maiden in distress, not a homeless junkie or an escaped lunatic (although those possibilities did cross my mind). Her weird clothes somehow added to her mystery and charm. I only saw that she was exhausted and needed a meal, and I admit I was glad of her company.

For the first year after Kate and I split up it was a novelty to eat alone, but that soon wore off, and I had begun to dread the click of my solitary key in the door. When you open the door of an empty room, silence wallops you. I had developed a habit of switching on the radio or television as soon as I got home to produce a numbing babble of voices or music; electronic companionship that left me feeling lonelier than ever.

Nina was such good company. Everything surprised and delighted her, and she made me look at London through new eyes. My dreary little flat was her Wonderland, and she thought my Waitrose convenience meal a banquet.

After supper that first night her tiredness caught up with her and she became weepy. I couldn't throw her out, so I made up the sofabed for her and primly unfolded the screen I bought in Tokyo to divide my one large room into two tiny ones. It's made of lacquer and paper, very expensive and rather beautiful. Waves and fishes and women in kimonos act out some scene from kabuki drama on translucent panels. I averted my gaze from even the shadow of her undressing.

When I came out of the bathroom I saw she had fallen asleep fully clothed on top of the summer-weight duvet. She slept on her side, with her arms crossed and the dark mass of her hair spread out around her, looking as if it might have a separate dream life of its own. Her face was calm and trusting, as if she had wiped out the tears and dramas of the day as Ben does. I stood over her, wanting to cover her in case she woke up shivering in the middle of the night, but I was afraid she'd think I was . . . a dozen melodramatic phrases came into my mind. Would she know a word like rape, or would she say, 'Unhand me, villain'? I was tempted to touch her just to see what she would say. I was tempted for other reasons, too, but in the end I just crept back to my side of the screen.

In the morning I woke at seven. The sunlight threw ambiguity on to the screen so that the fishes and waves and women seemed to be dancing. There was no sound from the other side, and for a moment I thought she might have disappeared. I could see the lumpy shadow of the sofabed but couldn't be sure that Nina was still lying on it. I got up and dressed, suddenly aware that my weekend would be ruined if she wasn't there. Then I heard a long, quivering snore. Can ghosts snore?

The sun warmed my face as I put coffee, fresh orange juice and *pains au chocolat* on a tray and carried it through. The thud of the tray on the wooden floor woke her. Nina opened her eyes and stared at me in horror, as if I were the phantom. Then she appeared to remember what had brought her here, and tears came into her eyes. I handed her a cup of coffee before she could start crying again. She lay in a tangle of dark hair, dark-green duvet and black dress, a personal forest that smelled none too sweet. Her washing habits were either of the streets or of another century. I sat back in my rocking-chair, out of olfactory range, and observed her as she twittered and gushed over our very simple breakfast.

'And did you prepare all this by yourself?'

'Yup. The butler's still off duty.'

'Your servants seem to have a great deal of leisure. Oh dear – you are laughing – do you really live here all alone?'

'Except when mysterious women invade my flat.'

'I do apologize. You have been so kind, my presence must be a dreadful inconvenience –'

'Nina, please don't be so polite.' She frowned, and I lost patience with the quagmire of mutual misunderstanding. 'The bathroom's free, if you want to use it before you go.'

'Where am I going?'

'Don't you think that's up to you?'

Forty minutes later she was still in there. I wondered if she had fallen asleep or slit her wrists or disintegrated back into my imagination. As my bathroom has no window the air conditioning comes on with a roar when you shut the door, and I couldn't hear any noise above it. I knocked on the door and asked if everything was all right, but there was no reply, only the sound of water running. Then water started to appear under the bathroom door, a trickle that rapidly became a large puddle. The very expensive antique-oak floor I installed here isn't waterproof, and I was beginning to think Nina was a suicidal maniac who had chosen my bathroom for some ghastly scene of self-sacrifice. Had she slit her throat? Drowned herself in the bath?

I shouted and thumped on the door, which opened – she hadn't even locked it – to reveal a wet, steaming heap of gigantic clothes, taps gushing wildly and Nina, about an inch away from me in the tiny space, very small and crestfallen, wrapped in my white bathrobe. I leaped to the overflowing bath, turned off the taps, slipped on the wet tiled floor and hit my head.

Above me I could hear Nina wailing that she had killed me.

'I'm not dead,' I said irritably, climbing carefully to my feet, furious at the damage she had done to my immaculate flat. Then I caught sight of her face, terrified and apologetic under her wilderness of hair, and started to laugh. I've always liked Chaplin and Laurel and Hardy; I didn't really mind finding myself in one of their films. The straight guy in his elegant flat overtaken by the forces of anarchy.

Nina's tears turned at once to smiles. I've never seen such rapid changes in mood in anyone over the age of seven. I told her to go and get dressed.

'I cannot dress myself.'

I looked at her sharply. 'So you're going home in my bathrobe?'

I don't know exactly when we both realized she wasn't going to leave. I lent her a pair of old jeans and a white T-shirt, explained, as if to a Martian, how they were to be worn and sent her to the other side of the screen. I tried not to think about the underwear she wasn't wearing, about the friction of my cotton and denim against the soft white flesh I had glimpsed.

When she stepped out from behind the screen Nina looked so young and slim and modern that I gasped. She was a pretty girl with a lot of hair, and instead of that formidable hour-glass the figure beneath my borrowed clothes was quite boyish. She shed some of her embarrassing gentility as she helped me mop up the mess she had made and seemed as amazed as me by the size of her corset and her black dress, the pod from which she had just emerged. The vast black dress, the corset and the elaborate white underwear filled my flat. She joked that she had brought her clothes to furnish my bare garret, and somehow this turned into a petticoat fight, a wild, giggling game that left us both weak with laughter. Once you've thrown a woman's knickers at her (however enormous and majestic Nina's version of that garment was), you can't throw her out. And she didn't want to go.

So I made more coffee and turned on the television. Nina's squeals of amazement and horror made me laugh again. I stopped asking myself if she could be genuine and just enjoyed her company. I've always thought it must be fun to be an anthropologist, looking at familiar worlds through fresh eyes. Nina was so upset by an item on the news about a car bomb that had killed eight soldiers in Basra that I had to reassure her that it wasn't true.

'It is a fiction? But why would anybody wish to write such a beastly, ugly story? It is the mission of art not to repel but to invite and please. Those poor men!' She sobbed, dissolving into tears again. She had already used up all my boxes of tissues and was consuming my loo paper.

'Nowadays people quite like ugly stories. There aren't any car bombs in London, you know. Not many, anyway. Basra is a long way away, in – I think you'd call it Mesopotamia. We're fighting a war there.'

'We? The dear old British nation?'

'Please, Nina, you sound like the BNP. Oh, never mind. Yes, there was this tyrant in Mesopotamia, and the Prime Minister and the President of the United States thought he was developing dangerous weapons, so they invaded his country.'

'So it is true? I thought you said – Oh! No! I cannot bear to look!'

'Oh, those are people in Sri Lanka – Ceylon – who lost their houses when there was a tsunami. A tidal wave.'

'How dreadful! That poor woman! She looks so sad, and her children are weeping. Their great eyes are beseeching me. They must need food. Can we not do something?'

I turned off the television. Nina made me ashamed of the cynical indifference with which I usually watch my daily dose of reality. What use was our reality to her anyway? She sobbed and writhed on the sofa beside me, grief-stricken. So I told her a story, just as I make up stories to comfort Ben when he is hurt by the world.

'As I said, it is all a fiction. These things only appear to happen, to remind us how fortunate we are in our prosperity.'

'They are not real people? Thank goodness! Last night, as I wandered through your London, I was so happy to see that you have banished poverty and sickness. I could not bear it if they lurked still in distant lands, if it turned out that the glory of your civilization was but a thin veneer –'

'It's all right, Nina', and I put my arm around her shoulder. To calm her down. Then withdrew it as I felt her shoulders and back tense as if she was still wearing a corset. No touching, no television, no exposure to unpleasant facts. Yet I didn't want her to leave. 'We could go shopping. Would that amuse you? We could take my car.'

She jumped up with a shriek of joy. 'To travel like the wind, as if by magic! I should like it of all things. Oh, Jonathan, my dear staunch friend, how good you are to me!'

I mumbled something and got my car keys.

'But I cannot go out like this. I have no hat or gloves. I am bare-foot and dressed like a street urchin –'

'You look fine. I'll lend you some shoes until we can buy you some.'

'Jonathan, I cannot possibly allow you to go to any expense. I have no money. I do not understand your money.'

Once you start lying it's so easy to carry on. 'Oh, we don't use money any more. We use plastic. Don't worry. We'll just pick up a pair of shoes while we're out.'

She looked baffled but delighted by the money-free economy I had just invented. I finally persuaded her it was socially acceptable to go out without a hat or gloves, but she was anxious about her hair. I gathered she usually had a maid devoted to brushing it and dressing her. She spent so long trying to force my comb through her tangles that I started to look at my watch. Nina was in a panic at the thought that she was keeping me waiting (Kate would have told me to sod off and mind my own business). In the end Nina produced some hair pins from the pockets of her voluminous dress and balanced a tower of hair on top of her head.

At about midday we went out into the dazzling sunshine in search of lunch. As soon as we hit the street Nina lost all self-consciousness. Nobody stared at her. What would you have to wear or do to attract attention on the streets of London? But she stared at everything, and her delight was infectious. I became a tourist in my own city as she walked beside me, Chaplinesque in my shoes, which were several sizes too big for her.

'How clean your streets are! And how free you all are – ladies and gentlemen both. Indeed, I cannot tell the difference. I wonder where the elephant is today.'

'What elephant? Oh, you mean the Sultan's Elephant?'

'Do you have a sultan now, instead of a queen?' Her face lit up, she smiled so broadly that I thought she was going to tell me another of her awful jokes. 'Now I understand why I saw so many veiled ladies yesterday. They must have been the inmates of his harem. How very exotic. I hope he is a benevolent despot. I thought it was some kind of religious ceremony, that perhaps you worship elephants now?'

'Well, in a way.' It seemed pedantic to keep correcting her. This new London we were concocting together was far more attractive than the lonely city in which I had been living.

'And you dine upon the pavement! How enchanting! My dear husband was in Paris many years ago and told me that they also eat alfresco. Does your sultan have French blood?'

'Um, I think he might,' I mumbled, wondering about her dear husband, whose silence was deafening. Was it really the silence of the grave, or was Nina just a wild fantasist?

We sat at a table outside a café on Marylebone High Street. It was so warm that most people were in summer clothes, a display of bare flesh that Nina found shocking. She couldn't take her eyes off the procession of tanned flesh, tattoos, tousled hair, cut-off jeans, shorts and short skirts. She stared at them, defensively clutching her arms, as white as the T-shirt I had lent her, while I stared at her. Nina's face expressed delight and amazement while her crossed arms seemed to be trying to protect herself from the hedonistic parade. She commented in a loud stage whisper as we ordered brunch.

'And this person is almost naked. Is she, or he, exceedingly poor?'

'No, she's exceedingly rich. Armani.'

'Oh, Jonathan, do look at that poor crazed fellow talking to himself. Should we offer to assist him?'

'I don't think he needs our assistance. He's telling his broker in New York to sell some shares.' I showed her my mobile and tried to explain the concept, realizing to my embarrassment that I have no idea how or why it works. I took some photos of her on my mobile and then passed Nina my phone to show her.

'And does this tiny box possess such power? To throw voices over the ocean and capture living faces in a frame hardly bigger than a postage stamp? What a fright I look.'

'You look good.'

'I do not feel good. Do you think I am very wicked to indulge in worldly pleasures, far from my husband and child?'

'Not at all.'

'I know Henrietta would say so. She would scold me and quote some horrid psalm.'

'Then I'm very glad Henrietta isn't here. And that you are.'

Our food arrived, a burger for me and an omelette for Nina. We drank Diet Coke, mineral water and cappuccinos. I didn't want to ply Nina with alcohol; she was quite overwhelming enough sober. My intentions, as she might have said, were honourable.

'That was the most exquisite meal I have ever eaten. Dear Jonathan, how fortunate I am to have found such a noble guide to your paradise. I think I owe as much to your manly kindness as Dante did to Virgil. And is that really all the payment that is required? Your visiting card? How glorious it is to sit here with you and bask in the sunlight of this pinnacle of civilization.'

This speech, declaimed in a loud voice, did turn a few heads. I shuffled off to buy a *Guardian*, needing a break from her exhausting earnestness. I looked at the reviews and handed her the news section. This was a mistake, as the headlines, of course, were all about war and suffering. Nina's post-prandial joy quickly turned to tears.

'Oh no! What a catalogue of woes is here! Jonathan, tell me it is not true.'

'It isn't true,' I muttered, wanting to finish reading a review of a Chopin concert. But it was quite impossible to concentrate on anything but Nina. Her modesty was as demanding as the most outrageous egotism. So I gave up trying to read and suggested a trip to the supermarket. This, usually the nadir of my dreary weekend, became a huge adventure.

We ambled through to Wimpole Street where I had parked my car. Nina lowered her voice, as if afraid of shocking passers-by. 'And do they still gossip about the elopement?'

'The what?'

'Why, Miss Barrett and Mr Browning. I understand her papa was quite heartbroken.' She gazed up at a large house, as if expecting a sad old man to appear at the front door.

'"Dear dead women, with such hair, too – what's become of all the gold / Used to hang and brush their bosoms? I feel chilly and grown old".'

Nina looked at me blankly. Her hair, not gold but almost black and full of red and blue lights in the dazzling sun, had come down from its mooring of pins and hung thickly around the small pointed breasts under her borrowed T-shirt. I couldn't remember when Browning had written 'A Toccata of Galuppi's'. I did feel a little chilly, and my head was spinning as if time was a wine I had drunk too much of.

My car delighted Nina, and I must admit her shrill admiration was gratifying. Buying a scarlet Lotus was my one big luxury after Kate threw me out, my way of advertising that I was single again. I usually drive it alone or with Ben strapped into the tiny back seat, so it was fun to show it off to her. I opened the doors with my key ring, pressed a button that made the roof zoom down and fed a Bach CD into the sound system. Nina's astonishment and whoops of joy enlivened the drive to the Edgware Road.

I usually dread my weekly trip to the supermarket. A middle-aged man shopping for one is making a humiliating public statement that nobody wants him. Me. I've failed at family life and can't even find a partner to defy bourgeois conventions with. I imagine critical eyes judging the seedy contents of my basket and sniggering at the banality of my appetite. Of course, there aren't any such judges; most people who shop in that supermarket are single, and the mothers with screaming brats certainly don't fill me with envy. Anyway, Nina's presence transformed this boring ritual.

'What a magnificent emporium! And is this another car, to whisk us through the dazzling array?' She tried to sit in the trolley.

Nina explored each aisle with shrieks of wonder. Embarrassing, but a lot more fun than schlepping around on my own. 'And to think that all these riches on display are free! That all may enter here and fill their cart according to their needs. Are they Chartists, these wonderful men who have abolished property? Truly I think you must be governed by angels not by men.'

'I wouldn't call them angels exactly. Definitely men, although as a matter of fact there are quite a few women in our government. One of them even became prime minister a few years ago.'

'A prime ministress? Is it possible? And was she wiser and more benevolent than a gentleman?'

'Not at all. A very tough old boot. All the men in her cabinet were terrified of her.'

'I wonder she had the effrontery. Oh, Jonathan! How glorious this is, like a harvest festival in Heaven itself. May I?' She filled our trolley with pineapples, melons, aubergines, green and yellow peppers and purple grapes – more fruit and veg than I'd normally eat in a month. I humoured her. They did look pretty, and it was my own fault for telling her it was all free. 'If I had my paintbox here I would compose a *nature morte*. I have never seen such fertility. And I would paint your portrait, dear Jonathan, as a souvenir of our friendship.'

'To show to your dear husband?' I couldn't resist asking.

'Charles is – I mean, he was – I know he would understand our situation.'

'I wish I did.'

Then I felt like a curmudgeon because the clear bright stream of her joy stopped flowing. She was even silent for a few minutes.

Nina caught sight of the escalator at the back of the food hall, and that, of course, was another celestial vision. So I decided to be an anthropologist again. I stopped trying to rationalize and just laughed.

'Chickens! You still have chickens!'

'Of course we do.'

'Why is a hen walking like a conspiracy?'

'I don't know.'

'Do you give it up? Because it is a foul proceeding.'

I enjoyed her raptures at the cash desk when we were 'given' five bags full of food.

'Now we'll go and find you some shoes. Mine are far too big. You must be terribly uncomfortable.'

'I think I was never so much at ease in all my life.'

I took her arm and guided her to a tacky boutique near the supermarket, full of cheap clothes, shoes, rugs and brassware. Nina was delighted. 'Why, it is like a scene from the *Arabian Nights*! If I take that coffee pot home and rub it, do you think a genie will appear?'

'You might get arrested for shoplifting. Do you like any of those shoes?'

'How brilliantly they sparkle!' They were covered with nasty glitter, like the stuff Ben sticks on Christmas cards. 'And how kind of this gentleman to offer me a pair.'

The shopkeeper plied us with shoes and brought us some mint tea. Despite Nina's protestations, her feet, when she took off my shoes, were red and raw with blisters.

'You must have been in awful pain, Nina. You should have told me.'

'It's nothing. Only my feet. You cannot imagine how wonderful it feels to have no beastly corset biting into me.'

I couldn't imagine it. Pain, even the mildest headache, fills me with indignation. As I paid for the demure, flat black slippers she chose I felt the feebleness of my imagination. I also wondered why I was buying her shoes when her visit, if that's the right word, could hardly last much longer. Yet while Nina was here I wanted her to be happy. I suppose I made Kate happy once, but it was so long ago that I can hardly remember.

'We'll get you something for your feet.' I led her to Boots, asked the pharmacist for advice and bought Nina some kind of jelly popular with dancers.

As I handed her the bag she thanked me effusively, and I realized I had never felt so protective of anybody, except Ben. Kate would have despised me, would possibly have even shot me, if she had known that Nina's gentle helplessness appealed to a side of me I wasn't even aware of. As if I have always been an outsider in my own time, a silent and futile critic of the prevailing amorality, a critic who flourished and kept his mouth shut – not one who risked anything. My marriage with Kate broke up because I had a fling with a colleague who I certainly wasn't in love with, so I stood on the same moral quicksand as everyone else I knew. But Nina's innocence and integrity were so touching. I wanted . . . why am I burbling on like this? What happened later that night was what I really wanted.

As we drove home I took the roof off my car again, and Nina's hair flew around her face. I parked in my mews (my richer neighbours were all away for the weekend) and locked the car. Nina stood beside me like a windswept Ceres, carrying four bags full of fruit and vegetables. I was totally charmed by her and by the city we had created together and grew shameless in my embellishments.

'How strange that all the horses have gone. What charming little houses you have made of our old stables. And are you all architects and artists here? A community of idealists?'

I thought how much more sympathetic that would be than being surrounded by plastic surgeons, artists of breast and nose jobs, who disappeared in the evening and whose names I did not even know.

'Well, I suppose it is a bit like that.'

'I knew it! And since you have abolished the demons of Mammon I expect you all live together quite contentedly, without rivalry or malice?'

It sounded wonderful. How could I resist? I smiled vaguely, and Nina said passionately, 'How I envy you your purified city. The cleanliness of your streets is mirrored in your beautiful minds.'

It would have been callous to disillusion her. So I just smiled, beautifully I hoped, and we carried the shopping upstairs. As I stowed it away Nina gazed at me admiringly as if putting cheese and eggs in a fridge was a recondite skill. I was growing rather addicted to her admiration and no longer mentioned her husband. Nothing had been said about her staying another night, but I assumed she would. Hoped she would.

Nina asked if there were still theatres and opera houses and museums, so I tossed her the 'Guide' section from the newspaper.

'Soulmates. Is this part of your new religion?'

'It's where lonely men and women try to get together.'

She blushed and turned the pages quickly to 'Clubs'.

Four months ago now.

Ben is coming tomorrow. I must get that ridiculous corset out of the way and bring his toys and books down from the loft. If I see Annabel at the gym tonight I'll invite her out to supper. All this fantasy has become a kind of drug. Living alone isn't good for me. I feel as if I've regressed to my adolescent self when I felt an outsider both at home and at school and retreated into a kind of Victorian daydream. Why Victorian? Alice, I suppose, and my unfashionable taste for Pre-Raphaelite art and Tennyson and Browning and both the Scotts, the novelist and the architect. When I was sixteen I dreamed of creating magnificent Gothic palaces like Pugin and hand-crafted interiors like Morris. Sentimental kitsch, as Kate used to point out in disgust. She was always perfectly at home with modernism, and she argued me out of love with romanticism or at least into love with her. But even in my marriage I felt lonely. Solitude is a deserted corridor I sleepwalk down, hoping to encounter another face from another time.

Nina's awful jokes and puns, her disgusting habit of not flushing the loo, her infuriating tears and swoons; since I met her Nina's London has become quite solid. It stands behind my own city like a puppet master behind his marionettes, and I am hungry to smell her fog, to walk her streets by gaslight and see her still Georgian city sprout with the glorious fruits of Victorian architecture. When I told Nina she was a Victorian she looked bewildered. I wonder what they will call the present age when I am dead. I think I've always been a temporal misfit. I'm too dreamy, serious and romantic for the twenty-first century.

That desultory fling with Kerry or was her name Carrie? How could I explain a one-night stand to Nina? I wonder how people talked about sex and love before Freud. Perhaps they didn't. What happened between Nina and me was brief, but it certainly wasn't casual. She has changed my way of seeing myself and my city. I can't switch on the television without wondering what she would think of the invariably harrowing news. She would cry, of course, once she realized these horrors are our reality. Perhaps we should all be crying, every day, all day, until we stop torturing and murdering and starving each other.

Silky hair. Captain Silk, the fittest name in the world, for silk never can be worsted. To be haunted by awful jokes is even more ridiculous than . . . last night at the gym I thought I saw her. Not thought so much as sensation, hope, craving. I'd finished my workout on boring machines and was in the steamroom, trying to sweat out a cocktail of toxins from my drinking bout with colleagues the night before, from the cold I had last week and the more deadly poison left over from my marriage to Kate. The steamroom is like a small tiled shop where we all sit on shelves, most of us past our sell-by date. As it's mixed, we primly wear swimming-trunks and bikinis or swim-suits. Half-naked, we sprawl in the heavy swamp-like air and eye each other through the flattering mist.

I felt my skin grow taut as the heat invaded it. Sensuality returned after the cool detachment of my working day and the grimly puritanical gym. My quest for health ceased to be self-punishment and became pleasure as my eyelids drooped, my nipples tingled and I felt an erection fill my tight swimming-trunks. I lay back on my marble shelf; specks of colour and light floated behind my eyes and gradually settled into recognizable images like beads in a kaleidoscope. Someone threw sandalwood on the hissing steam machine and transformed a cell off Baker Street into an erotic Alma Tadema phantasmagoria of nymphs and fountains. Nina was lying in one of the pools behind my eyes. I could see her soft, white naked body, her hair spread out above it like seaweed.

The door to the steamroom opened with a click, cooler chlorine-scented air rushed in from the pool, and I opened my eyes. She was there, a pale, beautiful phantom with a mass of dark hair gliding through the steam towards me. I sat up with a gasp and opened my arms to her.

'Fuck off,' said the phantom.

# BEDLAM

WHEN CHARLES SUMMONED me down to the drawing-room I did not know what I should find there. I thought it was some kind of tea party I had not been notified of and that the gentlemen were his friends. I remembered Dr Porter from our dinner party and tried to be pleasant, although he seems to me to be a weaselly sort of fellow.

Charles said, 'These gentlemen have come to ask you a few questions, my dear.'

At once I felt like a criminal, and when Charles withdrew from the room I longed to follow him. It is a long time since I have been his dear. He wears his disapproval of me like a great wide-brimmed hat that hides his eyes. We used to sit on the sofa hand in hand for whole evenings and gaze into each other's eyes and talk. I could still paint his eyes as they were then, softest grey, tenderly reflecting the rounded image of his beloved. His little bird that flew away and could not find her way back into her cage. I did not mind being in a cage with Charles when he was gentle and kind, but now there is no more kindness in him, and those doctors who barged into our drawing-room were not kind either. Although it was a sultry afternoon I felt their chill and folded my arms over my plain black dress to hug my soul deep within me where they could not harm it.

Dr Porter behaved as if he were the umpire in a game of croquet and I was the ball that would not pass through the hoops. He thinks himself handsome, but I see the weasel behind his mask. Dr Morris was very red with a veneer smile and piggy eyes. He sprawled fatly on the sofa, and he was all stuffing. Dr James sat beside him and pretended to be my father, but I wasn't taken in. My father is dead and would never have sent me away. Rub-a-dub-dub three doctors in a tub. All great chums and members of the same club.

They shook my hand and were so polite that I shivered. Dr Porter was very gracious and invited me to make myself at home in my own house. 'Sit down, Mrs Sanderson.'

I sat on the green wing chair, which is Charles's chair, and laid my arms over the green velvet arms. I wished I had Charles's arms to support me still, but I was alone with them. They surrounded me on three sides like a medical fence. Then I saw that Dr Morris had a copy of the letter I wrote to Charles after my visit to Jonathan's London, and I wondered how Charles could have taken that piece of me and handed it round to his friends like a slice of pie. I understood that they had come to devour me and that whatever I said they would tell clankers about me, and then I felt very much afraid.

'Don't be nervous, my dear. We won't hurt you,' said Dr James like the wolf in *Red Riding-Hood*.

'Why are you here?'

Dr Porter thought this was a good opening shot. 'Let us come straight to the point. Your husband is very concerned about you and has asked these two distinguished gentlemen to examine you.'

'And if I fail your examination?'

Dr James has grey mutton chops and a voice like gravy. 'Let us not speak of failure. William, you have alarmed Mrs Sanderson. Would you like me to examine you alone, my dear?'

'I would prefer not to be examined at all.'

I stared out of the window at a nursemaid moving through the dusty heat haze with her two charges. Whenever I see two children I think they are Bella and Tommy. When Bella died a part of me slid into the grave with her. A slice for Bella and another for the doctors. Perhaps that was why I felt so insubstantial on my chair. If I stopped holding on to the arms I thought I might float away and be very little missed by anybody.

'Mrs Sanderson?' said the fatherly wolf.

I wondered who Mrs Sanderson was and continued to gaze out of the window.

The three doctors fussed together on the sofa. They whispered and coughed and egged each other on like pancakes. Then I felt Charles come back into the room. I looked around, and there he was just inside the door staring at me. I knew from his red face and awkward gait he had been drinking in his study again. He keeps bottles of brandy and whisky there and drinks a great deal nowadays, but it was I who had to be examined.

'Now, Nina, be a good girl.' He spoke to me as if I were Tommy, and I knew I ought to be cross, but the sound of his voice was so dear and familiar. I wanted to be touched by him, not examined by the other men. Then I remembered that he had showed them my letter and tried to stop feeling again.

Charles and Dr Porter sat on the gilt chairs as if waiting for a play. I was the play. Dr Morris and Dr James stayed on the sofa and looked at me in a distinguished way.

Dr James poured more gravy into his voice. 'Now, Mrs Sanderson, Dr Morris is going to examine you first, and then I will examine you. Your husband and Dr Porter will remain in the room to make quite sure that our examinations are fair and independent. Is that satisfactory?'

'You speak as if I had some choice in the matter.'

'My dear lady, we are here to help you.'

'And if I do not want your help?'

'Nina!' Charles said in that tone that still flies straight to my heart although I tried to bang the gate shut against it.

I turned away from the window and looked straight at Dr Wolf who stood up and left the room. Dr Pig stared at me with suspicious little eyes while Dr Weasel watched us furtively, and Charles . . . I wish I could think of him as a silly animal dressed up in clothes. If he were in a menagerie I would throw a bun through the railings at him and go home. But he is always a man. And I was already at home.

Then Dr Pig held out my letter, and I hated to see his fat fingers slime all over the words I wrote only for Charles.

'Mrs Sanderson, I believe you wrote this, ah, document four months ago.'

'Yes. It was a private letter to my husband.' I turned and glared at Charles, who lowered his eyes and would not meet mine. He did not blush, for he was already very red from drinking, and, besides, he does not blush now that his skin has become so thick.

Dr Pig tried not to smirk as he read from my letter. The others quivered and snorted with suppressed laughter as he read several pages aloud. His monotonous voice transformed all marvels into medical formulae. I felt half-dead with mortification, and my eyes were so full of tears that I could not even see Charles.

When he had finished crucifying me Dr Morris said in the same calm porky voice, 'Now, Mrs Sanderson, this elephant you saw. How large was it?'

I knew there was no right answer. Whatever I said now I was condemned to sound mad. I decided to be a truthful idiot. 'It was a little taller than this house.'

Dr Weasel could not resist sticking his sharp snout in. 'And was it pink by any chance, Mrs Sanderson?'

'No, Dr Porter, it was not. Pink elephants, I believe, are a common symptom of delirium tremens. I do not drink alcohol. You and my dear husband are more of the pink-elephant persuasion than I.'

Although my voice shook, I held back my tears of rage and triumphed to think I had clawed back a little of my dignity. But I was not able to hang on to it for long.

Dr Piggy Morris did not care whether or not I liked him, and indeed I disliked him intensely. 'Now let us be frank, Mrs Sanderson. All this stuff about dancing girls and goblins and footmen in claret velvet and giants and freed slaves and fairy music and an enchanted garden of Eden – it is all so much twaddle, is it not? Concocted from dreams and tales you have told your children. We are not children,

Mrs Sanderson. Now, your husband tells us that you discharged your domestic duties quite satisfactorily until your mysterious disappearance in May.'

I stared incredulously at Charles who had discussed me with this repulsive stranger as if I were an unsatisfactory parlourmaid. Charles would not look at me. He sat on his chair – guilt on gilt – and muttered to his weaselly friend.

Dr Morris was enjoying himself. Perhaps he is tired of being a doctor and relishes being a barrister, and now I was in the dock. He waved my letter at me contemptuously. 'Here is more moonshine and foolishness. Multicoloured angels and Scheherazade and even a pirate ship! But there is darkness in your faery realm. Semi-naked people and centaurs and men. I see that there are men in paradise.'

He read again from my letter and tossed my own words back at me like bones he had picked and stripped of all goodness. He stole my beautiful interlude with Jonathan and turned it into something vile and degraded. I think I became hysterical, but Dr Morris's voice did not stop. Every time I said something he wrote it down in a brown leather notebook, and this made me even more nervous.

Then Dr Pig left the room and Dr Wolf re-entered it. Now he was holding my letter to Charles as if my private thoughts and feelings were the prize in a secret game they were playing together.

'Mrs Sanderson, please accept our sincere condolences for the tragic loss of your daughter.' Dr James was all greasy chops and buttered eyeballs, and he wanted to spread his butter over me, but I only glared at him. 'In my work as an alienist I have come upon many cases similar to yours. Ladies have weaker brains and more tender hearts than gentlemen, and so they very often lose their wits from love or grief. It is up to us to find them again.'

He beamed as if expecting me to be grateful for being told I had windmills in the head and was weak-brained. I was not grateful.

Then he adjusted his sheep's clothing so that his teeth and eyes looked very sharp.

'Perhaps you could tell us more about this fellow Jonathan? Are you in the habit of accepting the hospitality of strange men?'

'I was very tired.'

'Exhausted. I don't wonder after all your travels in time and faery realms. However, those of us who have no magic carpet and must live ploddingly in this nineteenth century cannot resist a few questions.'

I do not remember exactly what happened after that. He asked his questions, and they were very insulting and presumptuous and upset me. I looked around for Charles and saw that he had left the room again. Phrases like bullets flew around the room until my heart was so full of lead I could not speak, and I put my hands over my ears to keep out his voice.

Then Dr James said he had finished examining me and Dr Morris came back into the drawing-room. My letter lay on the table in front of them, its pages crumpled and scattered like a toy they had finished with.

They muttered together, then turned to Charles and said they were ready to sign the certificates. I kept my hands over my ears and shut my eyes against their cruel faces, but their voices crashed through my hands and eyes to invade me. Their voices chanted the words to disenchant me:

moral insanity
singular wayward eccentric
strange humours and escapades
aversion to those she formerly loved
disturbance of the natural domestic affections
confusion and dismay in this once happy household
she has betrayed her affectionate and honourable husband
*non compos mentis* to be confined to the Bethlem Royal Hospital

I fell at the foot of their pyramid and sobbed. My father had a book of old Hogarth's prints. The rake in *The Rake's Progress* ends his life in Bedlam, and I knew that I should find it full of lost souls and depravity and wickedness and brutality. I shrieked and yelled and begged for mercy and was so terrified of being sent there that I fainted.

When I opened my eyes I was still in our drawing-room. I lay on the sofa and could not move my arms. Faces floated above me. I could see the farmyard doctors' and Charles's, too. His cheeks were all scratched and he had a bruise over one eye. He stared back at me with an expression of fear and anger, and I wondered if I had put the scratches and the bruise there. Not me but the other Nina who sees and does strange things. Singular, wayward, eccentric Nina.

I opened my mouth, but no sound came out, for words had failed me. I will not trust in them again. I discovered my arms were tied to my sides and I was wearing a strait-waistcoat like the one my father used to put on patients he said were crazed. It was made of harsh canvas and stank of madness and death, so I started to weep again. I heard Charles say they should wait until it was dark, and I felt more than ever like a corpse that had to be buried in the night. Lucy came in and silently handed my small black suitcase to Charles.

Suddenly I wanted my naughty little boy. I thought of all the times Tommy had been punished because he was bad when perhaps he had not intended to be bad at all. I longed to hug him and tell him I was sorry for loving Bella more than him. I forced myself to speak again and asked Lucy where Tommy was.

She glanced at me and looked frightened as if I were already a ghost. 'Master Tommy is in the nursery, madam.'

'I want to say goodbye to him. If you are sending me away what will you tell him?'

Charles said, 'Tommy must not be distressed.'

'Tommy is six years old. If his mama disappears do you not think it will distress him?'

Charles looked very cross as if he would prefer me to be a silent corpse. His injuries made him look ignominious, like a drunken ruffian who had been in a fight.

'I want Tommy!'

When Charles's face did not change and he did not even look at me I said it again. Then I screamed it and screamed again and Charles finally looked at me with hatred and I found I was screaming at him with hatred and then he made me drink something and I thought it was poison and there had already been so much poison that I did not care.

After that it was dark. I did not know if the darkness was within me or without me. Two people carried me, I think it was Charles and James. We went downstairs and there was a carriage waiting. I looked back at our house and thought I shall never see it again. There were two faces at the nursery window. One was Tommy's, and I could see Henrietta behind him. I wanted to swoop up there like an eagle and hover outside the window while Tommy climbed on to my back and fly away with him, but there were bars on the nursery window, and Henrietta would stop me – she always stops me. Now she has stolen my son and my house, and she will steal Charles if he lets her. But I was not an eagle and did not even feel like a girl woman lady mother wife sister as the dark carriage drove through the dark streets.

My terror was stronger than the stuff Charles had made me drink. I could not, would not, sleep but drowned in my horror of the place to which they were taking me. The angry pounding of the horses' hooves galloped in my heart. The hands grasping my arms dragged me down into the screaming inferno I was condemned to. I wanted this horrible journey to last for ever, because in this dark carriage I still recognized myself. In Bedlam I knew I would dissolve into the floodtide of madness and would not have the strength to separate myself from the howling chaos around me. I struggled to stay awake and keep the flickering candle flame of Nina alive. To sleep would be to die and lose myself and never find her again.

# HENRIETTA'S
# JOURNAL

As the carriage disappeared around the corner Tommy's sobs became quite hysterical. I fear he has inherited his mother's tendency to give in to his passions. He screamed and sobbed and flung himself down on to the nursery rug, thumping his legs on the floor like a demented rabbit. The floor, like the rest of your house, is not clean. Because of my sister's domestic republicanism you might write your name in the dust tracks on every piece of furniture.

Before I turn my attention to improving your house I must take your son in hand. I sat with my back to the window and watched my nephew indulge his wild and undisciplined spirits. Sobs shook him like a summer storm in the boughs of an apple tree; he quivered and gasped for breath and could not speak. Exhausted, he lay on the floor and looked at me through his dark curls, which have grown too long again. He looks so like his dear sister, but he was always the less brilliant child. His little face was red and swollen, slimy wet, as he regained his breath and wailed for his mama.

I took him in my arms. I used to watch Nina do this to her children and wondered how it would feel to hold another human being tight against my heart. The child struggled at first, but then he became still, and I cried a little for my poor sister who has lost so much. Then I said firmly, 'It is time for bed now, Tommy.'

'But where is Mama? Will she come back and kiss me and tell me a story?'

'She has gone to . . . a hospital.'

'When will she come back?'

'She is very sick.'

'Is she going to die, like Bella?'

'I fear it is all too likely.'

I had agreed with you that we should prepare him, for he will not see his mother again. Even if Dr Hood accomplishes a cure of Nina's delusions you naturally fear her influence upon Tommy. My sister has fallen out of the ranks of honest women and can never again be regarded as a wife or mother.

At this Tommy had another fit of histrionics. I saw, too late, that I should have waited before telling him of his mother's social, if not actual, death. I have always believed it is better to face the truth than be swaddled in the folds of silken falsehood. I sat and patiently waited until the child was capable of rational discourse.

His nurse, Emmie, knocked and entered. Nina has the strangest taste in servants. Emmie was our own nurse and to this day treats me with inappropriate familiarity as if I were still five years old. She glared at me like I was the source of all the uproar in your house, enfolded Tommy in her plump arms and cooed and rocked him, kissing him all over. I turned my head away, for it was painful to watch them. When tears appeared on her coarse cheeks I wondered if she had been drinking. She fussed over the child and persuaded him to take some bread and milk. Then she put him to bed, which I was glad of, for I would not know what to do.

When he had settled I dismissed the nurse and entered the night nursery. Tommy lay in a little white bed, a candle beside him. He looked very small and so like his sister, who died in that very bed. I remembered how I had come to help Bella to have a good death and how Nina had spurned me. I took Tommy home to Newington Green and tried to give him spiritual strength, although he was very wicked and ungrateful.

Now I am no longer a visiting poor relation but mistress of the house. I stared down at his angry little face, screwed up against me like a gargoyle on the white pillow, and tried to think of him as your son rather than as Nina's child.

'Mama used to read me stories at bedtime. Before her beastly illness,' he whispered,

'Then I shall read you a story,'

His voice brightened. 'Can I have *Mutiny of the Bounty*?'

'I think you have had quite enough sensation for one day.' I took the candle and searched his bookshelf for the books I had given him at Christmas from the Hofland Library for the Instruction and Amusement of Youth.

'Here we are! *Alicia and Her Aunt or Think Before You Speak.* Is not that an appropriate title?'

'What's proprit?'

'Suitable. Tomorrow we shall begin your education and prepare you for school where you will learn to be a little man.'

'I'd rather be a little girl like Bella. Mama and Papa loved her more than they loved me.'

'That is a very selfish and unwholesome thing to say.'

'I don't know why they did. She was spiteful.'

'Bella was a good little girl, and now she is better than she has ever been, for she is in Heaven. She is an angel. Soon your mother will be an angel, too. You must please Bella and your mama for they will be watching you always.'

'Where are they? I don't want them watching me. Tell them to go away.' The petulant tears came again. 'I don't want angels. I want someone to play with me. I don't want to go to school and be a little man. I want to stay here.'

'Now, shall I read to you or not?' I had to shout to make myself heard above the wild tempest of his weeping.

'No! Go away! I want Emmie! I hate you!'

'Dear Tommy, we must try to love each other.' Silence. If I had gone to Africa as a missionary I could not have found a more savage heart. But I determined to tame him. When his effeminate wailing had subsided I looked down and tried to feel affection for him. Gently I said, 'You must always remember, Tommy, that you are very fortunate to be alive. How easily might Jesus have chosen you instead of Bella to be his little companion.'

A sulky silence, punctuated by sobs. The beautiful words of Letitia E. Landon came into my mind. I spoke them aloud, hoping to inspire him with the finer feelings he so woefully lacks.

> 'His shroud was damp, his face was white,
> He said, I cannot sleep,
> Your tears have made my shroud so wet,
> Oh, mother, do not weep!'

I could hear him breathing beside me long quivering gasps. For a moment I thought Miss Landon's exquisite sentiments had conquered his pride. 'You're not my mother anyway,' he said at last in a sullen voice.

'Dear Tommy, you will not see your mother again. You must think of me as your mother now, and I will do my best to do my duty by you.'

At this he unleashed such a hurricane of weeping and screaming that even my patience was exhausted, and I fled. I passed Emmie on the stairs. She rushed into the night nursery and went to Tommy. I heard the two of them whispering and giggling like lovebirds. I do not think it good for the child to be so intimate with a servant.

I stood alone on the dark stairs, conscious that your mansion is now to be my home. I can let go of my rooms in Newington Green and preserve a tiny financial independence. I shall offer you my modest income, for you have told me of your financial worries. I wish only to be your help-meet, as Nina never was.

I sat alone in the drawing-room, waiting for your return. How strange to sit in your green velvet chair, where I have sat opposite you and watched you as a visitor a thousand times, my eyes unable to leave your handsome face. I do not think you noticed, for your eyes were always fixed upon Nina.

I longed to hear your deep musical voice confide in me the horrors my sister has made you suffer. Each carriage that passed in the street below made my pulse beat faster for thinking that you might be inside.

Hours passed, and you did not come. I fell to thinking of ways in which I may be of use. The demons in my sister's heart had made it impossible to hold family prayers that day, but I resolved that our little parish should not be disrupted again. I appointed myself the guardian of both your spiritual and domestic welfare. You shall not go without your comforts while I am under your roof.

Remembering that the dreadful scenes caused by my sister's intransigence had deprived you of both tea and dinner, I determined that you should return to a hearty meal. Bread and cheese will suffice for me, but you need regular well-cooked meals. I went down to the kitchen to give orders to Cook and found she had gone to bed, although it was barely ten o'clock. The kitchen was in disorder, and I noticed that a large bowl of dripping had been neatly wrapped. I daresay Cook sells it on. Pots and pans were stacked in the pantry all unwashed, and I almost slipped in the thick grease on the floor. A paradise for mice, and indeed I heard an ominous squeaking as I entered. I am well versed in domestic knowledge, the true science of a lady, and was outraged by the slovenly state of your kitchen.

So I marched up to the attics and roused the servants. Lucy and Rachel are not bad girls, but they are lazy and need to be constantly supervised. When I pulled them out of bed they rubbed their eyes and stared at me in bewilderment. They were both wearing my old nightgowns, for I always pass on my old clothes to my servant girls. As for Cook, I observed a strong smell of cooking sherry in her attic when I forced my way in. I have noticed the slatternly creature snoring during our family prayers, and at luncheon the gooseberry tart was burnt.

'How dare you go to bed before your master has eaten?'

'But I always goes to bed at half past nine, ma'am. I'm up again at five and must have my rest.'

She glared back at me with brazen insolence, and my temper rose.

'Your rest? Dr Sanderson is a hard-working professional gentleman. There is little enough rest or comfort in his life. You are paid to provide him with regular, sustaining meals –'

'But I'm not paid, ma'am.'

I looked at Lucy and Rachel in surprise.

'It is true, Miss Henrietta. We've none of us been paid since Christmas,' Lucy said, and I know she is a truthful girl.

'I will speak to my brother-in-law,' I said. 'But you must put on your apron now and come down to the kitchen. The principle –'

Cook had been tying on her apron with a very bad grace, but she suddenly turned on me, took it off again and flung it at me with a vile obscenity. Were it not for my philanthropic work I would not have known that such words existed.

'So I'm to eat — principles now, am I? You — old maids are all the same. Mrs S. had a few screws loose, but at least she had a sweet smile. As for you! Never had a good —, so you take it out on the servants. I'm not even a servant, might as well be a — slave in this house. Well, I've had enough. I'm off to my sister in Bethnal Green, and — you for a sour-faced old spinster, not that any man would want to. Now get out of my room while I pack.'

I was so shocked that I could not speak. Lucy and Rachel, who know how sensitive I am behind my brave façade, helped me out into the dark corridor. My candle had gone out, extinguished by the torrent of abuse, but I lit it again and saw that Lucy and Rachel were shaking, dumbfounded by the harridan. When the two girls had stopped quivering and were able to speak again, I asked them in a whisper if my sister had really been unaware of the chaos in her household.

'Missis never knew nothing about anything,' Lucy said.

We were almost knocked off our feet when Cook burst out of her room with her bags. It occurred to me that I ought to search them for stolen goods, but I was glad to see the back of the dreadful creature.

How unfortunate that it was just at that moment that you and James at last returned. Cook descended towards you, muttering and cursing, and the two girls and I trailed behind her. Tommy had woken up and could be heard caterwauling in the night nursery with Emmie's voice trying to calm him down.

The seamy side of domesticity should not bother men, for they are the Lords of Creation. This was not the sanctuary I wanted to create for you. Your face, illumined by the lantern James carried in, was pale and tight with a misery I longed to share. The cook pushed rudely past you and disappeared from our lives. I ran down the remaining flight of stairs and felt a powerful urge to embrace you.

But I could not. It was as if a wall like the one that separated Pyramus and Thisbe stood between us, invisible but very solid. You took a step back and said abruptly, 'I will talk to you tomorrow, Henrietta', before rushing up to your study and locking the door.

I told Rachel and Lucy to go back to bed and promised them that they would be paid in the morning. Naturally I did not mention that their wages would come out of my own savings. Then I went down to the kitchen and prepared a meagre tray with some bread and cheese, cold gooseberry pie and a glass of wine. I knocked on the door of your study, but you did not reply, so I called out that I was leaving refreshments for you and went at last to bed.

It was after midnight, and I was very tired. As I undressed I compared the day that had just passed with my empty days at Newington Green. Enough events in a few hours to fill a year of my previous existence. And I found that I was happy as I have never been before, happy to be living beneath your roof, to be a part of your life at last, to help and serve you in humble little ways.

When I kneeled to say my prayers, words of gratitude sprang straight from my heart to GOD. There was no wall between myself and Him. He saw that I was doing His work. I prayed for all of us, for

Tommy to learn self-discipline and prudence and for my sister's wickedness to be forgiven. Nina is not fully responsible for her actions. I think she is incapable of accepting Bella's death in the proper spirit of submission to GOD. But she must learn to submit. I gave thanks that He has forgiven me for my evil speculation in railway shares. I understand now that their failure was divine punishment.

## MONDAY

This has become my household. I get up at five each morning to supervise the servants and follow them from room to room, making sure that they clean properly and ambush all the spiders. Then I go down to the kitchen to plan meals around leftovers and give out stores from the locked storeroom. My sister's management was appallingly wasteful. She hardly kept accounts at all and seems to have delighted in buying coal and food out of season. The first law of good housekeeping is 'never throw anything away', and I observe this rigorously. Lucy tells me that Nina gave perfectly good sheets to the poor instead of turning them into dustsheets or bandages. She also threw away wastepaper, which I always make good use of in the WC or twist and use as spills to light the fires. I am keeping meticulous accounts, and one day you shall see how much money I have already saved you.

When I first arrived, a month ago, these rooms were untidy and littery, meals took place at any hour and in any fashion and all was noise, confusion and irregularity. Order is Heaven's first love, and I have imposed the most beautiful order on your house. I do not expect gratitude; I am content to take my *assiette*. It is not as full as Nina's once was. I have chosen my text for my sermon for this evening's family prayers:

> But Martha was cumbered about much serving, and came to him, and said, Lord, dost thou not care that my sister hath left me to serve alone? Bid her therefore that she help me . . . Mary had chosen the good part, which shall not be taken away from her.

I wonder if you will realize that I am talking about myself and Nina: who did choose the good part and who took it away from herself and has now lost it for ever. I fear it is unlikely that you will be moved by my sermon. You usually come late, if at all, and I am not deaf to your snoring. You should, of course, be shepherd of our little household flock, but you have delegated your spiritual responsibility to me. As you said last night when I handed you the family Bible in the hope that you would find some beautiful thoughts to share with us, 'That's really your territory, old thing.'

I hope you appreciate the improvements I have already made. The new cook, Mary, comes from the Society for the Encouragement of Faithful Servants in Hatton Garden, so we may be sure that she is of excellent character. I have spoken to her about the importance of using more seasoning, although I thought your remark about the vegetable soup tasting like ditchwater was gratuitously rude. Her food is plain and wholesome, and so is she. I have now paid all the servants until November, and you have assured me that your finances will be in order by then. I know that you and Dr Porter are working together now, and I am sure that you are making our world a better place. I am touched by your humility, for when I ask about your work with Dr Porter you lower your gaze, and I want to say, 'Let your light so shine before men, that they may see your good works.' There is so much I want to say to you, but there is a new shyness between us. Do you feel it, too? Oh, Charles, I wonder if you will ever read these words.

How sweet it is to spend my days putting your house in order. I have taught Lucy to sew and get up fine linen. We can dispense with Madame B—, whose extortionate dressmaking bills I found stuffed in Nina's wardrobe. We can also save money on the servants' food, for anything will do for them.

Nina gave them far too much time off. I met Lucy on the stairs yesterday, dressed above her place in a blue silk gown and a twelve-shilling parasol. When I asked where she had got hold of such an elegant dress (thinking she had been pilfering Nina's clothes) she told me she had bought it herself, and it was the Queen's Choice in Swan and Edgar! Then she told me she always had Wednesday afternoon off, but I assured her that under my regime she would only be allowed one day out every month.

I shall have to watch that girl. Her waist is expanding at a scandalous rate, and Rachel says she found Lucy's sweetheart, a very burglarious looking fellow, hiding in the coal cellar. I shall try to keep her on until Tommy goes to school, for he is fond of her, knowing no better. But I can see the day approaching when I shall have to dismiss her without a character and with a baby.

At eight I tell Emmie to rouse Master Tommy. This morning there was, as always, a brouhaha. The child had had bad dreams, he wanted to stay in bed and did not like the way Cook had made his porridge. As I prepared our lessons in the nursery, which is now the schoolroom, I distinctly heard him say to Emmie, 'I don't want beastly lessons. Why can't you teach me?'

And Emmie's voice, 'I am not clever like your aunt.'

'Auntie Hen smells of old rice pudding, and she's always cross, and she doesn't like me.'

The child's ingratitude is a cross I must bear, for he is your child, although, alas, he grows more like his mama every day.

At nine I began my daily battle.

'Have you learned the poem I set you, Tommy?'

Silence.

'Tommy, I asked you a question.'

'It's a horrid, gloomy poem, and I don't want to say it.'

'Soon you will go away to school where you will have to do many things you do not want to do. You know what will happen if our lessons go badly. Emmie will not take you to see the ostrich race at Batty's Royal Hippodrome this afternoon.' I confess that I have taken to offering sensual rewards to make our lessons go more smoothly.

At this he stood up, held his hands behind his back, pouted and gabbled:

> 'The coffin by the cradle
> Told the struggle that was o'er
> Hope whispered in the Mother's ear
> 'Tis but an angel more.'

'Rather mangled, Tommy. We do not have to catch an express train. Now say it again, more slowly. Try to put some passion into the beautiful words.'

But Tommy is only passionate when passion is not required. After three attempts I sighed and turned to our little catechism. 'What causes the rain?'

'Papa says it's when clouds bump together and water spills out.'

'And a more spiritual answer?'

'Oh, I can't remember. Something about angels.'

'The drops of rain are the tears shed by angels over the sins of the world.'

'Why do angels cry all the time if it's so wonderful in Heaven?'

'It is not for us to try to imagine Heaven.'

'I bet I can. Heaven's the steamboat wharf near London Bridge. When are we going to Ramsgate?'

'There will be no summer holiday this year, Tommy.'

'But we always go to Ramsgate!'

His face was red and contorted with rage. I hurried on with our lesson, trying to distract him.

'What is the date of the invention of paper?'

'I don't care. Why aren't we going to Ramsgate?'

'What is the longitude and latitude of Calcutta?'

'I don't want to go to rotten old Calcutta. I want to go to Ramsgate!' Tommy bellowed so loudly that I am sure the patients in your waiting-room must have heard and have thought you had a lunatic in your attic.

Emmie knocked on the door and pretended she had to tidy his clothes. He ran to her and sobbed in her arms, making me feel as if I had whipped him when I had merely asked a harmless question.

When the child was calm again I resumed my fight to save his soul. I fear that he may die young like his sister, and, as I frequently tell him, he will not enter the Kingdom of Heaven in his present state. 'Tommy, have you thought any more upon our little plan?' He glared at me sullenly. 'I mean, dear, our uplifting idea that you should renounce your baby books and toys?'

'It wasn't my idea.'

'But when I suggested it you seemed so eager to make the sacrifice.'

'You said you'd give me a tin of Everton Toffee.'

I sighed. I have attempted to explain to my nephew that virtue is its own reward, but he is a very greedy, sensual child. 'And have you made the sacrificial heap, as we agreed?'

'I'll do it now, shall I? Where's the toffee?'

'I shall buy it this afternoon. And tomorrow we will go together to distribute your gifts to a poor family who live near by. I want you to see how children less fortunate than you live.'

He raced around the nursery in his usual fever. 'Now, Tommy, this is not a steeplechase.'

When he had thrown books and toys all over the floor I examined them. 'And have you given away all your baby things? I do not see Bertie here.'

He was silent. I knew that he is very fond of Bertie, his toy rabbit, for he takes it to bed with him and even carries it with him during the day. Once, when I was attempting to explain the Holy Trinity and the concept that GOD is in everything, always, he facetiously asked, 'Will He come back as Bertie?' Naturally I was obliged to punish his blasphemy.

'Tommy? Where is Bertie?'

'He's in hospital.'

'Don't be foolish. You must give him away, too. There is no virtue in renouncing only the things you do not care for.' Silence. 'Very well, if you refuse to tell me where he is I shall go and look for him in the night nursery.'

Tommy flung himself at my legs and screamed, 'No! He's gone to hospital like Mama.'

'Now you know that is not true. You have told me a lie, haven't you, Tommy? I am anxious for your eternal welfare, for this may be only the first of a series of evils. Do not break your father's heart. Now, give me the rabbit.'

The sacrifice was made. I forgave Tommy, and Emmie has taken him to the ostrich races.

I sit in my pleasant room and gird my loins for tomorrow morning's battle. I am helping Tommy to become a new person in Christ, and I am helping you, too. How rich my life has become and how thankful I am that I have found my vocation at last, not in Africa but toiling in the spiritual fields of my own family. I no longer fear the future, for I shall not after all be a reduced gentlewoman, eating the bread of charity. I know that I have valuable work to do here, and my reward is to see you every day. How happy I would be to spend the rest of my life beside you.

# DR HOOD'S
# NOCTURNAL

I LEAVE MY dear Jane sleeping and pass through the door to my other
family. Our own children lie peacefully, surrendering themselves to
the loving darkness; but for these bigger, older children each night is a
monster to be fought. Not with swords but with groans, sighs, mutters,
snores, grunts and screams.

I take my candle and move through the long galleries, locking
and unlocking doors with my master key. Sleep will not come to me
until I have patrolled these other sleepers and made sure that they
are as safe as the shipwrecked can be.

Here in the basement lie the most desperate and violent. They
are no longer in cages or chained to beds of filthy straw, as in the all
too recent Monro past, but lie in cells padded with cotton where they
may not harm themselves or others. These suffering ones are given
harmless morphine to help them sleep, and I almost envy them the
deep ocean of dreams in which they bathe.

My insomnia began when I was a young doctor, on call day and
night, and my years in asylums have not eased my condition. I have
so much work to do, I cannot waste time sleeping. When I do, for
a few hours each night, my slumbers are punctuated by tables of
statistics and ranting voices. I hear these lost souls call my name and
summon me back to my duties. My Jane says that to lie beside me in
bed is as restful as taking a nap at Paddington Station. She calls me
her Puffing Billy and says I charge through sleep at fifty miles an hour,
in such a hurry to reach morning that I hardly close my eyes. But she
does lie beside me, thank Heaven, and in her arms I know my only
rest.

Here on the ground floor are the new admissions, with whom I converse at length. I like to hear them tell their own stories and do not accept what families and so-called friends say about them. If we knew more of their real lives many of their delusions would not seem so absurd. We all have our deranged intervals, and I believe that most of my charges may be cured within a year. Otherwise, what is the difference between a certificate of lunacy and a *lettre de cachet*?

Our patients have separate apartments at night, with a keeper to watch over them and to make sure that they do not abuse themselves or others. One of my colleagues, Stephen Wheeler, performs cliterodectomies on women who persistently indulge in manualization. In my opinion female masturbation is not a cause but a consequence of insanity, and it is most painful to witness the frenzied, almost convulsive transports of these benighted creatures, who frequently become epileptics, nymphomaniacs, hysterics or prostitutes. How noisy they are tonight. These corridors echo with their paroxysms, moans and soliloquies, which are frequently indecent, quarrelsome or both.

I love to watch their sleeping faces as I try to solve the mystery of consciousness. The sleeping may resemble the dead, but they are very much alive, vulnerable and open. My fellow insomniacs open their eyes as I walk past, and I glimpse their secret lives like clouds scudding across their inner skies. Others toss on their pillows in that enigmatic state between waking and sleeping. Sleep is a great leveller, melting distinctions of class and time. I have always believed that Shakespeare must have observed the insane, perhaps in this very hospital when it stood at Bishopsgate. Hamlet, Macbeth, Ophelia and King Lear are observed with such truth and accuracy that I often expect to meet them on my nightly rambles. Indeed we have many Ophelias here.

> Cupid is a knavish lad,
> Thus to make poor females mad.

Tonight I start on the women's side of the building. We have always more women than men, for mental alienation is of more frequent occurrence among females than among men. I believe there are a variety of causes for this: disorders of the menstrual function, pregnancy, parturition. In the male sex the active pursuits of business or pleasure more quickly supplant tender impressions. The development and decline of the ovarian and uterine functions at the two great epochs of a woman's life affect her mental and moral condition. Men and women do not experience madness in the same way, and females are more subject to a monomania of vanity: they crave praise, attention, admiration and homage.

Marriage is for women the point at which all future and past hopes congregate. For us men, marriage is a shield against ourselves and our passions, but for women it is all. Their susceptibility of mind and delicacy of frame make them tragically vulnerable to disappointment, and their education arrests the development of their bodies, leaving their mental powers untaught. It encourages sordid and selfish feelings and vapid sentimentalism instead of a realistic view of life. I have told Jane that I want little Louisa and our own daughters, if we have any, to have a rational and thorough education.

Most of my women patients have been maids or governesses, like dear Jane. She calls me her Perseus and says I rescued her. The fate that was nearly hers, to rot for the rest of her life in a squalid private asylum because a cynical young man took advantage of her, is never far from my mind. Many of these women have similar stories: they are all Jane. When I enter these wards during the day I am thronged by women who press my hand, ask my advice and whisper to me. I do not tell Jane that several of them are convinced I am their husband.

Here on the ground floor are the women who have recently been admitted and those who have been promoted from the basement. The structure of our hospital is a little like Dante's cosmology, although I like to think that we have no Hell. No, that is not true. Our inferno is in the criminal blocks beyond, and I have no control over them. But here inside the main building real progress is possible. By their own efforts my patients move upwards until they are ready to leave us.

I observe these new admissions, interview and examine them, trying to identify their secret past life, the real cause of their disease. In the document Jane and I are preparing for Lord Palmerston my patients are reduced to initials. But as I wander here among them in the shadows of the night I call each one by name, silently, hoping to protect them from any more evil than has already befallen them.

Ann Wells is mild in manner with a round face and gentle brown eyes. Now, as I watch her sleep, she looks like any other plump woman of forty. Her prevalent delusion is that the Pope follows her about and harasses her. She recognizes in many strangers, including myself and the butcher's boy, a likeness to His Holiness. She is quiet, industrious, attentive to all the requests of her nurses and thankful for every kindness. However, the delusions still continue, and whenever she speaks of the Pope I observe her eyeballs roll, and she stutters. Her husband, a carpenter, brought her here three weeks ago and assured me she had always been mad as a hatter and there was nothing more he could do for her.

But Mrs Wells has confided in me that her husband ill treated her, beating her and going with other women when drunk. As a young girl she worked as a maid in a convent in Brompton and became very fond of the nuns, who were kind to her and gave her some education. I believe some half-digested idea of an all-powerful male has fused with the husband she is terrified of.

Elizabeth Thompson is an imaginary thief with an imaginary fever with which she is afraid of infecting others. Now she is sleeping and looks calm, but during the day she will not employ herself in any way and sits before the fire with her hands covering her face, lamenting her miserable existence and all the trouble she has caused. She would be a pretty girl were it not for the cloud of shame and guilt that envelops her. Although she is only nineteen she is convinced she will meet some horrible death, either by fire or devoured by animals. This is to be her punishment for the sins she imagines she has committed. She is in the best of health and as far as I can discover has never stolen anything, but her self-belief has been stolen from her. Every day she tearfully begs to be allowed to remain one more night here. She is always on the look-out for cats, and when she sees one she goes and talks to it as if it was human. I have tried to discover more, but she is rambling in her ideas, constantly muttering.

Elizabeth was brought here by her father, a respectable-looking carter. Her mother died when she was very small. I have offered her the chance to visit her father at home, accompanied by a nurse, but she will not go.

One page in our vast admissions book is never enough for the infinite complexity of an individual, and here we have three hundred and fifty individuals. I must care for them all; I am in a sense their father.

Their delusions cannot be removed by joking or argument. One of Pinel's patients was convinced he had been guillotined during the Revolution but that judges demanded that his head should be replaced on his shoulders. He had got the wrong one, which he very much disliked. 'Look at these teeth! Mine were exceedingly handsome. These are rotten and decayed.'

Esquirol, on the other hand, humoured his patients: a woman who suffered from headaches was convinced that animals were burrowing into her head. Esquirol pretended to extract an earthworm from a hole he had made in her forehead. A man who believed he had frogs in his stomach was cured by purgatives and frogs placed in his night stool.

But I think such deceptions are immoral and quackish. I am suspicious of all miracle cures and want to cure my children by kindness and wisdom, not fraud and folly. Like all fathers I have my favourites, and one of the new female patients, Nina Sanderson, fills me with an interest I must hide from all but myself.

When she was first brought here, one night two weeks ago, she was hysterical. She made such a commotion that I heard her from our little house under the portico and came through the door into the entrance hall, where she lay on the carpet writhing and screaming. Our new matron, Mrs Dunn, tried to soothe her, releasing her from her strait-waistcoat and reassuring her, 'You will be in excellent hands here.'

Most unusually, her husband is a doctor, a handsome fellow of about forty. He and his manservant had brought his wife here in a carriage. I did not like the calm way he handed over Mrs Sanderson and her two certificates of lunacy as if she were a large and vociferous parcel. I returned the strait-waistcoat to him, for we do not allow any instruments of restraint inside our hospital now.

Dr Sanderson completed the necessary paperwork and told me that his wife had been suffering for some months, ever since the death of their daughter, from the delusion that she has travelled through time to the remote future. She actually disappeared for several days, and her husband has reason to suspect that she was abducted and that criminal conversation may have taken place.

He gave me this account in a flat voice as we stood over the prostrate, sobbing form of his wife. It was almost like looking at a mirror image of myself. How often have I taken refuge in professional unfeelingness to escape the painful ravings of patients. But this was his wife – I was reminded, most unpleasantly, of those scenes when I removed my own dear Jane from her incarceration. Having established that there was no history of insanity in Mrs Sanderson's family and no previous attacks I dismissed him rather curtly and turned my attentions to the poor lady. I administered two grains of acetate of morphia and kept her in my observation ward.

There has been much to observe. As I have always maintained, some of our patients are so reasonable that it is necessary to live with them, to join in their pastimes and talk to them extensively, before pronouncing them mad. I recall Roger Cuthbertson, a solicitor who appeared to be of the most respectable character, until one day he bit me on the nose and screamed, 'If you don't discharge me by tomorrow I shall issue a writ against you.' He proceeded to take off all his clothes and demanded to go out into the street. There are many twists and turns in the dark and disordered mind, and the causes of alienation must be understood before they can be removed.

For the first few days Mrs Sanderson was tearful, restless and fidgety. Then I gained her confidence, and she began to speak to me openly of the tragic loss of her little daughter Bella. She spoke fondly of her husband and then broke off with a puzzled air, as if thoughts had swept away the path of her words. Although no longer young – she is twenty-eight, the same age as I am – she is a woman of considerable charm and beauty (not that I would allow myself to be influenced by that in any way).

As soon as she was well enough to converse she assured me she was not mad. Then she proceeded to talk about and draw London in the year 2006. Her drawings are well executed and so curious that I mean to show them to Haydon and Richard Dadd. It is clear that these strange pictures proceed from an overheated imagination, and yet she is otherwise quite rational. I have told the nurses and attendants that she should be treated with particular tenderness and benevolence, and indeed she is already a great favourite with patients and staff alike. She helps in the women's garden we are making of the former airing-courts and is clever and industrious. Yet she remains under delusions as to circumstances which could not possibly have happened. Now she sleeps, protected by the arms of Morpheus, whose excellent drug is of such benefit to us.

I move upwards to the convalescent wards where my efforts to make the hospital more home-like have already borne fruit. We have coconut matting and bird cages in these long galleries now, and flowers and prints soften the walls. At Colney Hatch we exhibited the patients' artwork on the walls, and here, too, the ladies' watercolours and fancywork are displayed. Barred windows have been replaced by glazed ones, despite the tendency of patients to jump out of them.

The local glazier remarked last week that I am his best customer. I would rather have all the windows broken than tolerate a single bar or strait-waistcoat in my hospital.

In the little cubicles that lead off these long galleries most of the women sleep quietly, and those who are noisy are visited by attendants. My candle illuminates each sleeping head as I pass among them. How I wish it could light up the contents of those heads. We have no mentometer, to coin a word, which will indicate the thoughts that pass through the mind. The diagnosis of each patient is infinitely difficult.

Although I rarely sleep I have a vision: a spacious palace surrounded by beautiful gardens; a light and bright interior filled with laughter and music; men and women labour in the kitchens, gardens, bakehouse and laundry. Their work is pleasure, rewarded with approval. No bars on the windows and, above all, no whips, chains or chastisement.

Jane tells me that my utopian schemes are more fascinating than practicable. Yet I feel I have made a start towards creating an ideal environment here, based on benevolent and rational policies. It is not so long since Pinel freed the lunatics in the Pitié Saltpêtrière from their chains and only a year since I freed my dear children from theirs. I am not their judge but their guardian, and I believe that I can help them pass from darkness into light.

My system is based on moral treatment, on practical philosophical principles and the benefits of exercise, fresh air and occupation. Without employment they will only sink into lethargy or torment each other. Patients who can walk must not be allowed to stay in bed all the time. It is not enough to provide a large building and have medical advisers occasionally inspect inmates. 'Presumed curable' is the promise we make to all new arrivals, and we do cure three out of five within a year. Bleeding, blisters and baths cannot help; the lancet cannot relieve mania and melancholy. They thrive on hope, sympathy and interest in their self-created miseries.

Our little community must become a family. My own family are safely sleeping on the other side of the wall; they are the engine that drives me on. I am glad that my children will grow up here. It delights me to see little Donald and Chas play on the front lawn with the patients. At first Jane protested and admitted that she was afraid the patients would harm our children. Then I reminded her that she was once called a lunatic and abandoned in a far worse place than this, that we must all wear several masks on our life's journey, many of them false.

Then Jane wept and said I was right and turned with renewed zeal to our work. Without her help I could not achieve the half of what I do. The only thing my dear wife does not share is my insomnia. Now she is sleeping soundly after her long day tending our children and her evening work compiling statistics and editing the weekly journal for the governors. In her calm intelligence I see the proof that women do not have to be weak and foolish.

Yesterday was Jane's birthday, and she was horrified to find herself suddenly thirty. 'I am an old woman!' she said. I kissed her and told her that I shall always find her beautiful. Although I am two years younger I feel like some Old Testament patriarch, the father of several hundred children. Yes, they shall all be my companions. Instead of hiding them away in shame and darkness we will celebrate their lives: their triumphant rise through the building, their birthdays and, above all, the great Christian feast of Christmas. Together we will embrace the joys of family life.

And yet I know that too often it is families that destroy their members. I think of poor Sally Jones, who was perfectly reasonable here. After three months I considered her cured and sent her home. But three days later she came back to the gate in tears and begged to be readmitted. She told me she felt, after spending some days with her family, that she was about to become ill again. Said it almost with longing, as if illness were a desirable state.

My father wore out his life as a doctor among the poor here in

Lambeth. How often he used to say to me that most of his patients' problems were not in their bodies. He died of overwork while I was a student in Dublin, but I often feel that I am continuing his work and imagine his shabby figure at my elbow. In the old black coat he could never afford to replace, he takes my arm. His face is crumpled and faded like his youthful ambition; it wears a puzzled look as he says again, 'It's all in the brain, my boy.'

A common opinion still, but I do not believe it. If all our actions, virtuous as well as vicious, resulted from the condition of our brain, then we would have no more control over them than the paddle-wheels of a steamboat over the engine by which they are set in motion. It would be as cruel to punish a man for horse-stealing – if his brain impelled him to – as to punish a man for shaking his limbs in a fit of ague. Burglars and thieves might rejoice in their predestined career, police offices close and the Central Criminal Court adjourn *sine die*. We must trace all manifestations of the intellect and feelings to the higher power of the mind itself. The mind, independent in its own citadel, reflects. The brain is only an organ.

Here in the lonely night my own mind argues with my father; with Dr Morison, my predecessor here, who said my ideas about non-restraint were a young man's wild experiment and could never succeed; and with Lord Palmerston. I wish I could show those gloomy old men how optimism, humanity and common sense have already succeeded. As Dean Swift said, 'The best doctors are Doctor Diet, Doctor Quiet and Doctor Merryman.'

The study of mental disease is now at last recognized to be a distinct and legitimate branch of medical science. I want this hospital to be a place where students have the opportunity to study all the different forms of insanity, to dismiss book-taught theories and learn to appreciate the value of facts. As I pass down these long galleries with my candle the attendants smile and nod. I interviewed them all and trust in them, for all are well educated, gentle and humane. Together we are making a new world, complete with kings, queens, bishops and deities. At the last count we had eight Napoleons, six Queen Victorias, three Marys, Queen of Scots, two Christs and a Buddha. A most distinguished little community.

But here on the top floor my delight in the utopia I am creating fails me. I stare out of the window at the male and female criminal wings where darkness reigns – and not only at night. Even in daylight I dread my visits to those dismally arched corridors feebly lit by small barred windows. The lost ones stare out at hopelessness through gratings like cages in the zoological gardens. To step inside this purgatory of punishment is to step back fifty years. It is lamentable to see healthy, strong men sauntering listlessly about the wards or airing-courts, lounging away in idleness the remnant of their existence. The only exercise available to them is fives and running in the exercise yard. If our criminal lunatics were employed in any outdoor work they would come into contact with other patients.

These criminal blocks are run by the Home Office, run without any respect for dignity. Although I have no responsibility for these patients I think of them all the time. They are my failures, and I shall not rest until Dadd and the other – I can only think of them as the more refined and civilized lunatics – are safely installed in our enlightened wards. Educated persons of good family find it a great hardship to associate with convicted felons, whose insanity has only exaggerated the more revolting features of their character.

To myself alone I confess that I do not dare to go inside the male criminal wing at night. And, yet, what to do? In cases where murder has been committed or attempted the man or woman must be perpetually confined. Britain has more homicidal maniacs than other countries, just one of many ways in which we lead the world. Perhaps our dog fights, bull-baiting and pugilistic contests encourage violence in the lower orders. However, there are said to be more lunatics in America than any other country, possibly as the result of the acquisition of independence. Well, I cannot speculate on international lunacy. I have quite enough work to do here in London.

The male criminal block is a little hell because the heartless, nameless officials at the Home Office refuse to spend a penny on improvements. Criminal lunatics must be isolated to protect society, but if they never see any other persons than lunatics, how are they ever to recover? They are totally excluded from all rational society, breathing only the contaminating atmosphere of insanity.

As if those dank and filthy walls were transparent I can see through them to the benighted ones within: Joseph Felden, who, while awaiting transportation as a convict in Millbank Prison, murdered one of the warders. If any of his wishes are opposed he threatens the wardens or fellow patients and has twice nearly murdered other men. Worthless and depraved, he has spent most of his life in gaol. There is no sign of the mental disease, on which ground he gained his acquittal. He was sent back to Milbank for three months, then the governor of that prison sent him back to us, not because he was insane but because he was neither a prisoner nor a convict. Gentleness and kindness are impossible with such men as him around. Stern discipline is needed for the few like him, and this invades the general morale of my hospital.

The gallows was cheated of another victim when John Patterson, an expert thief, being seized with delirium tremens, was placed in Westminster Workhouse where he committed murder. At the time of his reception here he was sane but brutal, and no amount of kindness or advice can temper his vicious tendencies. Such men refer to our criminal block as the Golden Bank, for the same conditions I abhor are comfortable and easy compared with a life of hard labour or transportation or even the gallows. Many, I know, pretend to be mad, and these counterfeit lunatics are always trying to escape. But they cannot, for the criminal block is secure as a place of detention.

As if there are not enough genuine lunatics to occupy me for a lifetime. Some crimes never lose their power to shock. For many years the Romans had no law against parricide, for they thought it impossible, the stuff of mythology. I think of Horace: 'Do you imagine that

Orestes grew mad after the parricide and was not distracted and haunted by execrable furies before he warmed the dagger in his mother's blood?' Whether the blood be of the mother or the father, the crime is equally terrifying. Yet I must understand this form of lunacy, like all the others.

I have confessed that I have my favourites. Chief among them is Richard Dadd, parricide and genius. It moves me to tears to see him calmly draw or play the violin, squalor and pandemonium all around him. With a few other inmates of cultivated tastes and tragic histories he plays chess and discusses religion and theology.

For some years after admission Dadd was considered a violent and dangerous patient, for he would jump up and strike a violent blow without any aggravation and then beg pardon. Even now he often pays no sort of attention to decency in his acts or words. After murdering his father he escaped to France with the intention of killing the Emperor of Austria (who is now here, together with several tsars). Hayden, my steward, shares my fascination with Dadd. Whenever we can, we pluck him from Hades and smuggle him into the comfort of the steward's room. This is against all the strict Home Office rules, but the keepers in the criminal block are so harassed that they are grateful to see one of their charges disappear, if only for a few hours. There, before Hayden's fire, with a pipe and a glass of port and a plate of good food, Dadd thaws, and the three of us have remarkable conversations.

Ralph Kenyon, a carpenter from Yorkshire, also murdered his father. He mutters to himself frequently and swears as at some imaginary being. Someone who tries to kill his sovereign is also a kind of parricide. Edward Oxford tried to assassinate our Queen in 1840, when he was only eighteen. He fired two pistols at her as she drove in Hyde Park with Prince Albert. Physicians described him as 'sane', and he was sent here under Royal Warrant for twenty-four years.

Margaret Nicholson, who tried to assassinate George III with a blunt table knife, was also sent here. The King said, 'Do not hurt her, for she is mad', touching, when you consider his own future. She lived to be ninety-eight; indeed, many of our patients live into extreme old age, which I take as proof that this is a healthy place. There has been no cholera here, even now when it is raging in nearby Lambeth and Vauxhall. I believe that God watches over us. Practical Jane says it is our artesian well that protects us.

Insanity is curable and is indeed less contagious than many fevers. I have no doubt that lunatics are capable of some form of reasoning, for the mind is never totally eclipsed; there is always some lingering ray of light. Dadd often penetrates deeper into my mind in the course of our conversations than I do into his.

These criminal lunatics cannot but be unhappy, for they know they will never recover their liberty. Yet they remain curious about each new arrival, and some, like poor Dadd, continue to pursue their intellectual interests despite being surrounded by manners and language of the most revolting description. Oxford spends his time learning French, German, Italian, Spanish, Latin and Greek.

As Jane and I argue in our petition dedicated to Lord Palmerston from 'His Lordship's very humble servant' (humph!), we need to organize a Central State Lunatic Asylum for their safe custody or put criminal wards in the existing county asylums. Asylums should be curative hospitals not prisons. Many madmen deserve pity but none punishment. Meanwhile, I long to remove Dadd and the forty or so others from the Home Office block to my own wards where I can care for them with respect and compassion.

We must solve these problems, for they will not go away. Insanity is greatly on the increase. The frenzy of modern life, the dreadful materialism and cut-throat competition all around us, bring increasing numbers to our gates. How fragile is the human mind!

I look down at the female criminal block, a less terrifying place but just as heart-rending. The most amiable and gentle of her sex may, in the agonies of childbirth, be attacked by puerperal mania and commit infanticide. I cannot consider this issue without thinking of my dear

Jane, who did not. All alone and abandoned in her remote circle of hell, she gave birth to Louisa and refused to give her up. When we married we agreed to pretend that Louisa is Jane's little sister. It is a nod to the social conventions, and I do not think it does any harm, for the child lives with us and knows she is loved by us both.

But my Jane is strong and intelligent. Nothing can be more melancholy and pitiable than the position of a weaker woman when she recovers her reason only to discover that she has destroyed her child and so must be treated as a prisoner for the remainder of her life. The law is an ass to treat such a woman as a criminal; she should be taken care of until after the change of life when she may safely be entrusted with her liberty.

Others have as much blood on their hands as Lady Macbeth or Clytemnestra, and indeed there is more drama within those dreary walls than in all of Drury Lane. Margaret Baker murdered her six children, yet, according to her sister, twenty-four hours before these murders she was in a composed and rational state of mind. Sometimes she forgets that they are dead and calls out their names with such pathos that silence falls even in that society of outcasts. Such criminal lunatics should not associate with harmless unfortunates.

With Emily Weston, for example, a lady of rank and property, who, without the least conceivable motive, committed a theft in a public bazaar. She stole a yard of Brussels lace, although she had enough money in her purse to pay for ten times as much. Such crimes are pointless and in my opinion unlikely to recur. Yet crimes they are. Miss Weston's humiliation, her knowledge that in a few seconds of mental aberration she ruined her life, are pitiful. I would like to consider her crime expiated and the stigma attached to her removed.

I unlock the door of our Chapel and enter for a few minutes of solitary prayer. In these lonely nocturnal communions I feel closer to His presence than during our Sunday services. I am a father, asking another Father for guidance and for time to accomplish my work. I pray for the poor wretches in the criminal blocks, beyond my control yet always on my conscience. Kneeling here alone, my candle throws my shadow on to the white walls. How enormous I look, and how small I feel.

Attendance of our Sunday services is not compulsory, although desirable. The attendants decide which patients may join us in our prayers. Sadly, those who are most eager to attend are often the least suitable. Two Sundays ago Roger Fuller, a butcher from Clapham who is convinced he is Jesus Christ, became overexcited. The poor fellow believed we were all money-changers and chased us out of his temple, much to the terror of little Chas and Donald.

Usually, though, our services are soothing occasions. Our chaplain is careful to make the sermons short and dull and to avoid references to hellfire and apocalypse. I always find it a great comfort to have my family here beside me. Indeed, this is the only place 'on the other side of the wall' (as the children call it) that Jane will happily enter. The rest of the building revives distressing memories of her own captivity. She can smile graciously at the inmates from our pew but fears meeting them face to face. They must think her remote and haughty. I wish they could see her humble, tireless labour on their behalf as she strains her eyes late into the night, writing letters and reports and gathering information. Facts, she once said to me, are her fortress. She calls me her dreaming spire and says I would float away were it not for her practicality. Perhaps it is so. I know I feel securely anchored when I lie beside her and clasp her swelling warmth and wonder about our child budding within her.

But before I can allow myself that luxury I must make sure that all is well on the men's side. It is quiet here. Women talk more than men, even in their sleep. If women in general harm themselves, men injure each other. During the day there are many more fights among the men than among the women. Many of these men are able to converse, play chess and read. There is a library here but not in the women's wing, for serious or exciting books would be bad for their more susceptible minds.

As I pace these corridors my candle dances in anguish on the walls. Here there is less suffering than in the criminal wards, but there is much to disgust in the furtive gasps and groans. Satyriasis is a loathsome and humiliating condition. How often do we forge the bolt that is to destroy us – many of these patients have led a debauched life, and Providence punishes the offence appropriately. Erotomaniacs live night and day in gross lasciviousness. Their voluptuous dreams poison our air, and I have trained my attendants to police their disgusting masturbation. I have learned to recognize the onanist, who is invariably thin and unhealthy looking, emaciated by his secret shame.

I pause outside the incurable unit. These are our failures, and there are too many. George Dadd lies in the cubicle nearest to me, *The Old Curiosity Shop*, as always, beneath his fingers. He has been reading it for ten years, ever since he was admitted. I do not know if he reads it again and again or simply needs to have it about him, as little Chas needs to hold his red knitted horse when he sleeps.

There is no family in the kingdom, from the domestic circle of the highest peer of the realm down to the humblest peasant, that may not be stricken with the calamity of insanity. But the Dadds! George's illness first struck a month after his older brother, the painter Richard Dadd, murdered their father. George was then but twenty, not possessed of his brother's talent but a clever workman, employed as a joiner in the Chatham Dockyards. His illness took a curious form: he fancied his bed was on fire and refused to sleep at home. He went out and returned home naked. When he was first admitted George Dadd was violent, but now he is only stubborn and generally silent. The other patients call him Tiger from the voracious manner he eats his meals (his brother Richard also has repulsive table manners).

As if their family history were not melancholy enough, there is another brother, Stephen, who now has a private attendant at home in Manchester. And I have heard from Haydon – a magnificent source of gossip – that their youngest sister, Maria, who is married to the painter John Phillip, has shown signs of mental instability. Miss Dadd, the aunt who brought up these ill-fated children after their mother and stepmother died, is in a private asylum on the Bow Road.

Last year I arranged a meeting between the two brothers in the hope that close observation would shed light upon their sad affliction. We alienists dream of a key that will open the locked door of hereditary madness. However, it was but a dream.

The two brothers greeted one another awkwardly and fell like wolves upon a simnel cake, demolishing it within minutes. Seeing the two men together I was struck by the resemblance. Both are handsome, tall, with light-brown wavy hair and large, powerful blue eyes. Richard's contain the stranger light. To be stared at by him is to feel seized by a brilliant power, as if Osiris (the poor fellow is obsessed by the Egyptian deity) really does gaze out from those enormous sockets. Despite the warmth of Haydon's snug steward's room the two did not thaw and had very little to say to each other. A few monosyllables, grunts and mutters were all they shared before sinking back into gloom and isolation.

A few days later I saw the artist again. He had asked me to sit for him in my evening clothes. I had thought he meant to paint my portrait to repay my encouragement of his work, and so, flattered, I gave him several sittings in Haydon's room before I asked to see the work.

To my surprise, the head upon the shoulders of the dinner jacket was not my own. I recognized an idealized version of the Dadd face, younger and more hopeful than either brother. The young man sat on a bench in a country garden, a red fez beside him. The background, which was as yet only sketched in, was curious. Beyond the familiar English landscape could be seen a Greek temple and a ruined city on a hill with cypress trees, as if the Mediterranean had crossed the channel.

'Whom have you portrayed here?' I asked Dadd.

'A young man full of promise. He has the world before him but wisely decides to see it only in his imagination. He wanders no further afield than Kent and lives at peace with his family and the world.' His ferocious blue eyes glittered with tears, and he asked me to take him back to the criminal wing, like a beast handing the knife to his slaughterer.

I do not know if there is still hope for the Dadd brothers. I do believe in Richard's talent, although the work he has done since his illness is bizarre and strange and vastly inferior to the charming landscapes and faery paintings he produced when he was sane. Some say it is the madness that makes the artist, but from my observation of Richard Dadd I have concluded the opposite: not that the bats make the belfry but that the purest, loveliest bells sound where there are no bats. There is only one Richard Dadd, and in his presence I am overwhelmed by his unique and powerful character.

But our hospital, like any other institution, exists to be of service to many not only to the individual. We aim to reseat the dethroned intelligence – genius is another matter, and I do not claim fully to understand it, although I confess that I am fascinated by Richard Dadd.

This evening, as I watched little Duncan in a rage because he did not want to go to bed, I thought how like to an infant a lunatic is: capricious, undisciplined, affectionate, as easily diverted by activity as Donald is by merry romps. Just as a good infant school will work with coaxing and persuasion, never with cruelty and humiliation, so do I wish to administer my little utopia. Let them labour but not by force. They can learn valuable skills by gardening, doing their own laundry and cooking. Their work should be rewarded not by money but by luxuries such as tobacco and privileges. Thus may my charges learn to look after themselves and each other. Their time here is not imprisonment but a reunion with society. They have rights and must discharge duties.

Walking here alone with the silent light of my candle and the thunderous machinery of my thoughts, I have faith in our progress.

# DANCING

One is dead and does not know it,
One is not yet born.
The third one sees me what I am,
My bright yet hopeless dawn.

'A VERY CURIOUS sampler,' says Marian, passing me with a basket of
dirty linen as I sit on my chair in the long gallery.

I have tried to do the towers and horseless carriages of Jonathan's
London in cross-stitch, in red and green wool. When I showed Dr
Hood my sampler and my drawings and watercolours of that wonderland he was not cross with me like Charles. He says fancy is free,
and I do feel free here with him to watch over me, like a Chinese lady
whose feet are no longer bound. Several of the ladies here think he
is a saint, but then they are prone to seeing saints, etc. We are all
smitten to death with him, for in addition to his beautiful nature he
is tall and elegant with dark hair and eyes, very handsome. I think
he looks like Mr Browning and would not blame any lady who ran
off to Italy with him. When he enters our ward we all rush up to him
and try to take his hand and whisper our secrets to him, but had he
as many hands and ears as a Hindoo god there would not be enough
for us all.

Dr Hood says my drawings are very interesting, and he is to show
them to Mr Dadd, a most fascinating monster who is incarcerated
(for the rest of his days!) in the dark and dreadful State Criminal
Asylum, a sort of Castle of Otranto in the London suburbs. Indeed,
Mr Dadd's prison is what I used to imagine Bedlam to be, only Dr
Hood says we must not call it that but the Bethlehem Hospital.

Where Christ was born and where many Christs now live, but they are in the men's wing and we are not allowed to speak to them.

I am in the most privileged ward at the top of the building, and from my little sleeping chamber I can see the horrid dank criminal block. Often at night when I cannot sleep I go to my window and look down. It is terrifying and a little thrilling. No lights shine in the barred windows, and nobody ever comes out or goes in there except the warders, who are oafish-looking fellows – not like our attendants, who are pleasant.

Mr Dadd was a brilliant young artist who killed his own papa. When we sit by the fire in the evening sewing together we often talk of him. It is a tale we long to know in every detail, but nobody will tell us. Dr Hood says it would excite us too much. Of course, we all remember the sensation in the newspapers about ten years back when Mr Dadd was arrested in Paris after he tried to cut the throat of a tourist. He gave his real name to the police and confessed to his father's murder. Hidden on his body was a list of those 'who must die', and his papa was number one.

In the evenings we piece together Mr Dadd's story. We have no need of ghost stories, for he is a kind of living ghost, among us yet unseen. I am very pleased that Dr Hood wants to show him my drawings, but I must not boast to the other ladies as Dr Hood does not offer to show their flower paintings and fancy work to our 'mad genius'. I can hear Henrietta's voice telling me I should not be proud of such a thing, and I do not want to make them envious, for they are becoming my friends.

So that is the night view from the back. At the front, when I sit drawing or sewing or chattering during the day, I gaze out of the window at a very different view. The windows themselves are a gift from Dr Hood. Before he came there were only bars, but he has replaced them with clear glass. He has let the light into our lives, and we love him for it. During the day I look down on lawns and on the gardens we are helping to make, those of us who have decided not to

172

be entirely mad. I used to enjoy helping my mama in the garden at Finsbury, but at Harley Street there was no garden. Is no garden. How strange that I feel so little connection with that house where I lived for five years. But darling Bella is dead, and Henrietta has stolen my place, and Tommy is away at school. I know this because Charles writes to me, not letters exactly but something between a laundry list and a prescription. I do not compare them with the letters he wrote when we were courting, for he is a different person now and so am I.

When I look down over the lawn at the front I often see Dr Hood there playing with his little boys. It is a glorious sight. When it is warmer I shall go down and make a painting of them if he does not object. If I am still here. I hope I shall be. I do not wish to get better, for better is worse. He plays with them very gently while they shriek and laugh and run around. They are happy children, and we feed off their happiness. We are so glad he lets us watch them, and if any inmate – one of those who is mad and bad – should ever harm Dr Hood or one of his children I think there would be a riot here. The miscreant would be torn apart before a policeman could be summoned.

Mrs Hood is *enceinte*. Her name is Jane, and she is not beautiful or young. The ladies say she is older than him. She is rather sallow with a snub nose and dresses very plain. We watch her swelling with hungry eyes, and in a few months she will have her baby for all of us. I know there will be no more children for me.

Mrs Hood is said to be very reserved, but I think she is only shy. I can see from my post at the window that she deeply loves her husband and sons. When I see her in chapel on Sunday mornings she looks ill at ease and does not return our stares.

Marian has just told me that we are all to spend Christmas with Dr Hood and his family! I think this wonderful. What need have we of presents when he gives us himself, and what need of a nativity scene when we can feast our eyes on this holy family? Marian says I am too sentimental, but I have need of such feelings, for I have lost so much of my little world,, and Dr Hood is a safe port for my frail vessel of love.

I think perhaps I will learn to love Marian. She is a most surpris-ing person. When I see her bustling in the laundry or weeding the flowerbeds she does not seem a bit mad. Yet she imagines Albert, her dead child, is constantly with her. She talks to him with delight and takes him to bed with her and feeds him at mealtimes. Her husband, a clerk in the city, could not bear these constant reminders of their much-loved only son and begged Dr Hood to keep Marian here until she is cured. But she is not cured. Albert was with us this morning when we were raking the dead leaves on the front lawn.

I said, 'Why do you tell him to step out of the way?'

'He is a heedless little fellow, always walking with his head in the air.'

I paused in my work and gazed into her rosy, charming face. Marian is plump and pink, and her face beneath her blue bonnet glowed with maternal fondness. Real feeling but not for a real child. I wanted to scream out that Albert is dead as a mackerel. I had to choose between humouring her and treating her as a rational being and chose the second.

'My dear, I know what it is to mourn a child. But would it not be better to accept that Albert is in Heaven?'

'He most certainly is not. He is here in St George's Fields, helping, or rather hindering, his mama. Albert! Stay away from Nina or she will tread on you and do you an injury.'

She glared at me and moved away, her mouth closed tight against me. I saw that she was the one I had injured but persisted in my mad doctoring. 'I cannot see him.'

'You should ask the nurse for some spectacles. That's right, darling, put them over there,' she added in a more tender voice to the patch of grass beside her.

We continued to work in silence until we had made quite a mountain of leaves in the corner by the wall. I do not mind working and indeed enjoy it. The heat and flurry of the kitchens makes me feel active and useful, and it is a pleasure to see our garden being born. It is more interesting to see how food and gardens are made than to give orders to a cook or a gardener.

Marian and I wore our outdoor clothes, for the air is Novembery now with that cold, smoky fragrance I love. We have asked Dr Hood if we may have a bonfire and fireworks, but he is afraid it would excite the other patients too much (for we are the pattern lunatics, trusted to behave well). I felt very cheerful as I stood on the lawn with my lungs full of richly rotting leaves. As Marian was not disposed to talk I drifted back to other Novembers.

When I was a child this time of year was both thrilling and terrifying. For Guy Fawkes was a Catholic, and our mother used to make us stay at home on the 5th of November in case there was a 'No Popery' riot and the Finsbury urchins wanted living effigies to toss upon their bonfires. I remember one evening when I was about seven I snuggled against Mama in the warm parlour and sang as she played the piano. Above the music I could hear the bangs and whoops and crashes in the darkness outside that could not harm me. Papa came home from visiting some gouty old merchant, and I ran to him at the door and buried my face in the cold fog on his black greatcoat.

'And you! You saw an elephant!'

Startled, I backed away as Marian strode towards me, brandishing her rake like a sword.

'But I really did . . .' I met her ferocious eye and could not finish my sentence.

She had won, simply by silencing me.

The elephant, Albert and Jonathan all exist. They are all 'real', although perhaps it would be wiser not to talk about them. If I had not written that letter to Charles and had not spoken of my experiences I would still be a matron living in Harley Street. If Marian had mourned her child inwardly and had not told her husband that Albert is still alive for her she would not be here either. In the other wards there are women (and men, but we are not allowed to meet them) who have truly lost their wits. They scream and slobber and hurl abuse and blows at all who pass. Marian and I have only little corners of our minds that do not fit in with the rest of the world. Our wits are not lost but only separated, like eggs: the yoke at our centre remains bright and healthy, but the white has been whipped up into peaks and troughs, and so the omelette . . . Charles always used to tease me about my mixed metaphors.

When I am alone in my room at night I search the darkness for Jonathan. I do not speak aloud to him as Marian does to Albert, but he is just as real to me. If I have changed it is because those few days with Jonathan showed me another way of life. If there is a future when women will be free as birds – free as men – then I do not need to squeeze myself back into the strait-waistcoat of Mrs Sanderson. I would do so for Charles if we still loved each other. But we do not. Perhaps it is not fair to say that Charles is 'dead but does not know it'. He is respected, admired, he hobnobs happily – far too happily – with the grandees of Portman Square. The Charles I loved is dead, but he died so quietly that nobody noticed – not even Charles himself. I am a kind of widow. The black dress I wear for Bella envelops me in its shadowy wings and flies me away from Harley Street.

At night the silence quivers and rustles, and I feel Jonathan beside me. His presence comforts me because he carries the wonderful future with him. We are all going to a better place, which is much jollier than Henrietta's Heaven because we don't have to die but have only to live hopefully. I won't live to see it, but I am so much happier now that I have caught a glimpse of it. Jonathan is part of the invisible army that surrounds us always; the beloved dead and the absent and the unborn and the longed for. I think it very strange that we are only approved of when we pretend not to feel or see or hear them. If Jonathan is a delusion he is as necessary to me as fresh air and cottage pie.

Dr Hood says I may draw and write whatever I please. I have the right to furnish the secret chambers of my mind as I like, and he will not pry or show this little book to Charles. He has set me free to put down whatever comes into my head, and so I will.

Last night I dreamed that I lay with Jonathan. We Said Good-night, and he did not feel a bit like a man who has not yet been born. We talked and laughed and delighted in one another, and it was very sweet and natural and not at all like disgraceful crim.con.

This morning Dr Hood asked if I wished to go home.

'You are almost cured, and I see no reason why you should not return to your family for a few days. Your sister will be able to look after you if necessary, and perhaps we could arrange for your son to come home from school.'

I was sitting in the long gallery sketching Jonathan's London. The doctor was beamish as he stooped over me, and his magnificent brown eyes were alight with kindness. I thought of Charles and Henrietta and burst into tears.

He handed me his pocket handkerchief – he has always a good supply ready – and I hid my face in the clean white linen. I was very glad of both tears and handkerchief, for they allowed me time to register my own thoughts. I do not want to see Charles or Henrietta. I long to see Tommy, but I know Charles will not allow me to. I heard him say to Dr Weasel in the carriage on the way here, 'My wife cannot be allowed to pollute our son. I will tell Tommy that his mother is dead.'

I was ashamed to explain this to Dr Hood lest he think ill of me.

'I hoped to please you, but naturally you do not have to go home if you do not wish to. Now here is something to cheer you up.'

He handed me a sheaf of my own drawings and watercolours. On the back of each one comments had been written in neat handwriting. For example: 'Most curious and interesting.' 'Are the immodestly dressed young ladies related to Titania?' 'I think you had better study perspective.' 'The shadow of the tall building would fall to the right, not to the left.'

'Did Mr Dadd write this?'

'He did. And asked me to tell you that you have talent and originality and that he is very glad you have not confined yourself to botany.'

They were the most encouraging words about my work that I

have ever received. It is true that they came from a madman but from one who has lived among artists as well as lunatics.

'Thank you so much! Tell him – tell Mr Dadd I should be so happy if he would be my drawing teacher. And I should like it of all things to see his work. Is he able to work in that dreadful place?'

'Indeed he does. All around him chaos seethes and the most vile ruffians brawl and riot. But he sits there, calm and patient, drawing and painting.'

'Poor man! Can he not be separated from the others?'

'He is under the jurisdiction of the Home Office. I have no authority over him, but I am petitioning Lord Palmerston to transfer Dadd and some two dozen others – scholars and gentlemen despite their tragic histories – to our more civilized regime.'

Now when I look out of my window at night my heart races with fear and indignation. I long to fly down into the darkness and rescue Richard Dadd. I imagine the wonderful conversations I would have with him if he were in the same building and we somehow contrived to meet – how I should tame him and win his confidence. It is strange to live only among women. Dr Hood and the jovial Mr Haydon are our only daily visitors of the opposite sex.

However, the other ladies are not dull. I never would have expected to meet such interesting people in Bedlam.

Susan was here just now. She is quite convinced I am her school-friend Eliza. Susan is old enough to be my mama and grew up in Sussex, but there is no arguing with her. So I allow her to pet me and try not to mind that she seems never to wash her clothes. Every evening she scolds Horatio Nelson and Christopher Columbus who are in her bed. Her cubicle is next to mine, and her language is so scurrilous that Mrs Dunn has deprived her of pudding for a week.

'My sweet Eliza!' A sweaty kiss. 'Come, let's run away from Jemima.'

Susan sees all the ladies here as people from her previous life when she was at a boarding-school in Chichester. I think she was happy there and has not been since. It is possible to have a sensible conversation with her as long as I allow her to pretend I am Eliza and do not laugh at her when she lisps and giggles and plays skipping games. She is a stout lady of forty-eight with leathery brown skin and grey hair, so the effect is rather comical.

We play cat's cradle and hopscotch and gossip about girls who must be grandmothers by now. Then there is a horrid screeching in our ears as Lavinia passes. She becomes incensed if we call her Lavinia, for she insists that she is Jenny Lind the Swedish Nightingale, although Marian calls her the Southwark Crow. Lavinia is tiny and withered – somewhere indeterminate between thirty-five and fifty – and has a truly hideous voice. It is so flat and so intrusive that I want to cover my ears and shut my eyes. Instead I smile and clap.

I tried to be honest with Marian because I like her best of all the ladies here, but it was not a success and now she is cross with me and says Albert is afraid of me. I do not like it when I am told that the things I saw with Jonathan could not have happened. I feel hurt and dizzy and want to cry, and so it is with all of us here. The truth is, I no longer know what the truth is.

Lavinia's caterwauling has disturbed Susan, who begins to be flighty again. She leans towards me and whispers (her breath is not sweet, and she is inclined to spit), 'How did she get in here? People often can get in through windows and keyholes.' This is true. I suppose all of us ladies have our keyhole lovers and all the gentlemen, too.

Susan has tired of being a schoolgirl. Her face is flushed and her eyes are wild and glistening. Is this how I looked to Charles? I move away from her, for last week she broke some vases on our ward and attempted to jump out of the window. She took the parrot out of its cage outside her cubicle and wrung its neck, and when the attendant restrained her Susan tried to bite her.

Before I can escape Susan grabs me and puts her hands on my shoulders and forces me to my knees. 'You must kiss my hand, Eliza, for I am the Empress of all the world except the East Indies, which is too hot, and you are only a chit of a girl.'

Fortunately Mrs Dunn is passing with a pile of sheets. She rescues me from the Empress and gives Her Highness a glass of Tranquillity Tea. None of us knows what is in it, but it tastes delicious and has a most magical effect. Susan abdicates and goes to lie down in her cubicle.

Sometimes I imagine I am the hostess at a Harley Street 'at home' with Marian, Susan, Richard Dadd and Jonathan. Lavinia would provide the musical entertainment. How the conversation would fizz and startle – there wouldn't be a word about the weather. And how surprised Jonathan would be, for he told me he thought the Victorians (his name for us) were boring and hypocritical and never said what they thought.

But none of us here is ever at home. Dr Hood is the only one among us who is comfortable in his own skin, and so we all love him and hope we may discover how it is done.

Betty is melancholy mad, and a peasouper of misery surrounds her. I am afraid to approach her. Once she asked if I was going to cut off her head.

'I do not believe in capital punishment.'

'Then how am I to be punished?'

'Why should I wish to punish you?'

'For my wickedness.'

She fell into such a fit of weeping that my own eyes brimmed with tears. Betty is tall and bony with sparse grey hair in a bun and dark eyes which are red where they should be white and sunk deep in shadows from all her weeping. Her eyes are like caves pulling me down inside a goblin mountain.

Betty was screaming just now. She can hear workmen erecting the scaffold for her execution tomorrow morning. Sometimes she is silent for days on end, and I have never seen her smile. Nobody seems to know what wickedness she has committed, although, of course, we are all dying of curiosity. I think of her as Cassandra, and then I remember that Cassandra was right. Betty does prophesy, and although she has not enough hair to tear she wails most alarmingly. After one of the assistants calmed her and told her the banging she could hear was only the water pipes being fixed Betty stopped screaming. Instead, she ran around the ward shaking us all and warning us, 'You must leave this place! All the houses are tumbling down, and everyone will be killed!'

Of course, leaving this place is the one thing we cannot do and most of us do not wish to. I would not wish to die in Betty's dismal company. She is quite an expert on Heaven and tells me she has been there lately and is going back in a day or two. Betty has just fallen over again, for she is near-sighted. Dr Hood provided her with spectacles, but she broke them because she said they hindered her salvation.

This has been a peaceful afternoon. I sit in the long gallery and work on the watercolour I am to show to Mr Dadd. My pencil and brushes fly over the paper since I received his message. It is so good to know that my work is appreciated and by such a judge – a man who has moved in the highest artistic circles.

How I long to speak with Mr Dadd. I feel sure that he would understand my vision of the future. Perhaps he would not find it strange at all, for artists move freely between phantasy and reality. I could tell him of Jonathan and of the wonderful future that awaits us. Mr Dadd and I shall not see it, but we could celebrate the happiness of generations to come who will live without poverty, war, ignorance or pain. I know Mr Dadd would listen to me and would not laugh as Marian did when I tried to tell her. She told me to get back to Cloud-cuckoo-land, which was not kind or helpful.

In the watercolour I am working on now Jonathan (how handsome he was! or is! or will be!) sits in front of his teavea in darkness illuminated by its weird blue light. His room is bare, but his mind is furnished with beautiful thoughts. He stares at moving pictures of horrible massacres,, but his expression is calm, for he knows that such barbarity is safely in the past. Our past.

A woman with dark hair sits beside him on the black leather sofa.

Her features cannot be seen in the shadows, but I know they are my own. The paints blur as I weep from envy of that future Nina. Her children will all live, and she will have machines to do the chores of servants and will be educated to use her mind to earn hard cash and be free. How happy she will be.

'More tears? Turn off the waterworks or I shan't dance with you tonight.' It is Marian. Although her voice is brusque I am very glad that we are friends once more.

We have an upright piano on our ward. Mrs Dunn says it a great privilege and we must earn it by our good behaviour. Last week Susan threw her porridge down it, and the keys are somewhat sticky. We practise dancing for the ball next month. I have not yet attended one, but I am told our balls are famous all over London. The great and the famous come to watch. We are all making paper flowers to decorate the ballroom, and many of the ladies are cutting and sewing their own ballgowns. Dr Hood lets them have lengths of fabric in return for extra work in the laundry and kitchens. Before she married, Marian used to be a lady's maid in an aristocratic household in Grosvenor Square. She is very dainty and fastidious and helps the other ladies with their dressmaking. Of course, Marian and I will have to stay in mourning even at the ball. I will send Emmie a note asking her to send my best black silk.

It is a little difficult to practise dancing without any men. Betty and I and the taller ladies have to dance the masculine steps. It is so many years since I have danced that I fear I shall have forgotten how and will make myself ridiculous by asking the gentlemen to dance and guiding them in an unfeminine manner. And what sort of gentlemen will they be? I do not want to dance with Jesus Christ or the Tsar, for I should not know what to say to them. We are all agog to know if Dr Hood will dance at the ball, but nobody has dared to ask him.

We all look forward to our dancing except Betty, who says it is frivolity and fiddlesticks and goes to bed early. There are three attendants standing by with Tranquillity Tea lest the excitement overcomes us. Lavinia accompanies us on the piano and screeches. We are all the teachers and try to remember what we can about dances we attended when we were young and beautiful and had men at our feet.

I am not at Marian's feet but mostly under them as we stumble around the ward. I imagine I am in the arms of Charles or Jonathan, but in order fully to imagine this I have to shut my eyes, and then I become even more clumsy. I discover that I would prefer the arms of Jonathan, but it does not matter since he is not here either. There is only Marian, whose hair smells of custard. She tells me to be careful not to tread on Albert's toes.

All of us are dancing now. Lavinia is playing a waltz that tugs at my heart strings, and the music floats us on a cloud of memory and romance. Around and around and around we whirl in circles of joy. A gaiety I thought lost for ever swoops over me as I fall backwards into the melody. We are dancing with the music as much as with each other, and while the music embraces us we are not alone. By gaslight our faces are softer and brighter and happier. I want all to share in our music as the piano's voice seeps through walls and floors. I want it to infiltrate the dreadful criminal block and soothe all those savage breasts – and most particularly Mr Dadd's.

# CHARLES

HENRIETTA STOPPED ME again as I was leaving the house to ask if I would return for supper. I am rarely at home; I suppose she eats and prays alone. A saintly woman, but I had rather not meet a saint on the stairs when I am going to discuss aphrodisiacs with William.

All this talk of the fatal passion is having a most unfortunate effect on my own passions. An appetite I can scarcely afford to gratify if I am to be a Bedlam bachelor for the foreseeable future, for I have no cash for a flutter outside the blanket. Indeed, I learned this morning that I have overdrawn my bankers by three hundred pounds.

In William's elegant library I felt the familiar acid of envy. It filled my mouth like poison, but I had to swallow it together with my pride, for William is my only hope of escaping from this detestable no-man's-land between respectability and insolvency. He let me know that he has a *petite amie* at the Drury Lane Theatre in addition to his house in Hanover Square and the country house where he conveniently stores his wife and children. He has no need to boast; his very presence reminds me of how little I have to boast about.

Over sherry and exquisite little almond cakes made by his Italian chef we discussed our patent magneto-electric box, the Elysium.

'Puffery is all, my dear fellow. We must advertise. *The Times* won't print this sort of thing, but we'll write a sizzling pamphlet. I count on you for that, Charles; you're a literary sort of chap. I remember how you used to read poetry and that kind of thing. Next week I shall order thousands – no, hundreds of thousands – of sticky labels. They will appear on every wall and railway arch in London, on wagons – and for a few shillings we can hire our own sandwichman to parade up and down Oxford Street. The Elysium will become a household name, like Pears' soap. By Christmas we'll have Tommy's school fees and Maria's dowry under our belts. Now, to work!'

William sat me down at a walnut davenport desk and pushed a large and alarmingly blank sheet of paper towards me.

'But how can we write of these things? Will we not be prosecuted for obscenity?'

'These things, as you call them, are of concern to everybody. There is nothing obscene about the propagation of the species. You have only to hint delicately at the marvellous efficaciousness of our invention. With the Elysium mutual satisfaction is guaranteed and pregnancy ensues.'

'But you know perfectly well that a few wires in a box can do nothing!'

'Charles, in a minute I shall think I have chosen the wrong partner.'

His threat was enough to liberate my imagination. As I puffed I sucked my pen and sipped my sherry. The more genteel my phrase-making became, the more I burned with lust.

'To restore a woman's response . . .' Nina on our wedding trip, after I had unwrapped her layers of frothy whiteness. She lay on the bed, so slender and pale and young. I felt like one of the coarse soldiers in a painting carrying off a Sabine woman; I felt ugly and hairy and expected her to scream or run away. She smiled at me with perfect trust and held out her thin white arms to me. I think nothing in my life has delighted me as much as that moment. 'Exhaustive satisfaction to both partners at the same moment . . .' Nina was both innocent and wanton; she gave herself with such sweet generosity. It was not a dance she had danced before, of that I am quite sure. Yet she enjoyed me, we enjoyed each other, with such frankness. Ramsgate, not a town usually associated with Elysium.

Memories inspired me to write a somewhat lurid description of a beautiful young bride driven to adultery because her husband was impotent. 'Lady Theodora writhed and thrashed alone in the night. She strove not to think of the dashing young Sir Percival and his passionate notes. Poor Lord Bruce lay beside his pulchritudinous young wife. All night he longed, he adored, but he could not act upon his desires. If only the Elysium had been available to them, to synchronize their yearning . . .' Why is it that titles lend romance to even the most sordid plots?

'The mere presence of the Elysium is the matrimonial bed will be enough to transport both partners . . .' It is a fairy-tale but a charming one. If only I could find such a magic box to restore my little Nina to me in all her loving freshness.

To lend my pamphlet some intellectual respectability I ended with a quotation from Galen: 'The pleasures of love, when they are moderate, and not indulged in until the body has had time to repair . . . promote gaiety, contentment and a sense of freedom in the female.'

William was delighted. 'Marvellous! Next year we will patent a machine to cure cholera. Professor Benvoglio has a great future!'

We have agreed to conflate ourselves into this illustrious quack, who has degrees from the Universities of Leipzig, Milan and Vienna and Testimonials and Honourable Mention from Their Imperial Majesties the Emperors of Russia and Austria and from the reigning monarchs of Italy and Transylvania. It would be foolish to use our real names in case one of our pamphlets falls into the hands of the College of Physicians.

'I am glad you like my literary efforts. By the way, William, we must discuss the financial aspects . . .'

'Hard pressed, old man? Let me see . . .' He took out his pocket book and produced two five-pound notes, which he handed to me with aristocratic vagueness.

'Thank you so much.' I tried not to grovel.

'Come on Thursday at about the same time and we'll discuss the manufactory of the box. I have to dress for dinner at the duchess's.'

I have the impression that William rarely sees an untitled patient now. No doubt the diseases of duchesses are more fascinating than ours. As I left the house in Hanover Square I distinctly heard my father turn in his grave at this thought. A very solid grave – he asked to be well weighted down, for who knew better than him the dangerous life corpses lead?

My father's voice came to me vividly. I had the sun very strong in my eyes, for I had helped myself liberally to William's decanter. Get yourself a good education, Charlie, and remember where you came from. When you're a doctor help the poor. The rich can look after themselves. And mind you look after poor Sam, as can't.

Conversations with the dead are apt to be disturbing. My lips moved in self-justification: I used to see the poor for free, but now I haven't the time, I have to provide for my son as you provided for us. I thought Sam would be well looked after in that private asylum. I'm sorry, Pa. Cholera, they said. I . . .

I stood in the raging torrent of Oxford Street, surrounded by horrible reminders of what happens to those who fail in life. After Hare was released from prison in Edinburgh he drifted down to London where the mob threw him into a limepit. They say he earns a living still as a blind beggar in Oxford Street. I always look out for him. If I found him I would buy him a meal, for he was not so much worse than the rest of us. But how to recognize one deformed human wreck among so many?

When sober I rush across Oxford Street, that stinking polluted river of accursed life. But yesterday evening my legs had no strength in them. I tried to squeeze between an omnibus and a hackney cab, but the cab's horse reared and nearly kicked me. Unable to move, dizzy, I reached out to balance myself on a heap of old sacking. My fingers clung to it as a swimmer clutches a rock when he feels the force of the cold treacherous current sweep him away.

But the rock moved beneath my hand. The heap of sacking stood up and became a man, a sort of man, a boozy wretch dressed in military rags. As his foul breath assaulted my nostrils I wondered if my own stank, too. His filthy grey claws gripped my arm.

'God bless you, kind sir. Will you give a copper to a poor old Peninsular officer, wounded at Barossa under the Duke?'

I gave him sixpence and shook him away. As if the flash of silver were a lighthouse, other human wrecks came sailing up and surrounded me. A destitute Polish refugee with long mustachios and a melodramatic cloak handed me a greasy letter telling me of his miraculous escape from a Russian prison and claiming to be a count of the Holy Roman Empire. Before I could read it he was pushed out of the way by a toothless old gypsy horoscopist who dribbled prophecies of my great future and demanded to see my palm, which I withdrew sharply from her stinking hand. I heard singing and turned to find myself being serenaded by an entire mendicant family. The mother was dark and pretty, the two children good-looking with dark curls and sweet voices. 'Sweet Lass of Richmond Hill', Bella's favourite song. The four of them were like a ghastly caricature of the family we once were. I reeled away from them, all of them, but my way to the road was blocked by an old man in seedy evening dress who stood pad, a ticket at his breast on which a piteous tale was written: 'Kind friends and Christian brethren! I stand before you ruined, victim of the breaking of six of the most respectable banking houses in New York . . .'

Had I broken one of William's fivers and distributed coppers to all of them it would never have been enough. Desperate to escape, I muttered, 'I am an officer of the Mendicity Society.'

To my astonishment they believed me and melted away into the pandemonium of shoppers. An old horse had fallen on the slippery road and was being soundly thrashed by an angry cabby. I could hardly cross through the traffic lock of spinning hackneys, ponderous omnibuses, jingling cabs, costermongers, newspaper sellers and bookies' runners.

Even when I had finally crossed Oxford Street and reached the calm prosperity of Cavendish Square I feared the beggars would follow me home. They are all distantly related to Professor Benvoglio, so why should they not seek bread and shelter at his house?

How sweet to stand at my own front door. To have a front door. James came to answer the bell, surly as he has been these last few wageless months. As I handed him my hat I glanced over my shoulder to make sure I was not being pursued by an army of mendicants. The empty street and the solidity of the hall reassured me. I was master again, with enough money in my pocket to pay James if I chose. But I did not.

'Charles!' Henrietta stood on the stairs, her face a burlesque of her sister's. 'How weary you look. I am afraid you have missed prayers again. You give too much of yourself to these paupers.'

When I go to see William I tell her I am going to help in the free dispensary in the St Giles rookery. I did go there once a few years ago but did not return as I was afraid of catching some infection and passing it on to my family. Now cholera rages in those courts and alleys, and I would not go near them, for as soon as cholera is a disease it is death. However, it is good I meant to do and still intend to do some day. I have no objection if Henrietta wishes to praise me for it.

They are very dismal, these tête-à-tête dinners with Henrietta. Hers is the wrong head, and her air of sacrifice depresses me. She is like a lamb that insists on lying on an altar, offering her throat to a vegetarian priest.

The lascivious thoughts that had besieged me in William's library returned after dessert. The prospect of spending the rest of the evening in the silent drawing-room, enlivened only by the ticking clock and the click of Henrietta's crochet hook, was quite unbearable.

'I have left a poor young girl in labour with only her mother in attendance. I must go back to her.'

'You are really quite heroic, Charles. Would you like me to go with you? I have considerable experience of visiting the poor.'

'No. Thank you, but I must plough my lonely furrow.'

I hurried out into the November fog. Apart from a few carriages delivering guests to smart parties to which I had not been invited, Harley Street was deserted.

How different London is at night. Hurly-burly and beggars meta-morphose into a girl-market, and how I longed to shop there. My testicles ached with disuse, my engine of desire was engorged with the most fatal passion that ever issued from Pandora's box. How long ago was it, that last passionate grapple with Nina on our sofa? Four months, at least. Night after night I have lain alone, longing to feel her again, remembering her warm soft tits and furry quim. To think that we two will never Say Goodnight again. Tenderness mingled with rage as I remembered her wanton mouth, the mouth of a joy-girl, not a young matron. I struggled for months, counselling myself as I would a patient against self-abuse: insanity, degeneracy, epilepsy, spermatorrhoea, consumption, premature senility and death; these are the wages of masturbation. But whereas women are, or ought to be, above carnal desire, we men must ejaculate to be healthy.

That was the last gasp of Reason, a dreary old crone who expired in the night. In Oxford Street there were women everywhere. Not crones but young and pretty, at least as seen by gaslight through the fog. I did not want some screamer or a diseased whore. I stared into the face of a shabbily dressed young woman, no doubt walking home from the shop where she had been working all day. She looked sweet and intelligent, and I wondered if she would keep me company for the night. I longed to speak to her. But what if she were respectable and called a policeman? Besides, I had nowhere to take her.

She passed, but there were hundreds more, outside every public house and on the corner of every alley. I remembered hearing at my club about the bedrooms to let by the hour above the shops in the Burlington Arcade. Would an expensive whore above an expensive shop be less likely to give me the clap? I stood like an idiot, paralysed with lust, longing for pagan pleasures but too damned cowardly to seize them.

On Bond Street carriages swooped down to bear elegant couples off to fashionable dinners and balls. I passed a beautiful young lady about to step into her brougham. I was so near to her that I could smell her perfume, hear the rustle of her silk and see the lovely curve of her cheek as it turned away from me. Such women are and have always been far beyond me. Yet in my lustful fever I imagined tearing her crinoline from her shoulders, stripping away her elaborate layers of lace and satin to reveal a body like any other.

In the Haymarket, that blazing sink of iniquity, rouged and whitewashed whores clutched at my sleeve as I walked past. One of them was very young, not more than thirteen, with a cloud of fair curls and soft blue eyes staring at me out of a dirty face. A little flower of the gutter, I knew that to go home with her was to court disease, yet I longed to fondle her small breasts where they pressed against her ragged finery.

I forced myself to turn from her and walked priapically away, hardly conscious of where I was going. Frantic with desire, I found myself outside the Argyll Rooms on Windmill Street. Like a hungry child lurking outside a pastry shop, I stood outside and watched the crowds being sucked in through the brilliantly lit doors. How I longed to be sucked – each painted mouth tempted me so that I could hardly walk. All the women here were prostitutes, not the repulsive harlot slaves of the Haymarket but their more prosperous sisters, respectably dressed with the bloom of youth still upon them. Like ripe peaches they flaunted their succulent flesh, and men followed them. I hardly saw the men.

A pretty girl smiled at me as she swept through the doors. It was the starting pistol, and I needed no more encouragement to pursue her. Gladly I paid my shilling entrance fee and let her draw me through the crowded casino to the ballroom, a large, luxurious room, well lit with huge mirrors, where a delicious pastiche of a genteel social event was enacted. To be sure, there was music and dancing and chandeliers and men and women in evening dress, but there were no dowagers or chaperones, and the embraces that began on the dance floor continued far into the night.

The girl I had been following, who was dressed expensively and quietly, turned around. I saw with a throb of surprise that she had large deep-blue eyes and a mass of dark curls. Perhaps Nina's is the only face I can ever love, even for a night. We danced and talked, and after the polka we shared a sherry cobbler with a single straw. I felt the heat of Sarah's fresh young mouth on the paper tip as she spoke of her life in a low sweet voice without affectation. This facsimile of my fallen angel was twenty-three, the daughter of a clergyman. They all are, I heard William's cynical comment.

'My mama died when I was six, and Papa was very strict with me. We lived as poor and shabby as church mice in a parsonage in Gloucestershire. I had no brothers or sisters and knew no more of the world outside our parish calendar than a fledgeling knows of the ground beneath its nest. It was not long before a tomcat came prowling. His name was . . . well, never mind, I dare say you dined with him last night. He was the youngest son of the squire who owned my father's living and all the land round about, so I thought him a great man and never doubted he was a kind one. When I was sixteen our warm glances in church turned into stolen meetings, and when he left our village to go up to Oxford we exchanged passionate letters. I have his still. I shall treasure them always and still adore the boy who wrote them to that foolish girl.

'The Christmas I was seventeen we met at parties in the village and then in secret. On New Year's Day he begged me to go to London with him so that we could be married. He said he would set me up in rooms where he could visit me until he had his degree. Willingly, wilfully, I agreed. We had a week of paradise in an hotel in the Strand before his father stopped his allowance and mine sent me a letter disowning me. Since that day I have never heard from my lover or my father, and so I have learned to shift for myself.'

I have no idea if this story of hers was true – it was hardly new – but she was so pretty and I was so intoxicated by lust and sherry cobblers that I was deeply moved.

At five to twelve the Argyll Rooms closed, and Sarah and I flowed out on to the pavement with the other flotsam and jetsam of the *demi-monde*. We had a light but very expensive supper at Scott's Supper Rooms in the Haymarket, and then she asked with admirable frankness, 'Will you give me a guinea to come home with me?'

We set off arm in arm, the best of friends. I asked her a great many questions, for I was very curious about her life. She told me she paid eight shillings for her room in Dean Street and lived alone because she did not want a bully boy stealing her earnings. I was naturally very glad to think I would not be robbed, for I trusted Sarah. The black streets, where I would never have ventured alone, seethed with howls, laughter, singing and the rhythmic thump of drunken violence. Sarah's cool hand drew me through the invisible inferno. She could have been leading me to my death, but my senses were so inflamed that I would have followed her anywhere.

Sarah stopped in a doorway and pressed herself against me in the dark. I kissed her on the lips and pushed my tongue deep into her hot, moist mouth. Inside that place where Nina had lured me, that place she should not have known. Sarah knew it well, and I almost lost control and had her in the doorway where we stood.

'Come upstairs,' she said, opening the door with a key and pulling me up some dark rotting stairs.

'Give me the money now,' she said when we reached the landing at the top of the house. Her voice had changed, the clergyman's daughter had fallen among the fleshpots. I was happy to press my guinea into her hand as we entered a tiny room at the top of the stairs. Sarah lit a candle, examined my guinea and put it in a hatbox under her bed. The bed was so dirty and malodorous that all pretence at gentility evaporated. It was not gentility I wanted.

Sarah took me inside her gladly, and for a few hours she was the best little bedfellow a chap could desire. After the wildest venereal transports we fell asleep together, and when I awoke her squalid room was grey. An inch away her large, sad eyes watched me.

'Stay here with me all night.'

In a few hours my first patients would arrive. There would be people about in these disgraceful streets. I might be recognized and my professional reputation might be compromised.

'Please don't go. When will you visit me again?'

I extricated myself from the tangle of our limbs and ignored her whining. Sarah got up, lit a candle and offered me a bowl of swamp-like water to wash in. I could not bear to touch her foetid offering, although my body was sticky and love-soiled. This is not love, I reminded myself as I hurried into my clothes.

'When will you come again? Kiss me before you go.'

Desire was cold as suet. I refused to look at her as I muttered goodbye and escaped down the stairs. I know my weakness for such women who enjoy the sensual arts frankly without cant or squeamish-ness. They remind me of the first girls I ever debauched with, when I was fourteen, in the brothel next to my father's house. My taste for them is as shameful as eating peas with my knife, and I must over-come it.

As soon as I stood in the dark street I became aware of the dangers around me. A pestiferous miasma of sickness and death rose from the muddy pavement like steam from a hot bath. In my fear I must have taken a wrong turning, for I found myself or, rather, lost myself in a labyrinth of foul alleys where scarcely human creatures lay sleep-ing in doorways or sprawling drunkenly in filthy gutters. The dawn that was refreshing the rest of the city could not penetrate this vile maze. The air was thick with sewage. I retched and thought I would choke. A villainous-looking fellow lurched towards me, glaring at me with gin-sozzled eyes. I turned and fled, running blindly until I came to a wide street where there was a pavement and a sky. I felt like Orpheus rising from the underworld, with the difference that I had gladly abandoned my Eurydice to the darkness.

I leaned against a wall and regained my breath, watching shabby men and women set out on foot for work. I joined the high tide of respectable poverty and let it sweep me to the elegant splendour of

Regent Street, where morning gilded the roofs and the sky was as blue as an expensive bonnet. In the Quadrant a young girl took my arm and begged me to take her home with me. I shook myself free and glared at her, having no more need of her.

Striding down respectable streets, my streets, in the golden light of the rising sun, I experienced a moment of pure optimism. There are so many Sarahs for sale, I need never again be racked by desire. In time, as my enterprise with William bears more fruit, I may set up a love nest with a jolly little bird whom I can visit at will. I cannot divorce Nina, but her absence need not be a tragedy or even an inconvenience. Henrietta will organize my household admirably. Tommy will grow up to be a gentleman, and my practice will flourish. As I approached Cavendish Square I felt that each solid building stepped forward to embrace me.

My epiphany was short-lived. I greeted the nightwatchman with a hearty good morning and a wholly unnecessary tale of an all-night deathbed scene in a slum to explain my dishevelled and unwashed appearance. I felt as if I carried the story of my night with Sarah on my back, like a sandwich man, to be read by curious neighbours and patients. In fact, Harley Street was slumbering, and I was at my front door when I remembered that I had no key. Lucy or James have always opened the door, but they were still asleep. I stared down through the railings at the area, wondering if any of the servants slept in the kitchen and would hear me if I rapped on the window. I could not face my patients until I had bathed and changed.

As I stood there anxiously the door opened as if by magic. My improbable good fairy was Henrietta, wearing a nocturnal garment so hideous that I assumed it must have some penitential significance. Her nose was inflamed, always a sign of emotional turmoil, and her bloodshot eyes warned me that she had been weeping. I braced myself for some saga of domestic woe.

# HENRIETTA'S
# JOURNAL

## SATURDAY

How stupid I have been. A foolish, ugly old maid. How could I imagine that I was loved? I cannot even love myself. How you must have laughed at me; how they will all laugh. Of course, I can never leave this room again. You prefer bright eyes to intellectual conversation. What man would not? Your disgust was so very obvious. As if some ghoul had arisen from the grave and embraced you. Well, the grave will come soon enough, and I shall welcome it.

Shall I create a temporary sensation by jumping off Waterloo Bridge? There is nowhere to go. I have no father, brother or husband to watch over me. What am I to do with my life? I know that I am neither clever, handsome or young. I cannot return to my dingy little rooms, for I have no more savings; I gave you all my money. I was so glad to be of service to you. This ink flows with the salt water to blot and blur the page. My diary, that was to have been a gift to you. How often have I imagined your delight as I showed it to you. How you would exclaim and laugh, and we would share our tenderest innermost thoughts.

Such stupid dreams. All the time you thought me plain and dull, serviceable enough when Nina went off to Cloud-cuckoo-land. You did love her, adored her, the nasty little flirt. She was scarcely out of short skirts when she took your heart and kneaded it like clay. I used to feel nauseous, watching you stare at her. Whenever she came into the room you blushed and stammered and hobbledehoyed and never looked at me.

That deathbed in a rookery was a lie, the kind men tell to maiden aunts and village idiots. You have found some tuppenny Nina to debauch, and every night I must watch as you go to her.

Once I thought I had an immortal soul and my fancy roamed the world. I believed that with brains and determination I could lead an interesting life and do valuable work. A governess in Bath, a missionary in Bulawayo: there was GOD's work to be done, and I was to do it. I would live a pure, simple and cheerful life, for I was determined that I would not be a nuisance, a drag upon society, but an active, bustling old maid. You were a secret shrine I worshipped at, tiptoed up to and never dared to touch. I should earn my bread in toil and pain.

But there was rebellion in my heart, and Satan, who is cunning, daring and cruel, saw it there. When you came to me that morning to ask for my help my soul leaped out to you like a salmon into a river of life. Such hopes I had, such hopeless hopes. A lifetime of faith I had built up brick by brick over twenty years came crashing down that morning, and now I can no longer hide behind it. A woman by herself in the world can do nothing. I am naked, indecent, as I was just now with you.

As soon as you left the house last night I began to fear that your strict principles and fearless integrity would lead you into danger. I heard Lucy and Rachel tittle-tattling about the cholera raging in the slums and thought – just a few hours ago I thought – that you were risking your life to help the poor. Without you the house seemed so vast and silent. After the servants had gone to bed I sat alone in the drawing-room and filled the shadows with my memories of you. I can hardly remember a time when I did not love you. Last night those beloved images of Charles Past surrounded me.

Like actors in a pageant they told a story I longed to hear: you and I have always loved; we belong to one another at a level far deeper than the marriage service. My sister's wiles and fripperies distracted you, but now that she is a lost woman, a poor seduced creature, we two are free to love.

For so many years I have lived with my secret wound. Last night I held out my hand for help and it was slapped. I have no place in the world. I want to think of spiritual matters, but I can think of nothing but you.

The clock struck three, shocking me back into the present. I began to be terrified that you had been set upon by a gang of ruffians or lay helpless with fever in some dreadful rookery. My heart thundered every time I heard passing horses – I remembered that you had left on foot but feared you would be brought back on a stretcher. I could not move. To go to bed would have been a betrayal of the love I yearned to prove.

I had to wait up for you. In those empty hours I was seized by the conviction that, if you did return alive and well, we must consummate our love. I looked at myself in the glass above the mantelpiece. I was wearing my faded old nightgown and my face was innocent of adornment. I wanted to be beautiful for you but told myself that you valued my honesty and simplicity. I am not a young woman, so it does not signify what I wear. In your shyness (the voice of Satan inveigled me in my head) you did not dare to declare your passion, and so I must be brave and offer myself to you.

Four o'clock sounded, and five, and still I sat on in a trance of love. All the passion that I have been starved of was distilled into those hours. I listened for you with every nerve. I felt like a tree waiting for rain, like a dog quivering for the hand of its master. I felt so intensely that I was quite certain you must be feeling exactly the same.

When at last I heard footsteps I ran to the window and stared out down Harley Street. I heard your beloved voice greet the night-watchman. The early sun shone on your beautiful head as you stood on the pavement and stared at the door, and I willed you to look up and see me. But you did not.

So I rushed downstairs to open the front door and hold you in my arms. But as the front door opened some other imaginary door closed, and you did not come into my embrace. You brushed past me in the hall, thanked me abruptly and hardly looked at me. I could not take my eyes off you. Your clothes were creased and grimy, and there was a strong smell of alcohol. Still I could not see the man who stood there, only the man I had adored all night. Convinced that you were nobly struggling to suppress your love for me, I took a step towards you and hurled myself against you with a moan. Our noses bumped. My mouth searched for yours, your arms held me tight, or so I thought. I shut my eyes and waited for paradise. I had never been so close to a man before. I could feel your heart beating against mine and smell your tipsified breath.

'Good Lord, Henrietta, whatever do you think you're doing?'

You pushed me away. On your dear face, which is like a map of my soul, I read disgust and amusement. I heard a rustle and a stifled giggle on the stairs above me.

You coughed and said, 'No, Henrietta, you must not be distracted from higher things. You are too good for me.'

Sobbing, I turned and ran until I reached my room. But it is not mine. I have nothing now, not even my dignity. This journal is my bloodletting, where I lance my boils and dip my pen in their pus. Now all the pages of this little book are filled with my handwriting, it is finished, and I think I am finished, too.

HE will not forget me when HE counteth HIS jewels. A flawed jewel. Perhaps HE will forgive me for loving you too much and not loving Tommy and Nina enough.

You gave me this laudanum to help me sleep. I hope it brings me dreams of you.

# CHARLES

I WAS VACCINATING a baby when old Emma appeared at the door of my surgery. The infant screamed in the arms of its pretty mama as my needle approached. Emma glared at me so ferociously that my hand shook, and I almost missed the baby's vein. I wonder where William finds his admirably faceless servants. A servant should not express any feelings, but Emma's face is large and red and as coarse as her voice. She was Nina's nurse but often behaves more like an aunt who knows far too much about us all. This morning her presence was most intrusive and attracted the attention of my waiting patients.

'I am working, Emma. Please come back later.' I glared back at her and vowed yet again to pay her the wages I owe her and replace her with a younger, more discreet servant.

'You'd best come now. The living can wait.'

Her words and tone were so ominous that I did follow her, murmuring apologies to the patients in my waiting-room. On the stairs we did not speak, but the old woman's back crackled with rage and grief. I was expecting to find one of the servant girls, Rachel or Lucy, *enceinte*. But instead of going up to the attics Emma led me to the door of Henrietta's room.

My sister-in-law lay upon her single brass bed, sprawled on her back, still in the hideous nightgown she wore when I returned early this morning. I knew at once that her sleep was eternal. I have seen many corpses but perhaps never one whose life was so unfulfilled. The phial of laudanum I gave her last week lay empty on her bedside cabinet, and one of her stiff hands clutched a brown leather notebook. Henrietta's eyes were open. She stared up at the ceiling with an expression of baffled indignation, as if the deity she had served so fiercely had disappointed her. As we all did. I pocketed her notebook and realized that Emma was silent in the doorway, staring at me with such hatred that I instinctively raised my arm to shield my face.

'Poor lady.'

'Is that all you can say?'

'It is not seemly to criticize the dead.'

Emma appeared to swell in the doorway, as if inflated by bellows. She shouted at me with the most brazen effrontery, 'Seemly, is it? I'll give you seemly, Dr Charles-bloody-dig'em-up-Sanderson, grew up in a knocking-shop with your pa who was lucky not to swing at Newgate –'

'How dare you insult my father's memory –'

'Your pa was a pleasant enough fellow, very simple and plain-spoken, though we all knew he did Sir Astley's dirty work for him. You're the snake in the grass. Don't think I don't know what you're up to with your sneaking in and out, and as for your treatment of my lovely young ladies, you packed Miss Nina off to Bedlam –'

'This is outrageous! Keep your voice down. My patients will hear!'

'Do you think I care who hears me?'

'Leave my house!'

'I'd of gone long ago, only I couldn't bear to leave Miss Nina and Miss Henrietta. Now you've locked up the one and done t'other in –'

Incensed by her effrontery, and beside myself with fear that our quarrel would be overheard, I told the old baggage that I could no longer tolerate her presence beneath my roof. Or words to that effect. Emma departed in a flurry of tears and vulgarity, and I had to return to my patients.

All day Henrietta's dead body hovered in the air between myself and the sick. I was afraid to revisit her corpse alone, so I sent James with a message to William, asking him to come as soon as possible to sign the death certificate.

After my last patient left I shut myself in my study and steadied my nerves with a decanter of sherry. Until Henrietta was safely at the undertaker's I knew there would be no peace in my house. Lucy brought in a decanter of claret with some cheese and biscuits and cold beef together with a pile of letters on a tray. A bachelor supper. As my household empties around me I feel more and more unmarried. I am sure I did not imagine Lucy's flirtatious wink as she turned to leave the room. Under Henrietta's regime such thoughts would have been smothered.

Most of the letters on the tray were bills and could be safely ignored, but I did open one with a Surrey postmark. It was from Tommy's school, enclosing a letter from him. His 'housemother', a Mrs Jenkins, wrote that I am not to worry about him as he will soon settle down. She has made some attempts to correct the appalling spelling and punctuation of my son's blotted and blurred epistle, proof that he is woefully in need of an education:

> Dearest Mama, [No mention of Dearest Papa, who pays his school fees.]
>
> I think they sent me here because I kild you. I think of you all the time so perhaps you think of me Thompson says you cant think becoz you are ded if you are not ples send me mony so I can buy toffy for the other fellows and they won't lauff at me and call me mammysick and spooneywally I hop you can read what I am riting they say my handriting is very pore and I am very stupid.
>
> Wen I was a littel girl and you wer at hom it was much more jollyer. I did put on Bellas nitegown but I dident mean to kil you I only thort you wud luv me. If you are not ded ples come and see me and bring me nice comfits with caraway seeds Mama ples I want to liv with you in the byootyfull sity with the laydees in pantaloons.
>
> Tommy

His signature dissolved into rows of red and yellow chalk kisses and hugs. I suppose I always knew that Tommy was the ghost that terrified poor Nina and made her flee our house. And our marriage.

Well, it is no use being angry with him now. There will be no more children, and I must make my peace with the one I have, however lamentable his spelling may be.

As I sat alone in my darkening study waiting for William to come and sign Henrietta's death certificate, my eyes played tricks upon me. I have been too long wedded to that cold-blooded demon called Science to believe in ghosts and all that bosh, but at times our buried life exhumes itself.

So it was this evening, when my study filled with shadows and memories of all the people who once lived in this house with me. I saw Bella, in her white frock with the pink sash, much loved and already half-forgotten. I strained to see the charming details of her face, but they eluded me. Bella held the hand of Nina, who was young and happy and gay as I have not seen her these many months. Tommy sat on the floor beside them, playing quietly with my books, building them into a tower that collapsed every few minutes. He still had his babyish long curls. I longed to stroke them but could not move from my desk. Henrietta stood behind the others, tense as always, staring at me with such reproachful eyes that I looked away and nervously fingered the brown notebook in my pocket.

Somewhere on the threshold between waking and dreams, sobriety and drunkenness, they visited me. I had not invited them and did not know how to behave in their presence. The silence grew oppressive and then ominous, as if words I dreaded hung in the air between us. It became so dark that I could not see where my visitors began and ended, but still I could not stir myself, not even to light a candle.

At last I heard the front door bang and footsteps came up the stairs towards me. Never have I felt so glad to see my old friend. William is so emphatically of this world, and his enormous absorption and devotion to Number One is a shining example.

'All alone in the dark, Charles?'

'All alone.' My voice sounded strange, as if it had returned from a long journey.

'What happened? Was it an accident?'

'My sister-in-law took her own life.'

'These spinsters! They have so little life to lose. Where is the corpse?'

We lit lamps and carried them up to Henrietta's small room. With William beside me I felt like a professional man again, exercising my duties. Henrietta lay at an undignified angle. Alone, I could not have touched her, but with William beside me I calmly closed the eyes no husband ever kissed and drew the shroud kindly over the poor withered breast where no child's head has ever lain.

'Poor creature. Did you not tell me, Charles, that she had conceived a secret passion for you? I believe I met her once. Was she not an exceptionally plain woman, of a dull or vinegar aspect with an I-have-seen-better-days air? But I dare say her mind was a perfect Augean stable of uncleanness and lustful thoughts of you –'

'Ours was a treaty of friendship, pure and simple.' Again I felt her diary in my pocket.

'Still, she lived here alone with you, the object of her adoration. Disappointed love results in *furor uterinus*. How often have I seen it!'

Now that she was dead I felt a strange urge to protect Henrietta from his cynicism. 'She was a most excellent lady, intelligent and full of energy. But she was a fidgety Christian that could not let her soul alone a minute, and the world had not the slightest use for her virtues.'

'A woman should only be educated enough to praise and sympathize with her husband.'

'She was too old for husband-hunting and hoped to find useful work outside the family.'

'As Hegel says, the individual is subordinate to the family. Without the family there is only the mob.'

I thought of Nina's muddled ravings of the future. 'Yet a time may come when respectable women do work and have a life outside the home.'

'Then I pray I may not live to see it! Who that ever listened to the confused inanities of ladies' chat would give females the vote or any serious responsibility? You know how I adore the sex, Charles, but women have neither heart nor head for abstract political speculation. Such matters may be safely left to us. The dear little things are our weaker, better halves, and home is the appointed scene of their labours. The superior strength of our reasoning faculties and bodies and the firmer texture of our minds are simply a fact, my dear chap. Why, the female cerebrum averages two ounces less in weight than the male.'

'There is no arguing with your science. And yet . . .'

'You are sentimental. Now, to business. What shall we write on her death certificate? I take it you don't want any scandal?'

'A doctor with a mad wife and a sister-in-law who has committed suicide is hardly likely to attract patients . . .'

'Quite. Then let us agree that she misunderstood the correct dose of laudanum and took too much . . .'

'Thank you so much, William . . .'

'Not at all. We are friends and must help each other.'

The old quack signed the document and twinkled at me, no doubt calculating the next favour he will ask of me.

We had a few drinks together in my study, and then William went home. It was late, but I knew I would not be able to sleep. I was reluctant to return to the upper regions of the house where the dead and the absent are so . . . present. I was very glad that the door of Henrietta's room was firmly shut. Tomorrow morning the undertaker will remove her, and I will know a little peace.

I took Henrietta's diary out of my pocket, where it had felt so heavy all those hours, and started to read. What a chronicle of pathos, frustration and wasted energy! To find myself the target of such hysterical arrows was quite exhausting. I did not wish Henrietta's pitiful scribbling to fall into the wrong hands, and so I burned her little book in the grate in my study. I sat in my old green leather armchair to watch the fire dance its mocking ballet. The orange tongues licked delicately at Henrietta's sad confessions, then devoured the book in greedy rage, subsiding at last into dark red caves of mystery. Each fire we make enacts a rise and fall, ending in a little death, *un petit mort* – no, I must not distract myself with sensual phantasy. I have my own ascent to think of and cannot waste any more time.

I shall not bring Tommy home for the funeral. It is better that he remains at school and settles down there. I must not look backwards but ahead to the time when my wild colt becomes a sleek racehorse: Master Thomas Sanderson, the accomplished son of a gentlemanly widowed doctor with no burking in his pedigree. Not Skeleton Sanderson, for he died when I qualified as a doctor. And what is it that Tommy will accomplish? My pa loved me dearly, but he could not advise me in the ways of a world he did not know. When I read Lord Chesterfield's letters to his son I felt a twinge of envy.

I decided to reply to Tommy's crude epistle. I turned away from the fire and rummaged on my desk for his letter. But it was not there. I rang for Lucy, who came looking flustered.

'What is the matter, girl?'

'It's Emmie, sir. She came to the door when you was upstairs with Dr Porter and said I was to pack her things. When I come down again I found her in here – in your study – I know I didn't ought to let her only I couldn't stop her, sir.'

Lucy looked frightened, and I believed her story. I searched the drawer in my desk where I keep my cash and found five pounds missing, Emma's unpaid wages and a couple of pounds more. She has been in this household so long that she knows all our secrets. I could report her to the police, but I do not know where she is and do not want to draw attention to my domestic upheavals. As for Tommy's letter, the old baggage must have stolen it out of mawkishness. I am well rid of her.

'Never mind, Lucy. If she comes to the door again, do not let her in. Go to bed now. I am not angry with you.' She looked relieved and left the room.

I sat at my desk and composed a letter to Tommy, the kind of letter I would have been happy to receive from my father. I flatter myself it is a wise letter, one that he will cherish in years to come:

My Dear Boy,

I hope that you are settling down well at your new school. How proud I am that you are taking your first plunge into the stream of Life. I offer these lines of fatherly advice in the hope that you will find them useful some day.

You will not see your dear mama any more. Your Aunt Henrietta has also left us. And so, my poor Tommy, you no longer have a mother, aunt or sister to love and guide you. You and I must be everything to one another, and so I hope that in future your letters will be addressed to your papa. I trust that your future communications will be better penned and spelled than your last.

Truth, Purity and Courage are the virtues I would place above all others. Choose your friends well, never utter an untruth and never applaud or utter a word you would be ashamed for your mother or sister (were they alive) to hear. You must be pure (you know what I mean). I am not myself a total abstainer from alcoholic liquors, but temperance is a noble thing, and I urge you to eat and drink only in moderation.

I am not a wealthy man, and after I have paid for your education there will be very little money. Marriage is an ennobling and purifying condition, and while I would not have you be a fortune hunter I would advise you to 'go where money is'. When the time comes for you to choose a profession, Medicine seems to me to be the noblest calling, elevating to its followers and beneficial to mankind.

Well, Tommy, I must return to my duties. You will be the architect of your own fortunes. You must please your dear mama, who is watching you always, and I hope you will also please

Yr affectionate Papa

# THE MARCH OF
# PROGRESS

HOW DELIGHTFUL TO see Emmie here! Like finding a lost toy. I gave her a bedtime bathtime hug and smelled her dear old coal-tar soap and lavender water as I rubbed my nose against the grey tweed coat she has worn for as long as I can remember.

She hugged me back. Nobody has ever hugged me like Emmie, 'Oh, Miss Nina, I've been so worried about you. I thought it was some kind of prison he'd sent you off to, but it's more like a bang-up palace. I never expected to see such homishness here. Pictures and books and birds in cages . . .'

'It is a palace, Emmie. You're not to worry about me here. They're kind to me. I feel like a princess, and you're my fairy godmother come to visit.'

'Well, here's your wishes.'

She handed me a brown paper parcel containing my best black silk dress. An envelope fell out – a letter from Tommy.

I read it twice and burst into tears, for I longed to see him and felt very bad that I had not loved him as much as I loved Bella and that he had known it all the time. I could see Tommy so vividly, sitting at his desk with tears and ink smudged all over his face, chewing his pen and wondering what to write to me.

So I fetched paints and crayons and sat down at once to reply. Not with words but with pictures, for I knew they would fly straight to his heart and he would understand them and the nasty school people would not, so they could not censor my letter. I ruled big squares all around the edges of the paper and inside them I drew the elephant we fed buns to in the zoological gardens and a child with long dark curls in a white nightgown and the towers and cliff-like buildings of Jonathan's London. I drew horseless carriages and people in strange clothes and a little boy sitting on the knee of a lady in a white dress. The last was a picture of myself with Tommy, of course, although it seemed as remote as a drawing of Good Queen Bess. In the centre I wrote, 'For my dearest Tommy from his mama who will love him always', followed by even more kisses and hugs than he had sent me and watered by tears – for who knows when I shall see him again.

Then I looked around and was quite surprised to find that an hour had passed and Emmie was over on the other side of the ward helping Mrs Dunn and Marian and Amelia to fold sheets. I was quite flustered and apologized for my rudeness, but they all laughed and said they were used to my disappearances when I was lost in a drawing. So it was all very jolly until I turned to Emmie and asked for news of home.

'Oh, Miss Nina, I know I didn't ought to say this –'

'But you will, Emmie. You know you will. Mama used to call you the *bocca della verità*.'

'I don't like to upset you, Miss Nina. For I know how tender-hearted you are, even if you are dicked in the nob.'

'Tell me, Emmie. I'll find somewhere private where we can go.'

I asked Mrs Dunn if we could go to the keeper's room where there is a fireplace so that we could be comfortable and talk in confidence.

Then Emmie told me what happened to Henrietta. I was so shocked that I could not cry. I stared at Emmie and hoped she would tell me it was a bedtime story, a horrid one. I have hated Henrietta all my life, and she most certainly hated me, yet how dreadful it is that she is no longer in this world. I would have liked for us to be enemies for ever.

'How did she die?'

'She took laudanum, ducks. Too much to sleep, enough to send her to paradise. I should imagine it would be paradise what with her being on such intimate terms with the Almighty.'

'Was it an accident, do you think?'

Emmie looked at me with a lugubrious face, and I knew she would not tell me what she really thought.

'But Henrietta was so contented with herself. So busy being good and better than other people. Better than me, as she always told me. Why should she be unhappy?'

Emmie would not be provoked into gossiping. I thought of Henrietta in my house that she had made her own. I wondered what passed between Charles and her after I left and realized that I will never know.

'I'm sorry to bring bad news, little Miss Nina, but I had to tell you.'

Then I hugged her again, and a few dry sobs came but no tears. 'Emmie you must tell my husband –'

'I shan't see your husband again.'

Then it all came out, how she and Charles had some kind of quarrel and Emmie left. 'I won't repeat the language he used to me, miss, for I should hope you've never heard such filth.'

Henrietta dead and Charles swearing like a fishwife and Emmie given in her notice. I could not imagine our family without Emmie. It was as if a hairbrush had jumped out of my hand and walked out the door. Then I remembered that I do not have any family, not any longer, and must stay here always.

'Wherever will you go now, Emmie? You must ring the bell at the workhouse and ask to be taken in.'

'No, miss. I have some savings, and I have my pride.'

'I shall give you an excellent character, although your organ of combativeness is rather large.'

'Don't you worry about me, miss. If you really want to know, I've had enough of being in service. Time to be of service to myself for a change. My sister has a boozing ken at Peckham Rye. She'll give me a room if I help out at the bar.'

'A boozing ken?'

'A public house, miss. Well, I must be off. Mrs Dunn says visiting time finishes at four.'

'Dearest Emmie! Will you make sure Tommy receives my letter?'

'I will that, Miss Nina. And I'll come to see you again soon.'

One last hug, and I did not know if I was embracing my old nurse or a new friend. People change so fast nowadays.

All the ladies here surrounded me when Emmie had gone and wanted to know more about my life. I had never told them that Charles and I lived in Harley Street, and now they imagine that we are exceedingly rich.

'Did you spend your life in ruby velvet and diamonds?' Lavinia asked wistfully. She has a supply of penny dreadfuls she hides from Mrs Dunn in her work-basket and is much given to romantic flourishes on account of being Jenny Lind in her imagination. 'Do you not long to return to your luxurious abode?'

'No,' I replied sharply. But I could not escape their curiosity.

Susan grew jealous of my supposed wealth and said crossly, 'When I was at boarding-school in Chichester I learned all the extras. Did you go to boarding-school, Eliza?'

'No.'

'Well then!' she tossed her elderly head as if she thought she still had pigtails and resumed her work. Mrs Dunn says Susan is too disruptive to help in the kitchen or the laundry, so she sets her a task that reminds me of Penelope's weaving: sorting coloured beads into different heaps. Each night they are dumped together again, and each morning Susan must begin again. I would not insult Tommy with such a mindless task, but Susan thinks that because she is the only one who does this work it must be a privilege.

Betty will no longer talk to the rest of us. She is grown very proud because her husband is about to transfer her to a private lunatic asylum where she says she will eat off gold plates and have ten attendants all to herself. She beckoned to me imperiously and summoned me to her chair beside the window.

'And will you remain here, Mrs Sanderson?'

'I hope so. I am happier here.'

'But this is a public asylum, and we must mingle with coarse people.' She spoke very loud, Marian and Susan and Lavinia heard her, and I was mortified for they are my friends. 'However, conditions here are much improved.'

'How long have you been here?'

'For five years. I am the senior resident of this ward,' she said with melancholy pride as if it were a title conferred by the Queen. 'When I first arrived here we were caged like animals and slept like beasts on straw that was hardly ever changed, and keepers thrust our food through bars at us. If we complained about our treatment or offered the least resistance we were bound with manacles, chains and leg locks.' Betty spoke in her usual monotone, but her sad, dark eyes glittered with tears. 'And now we are to have coconut matting and pictures given by Mr Graves, the well-known print seller of Pall Mall. Dr Hood is a great man.'

'Yet you are leaving us? When do you go?'

'After Christmas.'

All our talk is of Christmas now. There is the ball to look forward to, and Mrs Dunn says the steward, Hayden, who is very jolly, has prepared a magic lantern for us and we are to have apples, oranges, plain plum cake and negus. Some of the ladies are going back to their families at Christmas, but I do not want to return if I am not to be allowed to see Tommy. It is very painful to think I may not see my darling boy again until he is grown. Emmie will help me to write to him, and I must hope he does not forget me.

Marian saw that I was upset and came over to talk to me. We have both lost our little boys, whether to death or to boarding-school does not seem to make any difference. She is kind although a little peculiar.

'They are hiding from me again,' she said.

'Albert and his little friends?' I asked wearily.

'No, silly. Dr Hood and Hayden.'

'I am sure they would not play tricks upon you, Marian, for they are the kindest men alive.'

'But they do hide. I cannot see their mouths or the expression on their faces for the great bushes sprouting there.'

'Bushes? Oh you mean their beards and moustaches. They are the fashion, my dear. I expect all the men grow them now. Not that we ever see any other men.'

'My husband has not visited me for two months. And yours never comes. I wish we could leave this place for a day. Shall I ask Dr Hood for a day's pleasure? We could go to see the new concrete dinosaurs and the monstrous greenhouse at Crystal Palace. Do let's! We would have one of the assistants with us, but it would be almost like real life.'

Her ruddy cheeks glowed with an excitement I could not share. I did not like to disappoint her, so I looked away from her. I thought of those vast creatures that once roamed our earth and felt very like them. Old and lonely and out of my time. Tears came to my eyes.

'Nina, you must leave this place sometimes. It is not healthy to be always here, for they are all quite cracked, you know.' I thought this was rich coming from Marian who talks to her dead child day and night, but still I said nothing. 'Have you heard what happened to Georgina? She attempted to strangle herself with her handkerchief and the braid from her dress, and now she is in solitary confinement in the basement. And she will not be allowed back on our ward but must go to a bad one.'

We looked at each other in horror. We do not know exactly what happens on the bad wards, but there are many stories of screams and violence and howls in the night.

I saw that Lavinia was hovering near by and had been listening to us, the sly, sneaking little thing. She began to ask impertinent questions. 'Why don't you want to go home for Christmas if you have such a grand house? I'm sure I should even if I had Blue Beard for a husband. Better than no husband at all. Will you not miss your little boy if you stay here?'

I know Lavinia is a great tattlemonger, so I pretended not to hear and remained as secret as an oyster, although I was furious and would like to have her arrested under the Public Nuisances Act. What a puss she is.

Fortunately Mrs Dunn came in just then and said that if we had nothing better to do than gossip we could help in the laundry, and so we spent the time until supper up to our chins in soap suds.

It is as well that I have my little world within, for the world outside is shrinking fast. I do not want to leave, not even for a day's excursion. I feel safe here. Before my adventures I think I was not the same person. My mind then was like my work-box; it was divided into neat compartments with no shadows. Now there is such a jumble of threads and buttons and hooks and thimbles all hugger-mugger in the dark interior that I cannot find anything, not even myself.

At night when I lie alone in my tiny cubicle I feel that Jonathan is near me. I cannot see him through the wall as I did in my bedroom at home, but when I shut my eyes I do see his beloved face smiling at me.

Behind him I see the magnificent procession of the future when all our weaknesses and sins will be tales in history books and such places as this will seem as barbarous as the old Bedlam Betty told me of seems now. For the men and women of the future will be happy and good and will have no need of mad doctors. Their England will be so clean and safe and prosperous that the prisons will empty and violence and crime will be mere shadows on their teavees. The shimmering towers will rise to the skies, and the shops will offer cornucopias where all may help themselves to splendiferous banquets.

I confess I am a little jealous of these unborn people. I wonder how Henrietta and I would fare in such a place? A girl like my sister, who was clever but plain, will surely be appreciated there and flourish. I expect she will become a doctress or even a prime ministress and an even greater bossyboots. The thought of Henrietta fulfilled and contented brings tears to my eyes here in the dark where nobody can see them.

And I? In my imagination I see that future Nina. She is lightly clad in tea shirt and pettiloons instead of a corset and a long, heavy dress that sweeps the streets when it's dirty and gets draggled when it rains and trips me up when I walk and entangles me when I run. If she discovers that her husband has about as much warmth as an eel she will be free to leave him and make her own way in the world with Tommy. For she will have enough education to work and earn hard cash. Perhaps she will meet another gentleman and be free to marry him, and if she does nobody will call her a brazen hussy or a fallen woman, for she will be able to hold up her head and rise through her own efforts.

I lie very still and silent in the dark, but the March of Progress resounds in my ears, and I am there marching in step with those other felicitous ones, and Jonathan marches beside me.

# JONATHAN

WHERE DID IT come from? Just when I thought I was beginning to make sense of my life.

Supper with Annabel last night went off rather well. For a few hours I believed I had got over Nina and was about to embark on a new relationship with an actual woman: alive, here, now, available. We've been eyeing each other up for weeks in the gym as we performed on our various boring treadmills and torture racks. Annabel is about thirty, attractively energetic, with short reddish hair and green eyes. She works for a hedge fund, mysteriously serving some temple of money and being paid through the nose for it. Every evening she seems to be in the gym, pumping away masochistically and flaunting her long legs and beautifully toned bum. At first I thought she must have some immensely rich lover or husband, but her nightly appearances suggested she was as lonely as me, so after a few smiles and flirtatious chats we had a drink in the bar last week and arranged to have supper together last night at the new Turkish restaurant in Marylebone High Street.

Annabel was wearing a black velvet jacket with very tight black trousers and a white silk shirt. Her shining coppery hair contrasted beautifully with the dramatic velvet, and I wanted to stroke her from head to foot. It's so long since I've stroked a woman. I didn't, of course. We were both on first-date alert, watching and listening for danger signals, registering the interesting facts that we live and work so near to each other and are both interested in art and music. I had to fight my prejudice against people who work in finance and was agreeably surprised to discover that she loves Bach and Mahler and often goes to concerts at the Wigmore Hall. Over the meze we talked about the Cézanne exhibition and the 'Rebels and Martyrs' exhibition at the National Gallery about the romantic image of nineteenth-century artists. She turned out to be a lot more knowledgeable about the arts than I am about finance.

I heard Nina's voice as she disapproved of an item on the news about a contender for the Turner Prize. 'Pictures should awaken our reverence and admiration.' I shook my head impatiently to remove Nina and turned my attention back to Annabel.

'So how do you see yourself? As a rebel or a martyr?'

'Neither. I'm too old to die young like Chatterton, and I can't really kid myself that my shopping mall in Dubai shows a unique artistic vision.'

'So you're not destined to perish under the blows of the world like Gauguin?'

'I hope not. Do you like Gauguin?'

I must have sounded condescending because she said defensively, 'People in the City aren't thick, you know. We just need to make a crust.'

Her crust is better buttered than mine. Last Christmas she bought a flat around the corner from me, in Devonshire Place, out of her Christmas bonus. As we ate our delicious musakka we exchanged emotional histories. My version, of course, mentioned only Kate and no time slips; young women who work in the City can't be expected to understand temporal misfits – not that I understand myself what happened with Nina.

Annabel split up from her boyfriend, an economist, six months ago, and before that had a long affair with a married banker-wanker, as she put it.

We both admitted to dreading Christmas.

'Every year Kate and I fight over who has Ben for Christmas Day and Boxing Day. I don't know why we do it. It's so destructive, and Ben hates it. Last year he opened my expensive presents in floods of tears and then sat marooned in a sea of wrapping paper, wailing.

When I asked, rather irritably, what was the matter, he sobbed, 'I just want to be a proper family again.'

Improper, unhappy families. Annabel doesn't have any kids, but her parents are growing old disgracefully.

'They used to be boring, but that was OK – I mean you expect your ageing parents to be bores, don't you? Then last year when she was sixty-five Mum ran off with a Polish carpenter twenty years younger. I mean literally ran. They met when they were both doing a charity marathon. So poor old Dad was left alone after forty years of marriage, and he just fell apart.

'I went up to Shropshire to see him and found him living on digestive biscuits, surrounded by dog and cat turds. So I cleaned up a bit and told him to get a life. Then a month later the police phoned me to say a man in his seventies had been found wandering naked on a golf course near Bridgnorth, and it was my dad. He'd set off as usual one Wednesday morning to play golf, as he has every week since he retired, and then he just forgot who he was and where he was supposed to be going. My dad used to be a solicitor – he thought it was a scandal if my brother went out without a tie – so there he was stark naked on a golf course clutching his mashy niblett, or whatever you call it, and I had to go up there on the train and collect him.

'He has Alzheimer's, apparently. Just can't cope with the house any more, so we'll have to find him a home. I've looked at a couple, but they were awful, I wouldn't leave a dog there. Which is another thing. They've got two dogs and cat, all ancient and decrepit. They'll have to be put down now. Mum doesn't want to know. She's going off to an ashram in India with her Polish carpenter to blow our inheritance, so me and my brother keep having to take time off work to look at pricey gaols for the gaga. Have you got any mad relatives?'

'My parents died a few years ago. Quite considerate of them, although not very good news for me, genetically speaking. I sometimes think my ex is crazy, but she isn't really, just permanently angry.

I have a wonderful seven-year-old son I don't see enough of, and that's about it.'

We smiled at each other over the second bottle of wine and went back to talking about concerts we might go to together, as if we had used up our ration of personal history.

On the pavement outside the restaurant we exchanged an experienced kiss. My tongue pressed against her lips and stopped at her teeth, those elegantly capped cliffs that guarded the warm cavern of her mouth. Annabel's inner self, uncharted territory I hope to discover some day. There be mermaids and dragons. I hope not. I'd like a sensible, unmysterious love affair, and Annabel's straight back and tempting buttocks suggested that is possible.

I slept well – no dreams of Nina, thank God. There is one that I have dreamed so often it has become part of my inner landscape. I enter a tiny room, and she is there, dressed in a long black dress, smiling at me with unbearable sweetness. The room swells into a circular ballroom. We are dancing there, waltzing. I perform steps I don't know to music I have never heard. There are other couples dancing there, dressed in mid-Victorian clothes, and we are watched intently by a man with glittering eyes who draws us. Nina's body is warm and real, and I bury my face in her hair, inhaling her reality. I reach out to touch her face and try to raise her chin to kiss her. But I am never allowed to. She evades my dreamlust, and I wake up alone, exhausted, as if I had danced for centuries.

But this morning I woke refreshed, early enough to have time to walk to work. I love to avoid the rush-hour by cutting through the secretive back streets to the City.

Joggers and cyclists passed me, intent on their own escape from public transport and traffic jams. I crossed Oxford Street and strode through Soho and Covent Garden to the Strand, enjoying my walking pace, fast enough to get to work but slow enough to gaze up and appreciate the details of buildings. My long sight allows me to see curious chimneys and carved gutters and eccentric windows, all the embellishments that earlier ages had time for. Old houses look so solid and confident, yet so many of them are accidents, the lucky winners of a lottery of dreams. How I would love to build one great folly to be remembered by, but how far away from it I feel now.

Ghoulishly, I fantasized about some great apocalypse, a fire or a war, that would destroy most of London and give me the opportunity to fill the skyline with my own vision: towers jutting with terraces and roof gardens and garden squares in a car-free city with a 24-hour transport system, including commuter boats zipping along the river and canals. I'd like to see brick and stone everywhere instead of brittle glass and dismal concrete. Of my more imaginative plans, not one has materialized. Every building that does go up is the cemetery of architects' hopes, murdered by committees. London devours visions and spews them out again as profits for billionaire developers.

Crossing the shoppers' paradise Covent Garden Market has become, I remembered that after the war there was a plan to build a huge music-and-drama centre there. The Strand reminded me of Inigo Jones's elegant New Exchange, a kind of seventeenth-century department store that never did get built. I passed the newly restored and cleaned Somerset House with its riverside terrace and ice-skating rink. Like all illustrious buildings it has reinvented itself for a new generation, callously outliving its original architect.

After the Great Fire, Wren wanted to replace all those crazy courts and alleys off Fleet Street with great avenues and piazzas, which might have resulted in a duller city. Great architects are tyrants. There is a kind of democracy in muddle and inconsistency of style. In the forgotten streets behind Fleet Street London seems to juggle with its real and imagined pasts. It isn't fashionable for an architect to be as interested in the past as I am. Perhaps that was how Nina happened. Perhaps I'm too open to other people's dreams.

I'm lucky to work in the City because I have to confront its voracious heart several times a week. St Paul's looks so sure of itself and inevitable, but it might easily have been quite different, surmounted by a giant pineapple or a triple dome. Or it might have had to double as an observatory for Wren and his fellow astronomers. Thirty-six years Wren invested in St Paul's, and I've always wondered if he resented it .

I moved to this company two years ago when it became impossible for Kate and I to work in the same office. We're the London branch of a large American company, but hardly any of our clients are in this country. My office is on the tenth floor of a glass tower. We scurry around our open-plan office like the ants in a glass box I had as a child, highly visible to each other and to anyone looking out of the surrounding windows.

This morning at eight thirty most of my colleagues were already at work. I'm nostalgic for the days when architects produced exquisite drawings at easels, but now, of course, we all work at computers in a vast open space littered with plans and models. To discourage us from going out and wasting corporate time we have a breakfast bar, a sweet and doughnut counter to snack on and a pizza, burger and salad bar for lunch. It's all free and good; sylphs who come to work here rapidly become fatties. I helped myself to coffee, toast, peanut butter and a doughnut and carried them over to my desk, grunting at my colleagues, who grunted back. We compete to demonstrate total absorption in our work, for we are well paid and know that jobs here have hundreds of applicants.

My design team is working on the shopping mall in Dubai that is due to reach the ribbon-cutting stage in two years. The morning passed quickly. I had my usual lunch, quiche and a salad, then settled back to contemplate the logistics of incorporating a mosque and parking space into the basement. At first, when an oval appeared behind my underground car park, I thought my eyes were tired and took a break.

Twenty minutes later the oval had a nose and a mouth. It was a sketch of a face, as if a drawing from an earlier age was contemplating my slick computer graphics and subtly disapproving of my efforts.

Over the next half-hour the face developed a frame of dark curls and large deep-blue eyes that looked straight at me with a quizzical smile echoed in the curve of her lips. Nina had escaped from my head and pursued me to work. Feelings swept over me like a tornado as I sat there staring at my computer screen: terror, longing for her and indignation that she had so much power over me. I was afraid that my odd behaviour would be noticed and labelled as unprofessional and inappropriate, those kiss-of-death adjectives that could lose me my job. I have to finish my plans by Friday and can hardly complain that a woman who died in the nineteenth century won't let me work or ask Bob, our IT guru, to delete a ghost.

I sat there, paralysed, while my colleagues worked around me and the short December afternoon faded. The lights came on in our office and blazed in a hundred other glass boxes. Here we all sat in illuminated cross-section, transparent to each other and to ourselves. There was no space for a shadowy inner life, and I didn't know what to do with mine. Torn between my desire to preserve Nina's face for ever on my screen and my fear of looking crazy, I did nothing.

'You OK, Jonathan?'

It was Marty, a sweet-natured, very bright Canadian postgraduate who fancies me. After Kate I never want to have an affair with a colleague again, so I'm wary of her, although she is attractive.

'I've got a headache.'

All the women groaned. It's a standing joke in our company that the men are hypochondriacs and the women soldier on. But as soon as I said it it became true; my conflicting thoughts and emotions clarified into a tangible symptom, and I met it with some relief. If I was ill perhaps I was not mad.

Marty got up to come over with some Nurofen, and I panicked. What if she were able to see Nina, or Nina could see Marty? I logged off, clicked on 'shut down' and watched as Nina's face faded, perhaps for ever. I felt as if I had abandoned and betrayed her.

Marty stood over me with water and pills. I enjoyed her solicitude and the moment when her breasts touched my shoulder. 'You're so pale, honey. Want to lie down?' We have a sleeping capsule in the office so that we can stay here on the occasional nights we have to work late.

'I'll be fine. I'll just take a break.'

I walked over to the enormous window. The transition from day to night is beautiful here; I love to gaze out at all those other sparkling windows and feel part of the City's greed and dynamism. Over to my right the illuminated breast of St Paul's merges with the darkness, and the elegant span of Foster's bridge carries matchstick people over to Tate Modern. Seen from the tenth floor it is like a working model of a city, and I feel like a spoiled child allowed to play with it. The jagged skyline with its thousand years of architecture energizes me and gives me a dangerous illusion of power.

But my London was not there. Far below me, yellowish fog swirled and black smoke belched out of hundreds of chimneys into a filthy sunset. I had the feeling that if I opened the window I would be poisoned by the fumes and touched the window ledge to make sure I was still standing in my office, anchored in my time.

Down there the darkness squirmed with serpentine crowds and blobs of soft light. The great dome of St Paul's still dominated the view over to my right, but most of the buildings were unfamiliar. There were gaslit shops with awnings, and the crowds pouring out of them looked squat and dumpy, bundled up in heavy clothes like people in a Bruegel painting. Dozens of elegant spires and the black masts of ships on the river rose to the dirty sky. The horse-drawn traffic down there was chaotic and ferocious. I watched as a cabby climbed down from his perch and flogged a horse that was trapped between two carts and refused to budge.

Behind the triple glazing I could imagine but could not hear the whinnies and clatter and shouts and roar of the streets. I didn't feel that I was looking down at a different London. It was like the room behind my own where I once saw Nina in a dream, if it was a dream.

I've always felt it there, that older London, just behind the brittle shards and cheese graters of my own. I have spent my whole life flirting with nostalgia, romanticizing the past and longing for it. But now that it had finally come to claim me I was afraid.

Time sickness made my stomach lurch. I felt so dizzy that I had to stagger backwards to a chair where I sat with my head in my hands, afraid to look back at the window, thankful to be back in the now I have so often resented and despised.

'What's the matter, Jonathan?'

'Lie down.'

'Go home.'

I tried to speak, but my voice felt remote, as if I had left it over at the window. I took a deep breath and tried again, remembering that my colleagues were watching me and would discuss any eccentricities the minute I left the office. This time words came out.

'I think I will. I'll get the plans finished at home and bring them in tomorrow.'

The glass lift was its usual sleek self, shooting me down like blood in a syringe. The atrium soared and shimmered in the dark; more glass. It's as if we build our fragile world as the perfect target for the terrorists who fuel our paranoia.

On the crowded pavement I was relieved to see the familiar streets and buildings around me and told myself my hallucinations had been caused by an approaching migraine. I suffer from migraine only every few years, but the last one, just after Kate left, lasted for three days and forced me to lie in a darkened room. Like a Victorian invalid.

I promised myself an easy journey home, on the Central Line from St Paul's to Oxford Circus, before the rush-hour started. I would buy some mozzarella-and-tomato salad and a portion of lasagne from my favourite Italian restaurant, lie down on my comfortable sofa and listen to my new CD of Bach's *Mass in B-Minor*.

But somehow my feet turned away from the station, to the other side of St Paul's and down the shallow steps on to the Millennium

Bridge. In 1942, when the ruins were still smoking, there was a plan for a riverside stairway leading to St Paul's, and a committee chaired by Lutyens discussed the idea. This bridge was yet another visionary idea that finally materialized long after the architect who first imagined it was dead. When I'm in a good mood this is an inspiring thought, but most of the time it's just depressing.

My head cleared in the cold air. London's bridges always attract me like magnets; they are the wings of the city where its exhausted limbs rise up to elemental freedom in the water and the sky. Tonight the scintillating darkness was particularly seductive.

I felt compelled to cross the river. Walking is a kind of drug, a medicine for lost souls; it was good to move forward into the darkness and to feel connected with the crowds surging in both directions over the bridge. I inhaled the view: trains glittering across the river, cranes bisecting the sky and the operatic medievalism of Tower Bridge. Boats and helicopters carried inexhaustible Londoners onwards. Ahead was the Globe like an Elizabethan toy and the industrial campanile of Tate Modern. At the end of the bridge an enterprising girl violinist was playing Liszt's *Hungarian Rhapsody*, and a smell of caramelized peanuts rose from the bleak expanse in front of the gallery to join the histrionic music.

I turned right and followed the human river that flowed parallel to the Thames. Now Wren's dome was opposite me, supplanting three centuries of later architecture on the skyline. Strings of lights were reflected in the dark water, and the trees were illuminated for the Christmas I dreaded. At first, although I had nowhere to go, I walked fast, infected by the purpose of the anonymous crowds.

Then I slowed down and wandered on to the pier by the Oxo Building. Projected out on to the black river, I found myself alone with scavenging gulls and waves slapping on the beach. For a few minutes natural life pushed the throb of lights and traffic into the background, but the city pulled me back, and I opened myself again to its currents of energy.

I turned left just before the National Theatre, although I still had no idea where I was going. Behind the cosmetic surgery of the South Bank are dreary car parks, rotting concrete tunnels, stinking traffic and unplanned, unloved streets I usually avoid. I crossed the hideous Imax roundabout, where the drum-shaped white elephant sulks inaccessibly, and skirted the tangle of bridges and roadworks at the back of Waterloo Station. The last time I came here was when Kate and I set off on Eurostar for a romantic weekend in Paris that ended in tears and rows.

I didn't know where I was walking or why. I was cold and tired and thirsty but couldn't stop; movement had its own logic as if I were an ant following a path of invisible pheromones in the darkness.

Memories of Nina were acting themselves out in my head so intensely that I hardly knew what was in front of my eyes. I saw us in the shower together, that night we went to the club in Soho and got drunk. I felt her body against my skin for the first time, shampooed her glorious hair and soaped her breasts. Then I wrapped us both in the same vast green towel and fell on to my bed with her. Later, I dried and combed her hair, then wrapped myself in it like a sailor willingly beguiled by some mermaid.

I remembered Nina's laugh, surprisingly loud and sensuous, and her slightly husky voice as she primly recited her dreadful jokes: 'How must you spell honey to make it catch ladybirds?'

I took my mouth from her nipple for long enough to ask, 'Tell me, Nina.'

'M-o-n-e-y.'

We were in bed at the time, and I wasn't feeling too critical, so I stroked her hair and laughed. 'Nina, I'm going to report you to the pun police.'

She took this as a compliment. 'Do you like my hair?'

'It's the most beautiful hair in the world. Any world, yours or mine.'

'I know a joke about hair. Why is a bald man like an invalid?'

'I've absolutely no idea.'

'Because he wants fresh hair.'

Nina dissolved into infectious giggles; her shoulders and breasts shook as I lay beside her in the dark. That night we made love and talked for hours, but it wasn't enough.

A lorry swerved and just missed me. The driver swore at me in unmistakably 21st-century English. I ran across the road and found I was in front of the Imperial War Museum.

The last time I was here was when Ben was three and had a crush on aeroplanes, especially bombers. He must have picked up on my pacifism subliminally and found his first way of annoying me. Being a dutiful dad, I took him to the museum and let him hug the objects of his fantasy. It's the last museum I would want to visit. I walked through the black metal gates and stood in front of the museum, wondering how I had got here.

Two enormous illuminated metal guns pointed at me threateningly. Behind them loomed the graceful silhouette of the dome and portico. A party of belligerent primary school children came out of the bright mouth of the building, chattering and giggling. I moved out of their way, over to the right.

The park had settled into the cold night, and out here the sky, freed of the streetlights and dense buildings of the inner city, was reddish grey and wide. Old lamp-posts softly illuminated the path, and I was drawn by a flickering glow in one of the upper windows. I thought I saw a face up there and felt compelled to walk towards it over the frosty lawn until I stood, staring up, beneath the illuminated window. A face stared back at me.

I felt Nina before I saw her. My heart galloped with fear and excitement as her face became more vivid; not the one-dimensional sketch of an oval I had seen on my computer screen but a real woman, smiling down at me and waving, with dark curls around her shoulders. Her lips moved behind the glass, and I longed to touch her and kiss her and talk to her.

I rushed towards the entrance, convinced that if I ran up the stairs to the top of the building and turned right I would find her.

'We're closing now, sir.'

I backed away from the closing doors and ran back to the window where I had seen her. But the building was dark, and I couldn't even remember at which of the blank windows I had seen her.

Disappointment chilled and paralysed me. I couldn't leave and sat for a long time on a bench under a tree, staring up at the dark top floor. I had some crazy idea of staying all night there. The last of the visitors left the museum, and I noticed there was a way into the adjoining park through some bollards. I got up, so stiff and cold that I could hardly walk and stood on the path waiting for her to appear again. But she didn't, of course. I was alone again, a fool chasing shadows and stumbling away from dreams.

# CHARLES

To St George's Fields for the Bedlam Ball. I hired a brougham for my transpontine excursion – a rare extravagance, but one can hardly walk in full evening dress. I felt very grand in my white trousers and waistcoat and black tailcoat and hoped a few of my distinguished neighbours saw me climb into my carriage. I usually say that I walk everywhere for my health. The health of my bank balance.

Seen from the comfort of a leather seat, nocturnal London is a whirl of colour and gaiety, and I passed hundreds of elegant people flocking to parties. For many of my fellow Londoners every night is a social event, but I am a martyr to Mammon and must work far more than I carouse. This thought made me recall some lines of Wordsworth that drummed in my head:

> Such pains she had
> That she in half a year was mad
> And in a prison hous'd
> And there, exulting in her wrongs,
> Among the music of her songs
> She fearfully carouz'd.

Nina, however, is not in prison but comfortably housed. Many a husband whose wife had connection with another man and returned with misty moonshiny tales of the future would have cast her out into the street. Instead, I am paying to have Nina cured and have even offered to have her under my roof at Christmas. She has rejected my generosity and refuses to reply to my courteous notes. Tommy and I must be motherless and wifeless for the festive season in the home she has laid waste. I shall continue to tell my son that his mama is dead, for even if Dr Hood pronounces her cured I cannot ever again trust such a wife. And so I am condemned to solitude and mutton cutlets at home, unless Professor Benvoglio makes a fortune.

That night last summer when I delivered my fallen angel to the gates of the asylum, trussed and chloroformed, I was too grief-stricken to observe the building. Last night the hospital was illuminated by flaming torches, and the blaze of elegant carriages and bejewelled females was quite magnificent. Hood has succeeded in making Bedlam the toast of clever London.

What a graceful madhouse he reigns over! I suppose this is the moral architecture we hear so much about. It is not nearly so large as Colney Hatch, that great monument to modernity and progress, which is the size of a town. Well, this favoured island is the most civilized and advanced country in the world, and so we naturally produce more mad people than the inferior nations. We are all galloping too fast, demanding too much of life, and our nation is changing with such speed that it is not surprising that frail womankind cannot keep up with the pace.

I admired Cibber's statues in the grand entrance hall. Acute Mania is chained and naked; I am surprised the Archbishop of Canterbury has not campaigned to attach a fig leaf to him. Dementia looks vacant and lost; his face reminds me of Nina's after her disappearance. Pope called them the Brazen Brainless brothers. Well, she is brazen, I suppose. My heart thundered in anticipation of seeing Nina again, and I lingered downstairs.

For a few moments I felt as confused as a schoolboy at his first evening party. Hood has hung some watercolours and embroidery by his patients, including some very singular works by Richard Dadd, who is to be confined there for the rest of his days for murdering his father. Inside niches there are two old painted wooden statues – a young man in short breeches and a bare-breasted female – holding out bottles as almsboxes. 'Pray remember the poor lunaticks, and put your charity into the box with your own hand.' I did and felt a pleasant glow of virtue. This hall is something of a museum to madness. I felt a twinge of envy as I always do when reminded of my own aspiration. As yet mine is only a museum in the air, but one day, with hard work and William's help, I will build the Sanderson Hall of Curiosities on solid ground. If I have sometimes compromised my medical ideals this wondrous exhibition will make Tommy proud to bear my name.

I climbed the grand staircase to the large glass-sided ballroom on the top floor, where homemade paper flowers and chains decorated the walls and ceiling. Trays of wine, ale, cakes and biscuits, which were also no doubt homemade, were passed around .

On the other side of the ballroom a group of about thirty patients, presumably the exemplary maniacs, stood around in evening dress. I could not see if Nina was among them. Their costumes had a slightly neglected and lopsided look, and there was the atmosphere of a school concert. We were the parents and relations, desperately hoping that our children would not disgrace us. They stood far away from the guests, silent and awkward, surrounded by scribbling journalists. I felt suddenly ashamed and confused; Nina might be here, in the same room with me, yet we did not speak or even know one another. I wondered how many others here had spouses and relations among the inmates.

Looking around me I was struck by the distinction of the guests. Yes, Hood is making a very good thing for himself out of the mad business; they say he is anxious to attract a better class of lunatic. Well, God heals and the doctor takes the fee. I wonder if William and I could set up a private establishment. I oughtn't to throw away such a chance of extending my practice.

Sir Thingummy Whatsisname was there, that barrister whose opinion is always blazed all over the letters page of The Thunderer. He has an opinion about everything, it seems, and I saw him sniffing around the asylum, no doubt forming yet another. I also recognized

Lady D—, who is so massive and so addicted to good works that I wonder if she devours the orphans, widows and lunatics she patronizes.

Charles Dickens, the popular novelist, was standing in the centre of the ballroom as if about to dance, surrounded by toadies. I was surprised by his ungentlemanlike manners, his cockney voice and flashy clothes. He did not actually waltz but spoke very loud, as if on stage. 'Yes, poor old Dadd. He grew up in Chatham, you know, like me. Never met him, and it's too late now.'

Mr Dickens proceeded to act out Dadd's murder of his father, playing both parts, for the amusement of his friends. I thought this in very poor taste and turned away in disgust. No doubt his next novel will feature a brilliant painter who stabs his papa and is locked up in a madhouse.

Hood made a speech before the official opening of the ball. He is dark, more like an Italian hairdresser than an English doctor. The women in the audience looked up at him adoringly, and the little group of mad folk waiting to dance surged towards him. I have seen fashionable preachers in West End churches exercise the same magnetism over their congregations. There was hysteria in the air and a sickening fever of admiration. The fellow gazed at us with complacent eyes and proceeded to make a conceited speech praising his own methods. He held up large photographs to illustrate the success of his methods: Lilian B—, who has learned to spend her time making clothes instead of tearing her own, and Margaret J—, a cowering, depressed skeleton who has become plump and cheerful. I hoped that these ladies were not among us. Or perhaps they were and relished their peculiar notoriety.

With a theatrical flourish Hood held up a pair of manacles that had been converted into stands for flat-irons and declaimed, 'Sympathy, courage and time can release the manacles of the spirit.'

His speech was rapturously applauded. It never fails to astonish me how easy it is to bamboozle the general public with scientific twaddle.

Then we all stood in a circle and watched the ball. A lady at the piano struck up a waltz, dreadfully fast, as if she were a Pianola being wound too swiftly. The assembled lunatics chose their partners suspiciously quickly, and indeed as they danced towards us I saw that each wore a small number around his or her neck on a chain. Rather like Bread and Butter, a game popular at Tommy's juvenile parties.

Several of the inmates rebelled or lost their nerve and clung to the walls. One chap, very short with an enormous red beard, wandered around the edge of the ballroom like a peripatetic bush. An elderly lady, whose black dress had slipped off her shoulders, was unable to find her corresponding number. She burst into tears and stood sobbing into her bouquet of paper flowers until an attendant led her away. A gentleman with white hair and a mild countenance hugged himself and swayed all alone. Although he was at least sixty he reminded me painfully of poor Sam, who used to stand in the corner of our parlour for hours in just such a private universe, humming and singing softly to himself. He was not put there as a punishment, for our kind father never punished us. My brother had sentenced himself to solitude, and nobody else could release him.

The dancers did not look at each other but kept their eyes fixed on Hood as if he held the key that wound them up and produced their disturbingly mechanical oscillations. During the mazurka and the polka the speed of the music and dancing became positively dervish-like. The watching crowd murmured encouragement and appreciation, but the dancers did not speak. It was a grotesque parody of a ball. The main ingredients were there but something was wanting: pleasure, gaiety, joy.

Of course, I saw her at once. I could not move towards her, and she did not look at me. Once it would have been agony to see her in another man's arms, but I did not, could not, feel anything at all. Our encounter had the atmosphere of a dream, an unpleasant one. She was dancing with a tall, bald fellow, who held her as stiffly as if she were indeed a mechanical doll. They came waltzing towards me, and

I could not take my eyes from Nina's face, which was like a waxen mask of her real one. She stopped in front of me and her partner waltzed off alone, perfectly content to hold an invisible partner. Nina stood a foot away from me, and the watching crowd parted around us as if aware that we needed to talk. We did, but no words came. Her enormous dark-blue eyes were as cold as the charity she must live on for ever, and I knew we were not even in the same dream. How often have I grieved alone in my bed, aching to lay my head on her breast and be comforted. Well, I must find some other breast. Nina has her own crow to pluck.

At precisely nine o'clock a whistle blew, and, as if it were the signal for an express train, the lady at the piano played 'God Save the Queen'. We all attempted to keep up with her, but she rushed off without us and left us quite breathless, still singing our praises of dear Victoria after the train had fled.

There was rather a stampede to get down the stairs. I think we were all relieved to go back to our own lives and to leave Hood with his truant minds. Nina is in the best of hands, and there is nothing more I can do for her.

# AFTER THE BALL

W<small>E LEFT THE</small> ballroom in a twittering flock as if our lives had started again when the whistle blew. Lavinia was flushed with triumph as if she had just performed in the Hanover Square Rooms to great acclaim, although I thought she had jangled and rushed even more than usual. In the ward they stood around like mawkish schoolgirls giggling and prattling about their partners and the great folk who had come to watch us. Our paper flowers drooped, and our voices sounded shrill and gushing. I could not bear to join in and stood alone at the window where I had seen Jonathan, looking out at the black velvety lawn. My eyes painted his strange garments and dear upturned face on to the night. But there was nobody there. Only the frosty grass desert and the high wall that keeps us in our place.

All the time I had been dancing I had felt quite certain that Jonathan would be waiting for me. I was so confident of my imminent departure for the future that the ball had seemed quite insubstantial. When Charles's face loomed out of the misty crowd I could see it only as a blob among many blobs. I thought, your eyes have shrunk and James has not put your collar on quite straight. I shall not see you again, and it is of no importance since I am going to be with Jonathan, and you will be quite worm-eaten, and one cannot yearn for a skeleton. I did not yearn a bit. I stared into his face and wondered that I had ever thought him handsome. He has grown very thin and looks like a death's head upon a mop-stick. He did not speak to me and indeed seemed quite spiflicated by the sight of me. Charles stared at me as if I was something odious under his microscope, while number twenty-three, my partner with the grogblossom nose, danced off and seemed quite happy alone.

I was so sure that Jonathan must have found a way into the building that I went into my cubicle and looked under the bed for him. Bella used to do this before she climbed into her little white bed in the night nursery, looking for tigers escaped from the zoological gardens. That reminded me of Tommy, and I thought how cruel it would be to abandon him just after sending Emmie off with that picture letter.

I do not wish to escape from my zoo unless I can go with Jonathan to his wonderful city where men and women live quite freely and without lies and hypocrisy. It will be like living in a novel by George Sand where the only sin is to deny love. I will draw more pictures for Tommy of the shimmering glass towers and the people who look more like broomsticks than hour-glasses sitting at chairs and tables in the clean streets where they celebrate an endless victory. He will understand and be happy for me, and when he is asked what his mama died of he will reply that she died of joy.

The other ladies have gone to bed now after feasting on every morsel of that sham ball. The marionettes have finished their dance and must be laid in their boxes. All around me the hospital sleeps.

Now I can hear feet rushing down the corridors towards me as the real ball begins. The ceiling of my tiny cubicle soars up to the night sky, and the walls stretch like membranes of desire.

My mother sits at the pianoforte that has sprouted from the floor. Her dark hair is drawn into a bun at the back of her long neck as it was when I was a little girl, and she smiles as she picks out my favourite ninna-nanna with one finger. I never could go to sleep without it. Papa leans over her and caresses her hair.

As the room swells it fills with people. People who have died and people I have known and people who have not yet been born. Bella runs up to me as if she has just been playing in the garden and seems disgusted by my tearful kisses. She runs over to sit on her grandmother's knee on the piano stool and slowly picks out 'Three Blind Mice' on the high notes.

I am not hurt by Bella's insouciance because I am in Jonathan's arms. He must have been here all the time, but I do not ask questions because I know he will always be here now. I am beyond words, and my visitors do not expect them. Jonathan stands beside me with his arm around my shoulder as I turn to Henrietta who glides in. That in itself is odd, for she has lost her scratchy gait and uppish manner and spoilpudding face. Perhaps I am also improved, for she smiles at me and takes a step towards me. We do not quite embrace, but there is no hatred in the air between us.

Dr Hood stands in the doorway and watches us all benevolently. Richard Dadd squeezes in behind him, and although I have never seen him before I know him at once by his luminous eyes and the sketch pad he holds. He is like the King of the Elves pointing his wand at us as he finds an empty page and starts to draw.

Lavinia dug and gouged at her piano, but Mama strokes hers as her tapered fingers caress the keys into a gentle waltz. Our feet stir and tap, and Jonathan has to be taught how to dance. They all watch as I show him how to hold me and give himself to the music and rise and fall with each triangle of melody. He is smiling, perhaps he thinks our gentle dancing ridiculous and his mind is still in the future, but I do not care because he is here and now and mine. We each keep our own time as Mr Dadd draws us all and gives to each of us our own particular reality.

*Also published by Peter Owen*

# LOVING MEPHISTOPHELES
## Miranda Miller

978-0-7206-1275-2 • paperback • 312pp • £11.95

'A wonderfully generous novel, several
books wrapped into one, and I would
have been very happy to stay with any of
the strands or in any of the places it takes
us to – I was particularly struck by the
recreations of Edwardian London and of the
London of the modern homeless. It's an epic
narrative full of energy, with the wild and
joyful inventiveness of an Angela Carter
story. It is enjoyable and ingenious, and I
hope it will find many readers.'
– Hilary Mantel

When Jenny, a third-rate music-hall chanteuse, remarks to her mentor
and lover Leo, aka the Great Pantoffsky, that she never wants to grow
old, she doesn't know quite who she's speaking to. Her contract to love
him will reside at the Metaphysical Bank in High Street Kensington –
for ever.

As Leo gleefully exploits the rich offerings of twentieth-century
London – as a magician, fighter pilot, coke dealer and City banker –
Jenny finds that the joy of eternal youth is more ambiguous than one
might think. With the strain of constantly having to reinvent herself
as her own offspring and watching friends, lovers and family pass, she
begins to regret her decision. But it is when she becomes pregnant with
a daughter that Leo's true nature and that of her pact is revealed.

Peter Owen books can be purchased from:
Central Books, 99 Wallis Road, London E9 5LN, UK
Tel: +44 (0) 845 458 9911 Fax: + 44 (0) 845 458 9912
e-mail: orders@centralbooks.com

**www.peterowen.com**

*Also published by Peter Owen*

# NOT BEFORE SUNDOWN
## Johanna Sinisalo
978-0-7206-1350-6 • paperback • 240pp • £9.99

'A sharp, resonant, prickly book that exists on the slipstream of SF, fantasy, horror and gay fiction.' – Neil Gaiman

'Chillingly seductive' – *Independent*

'A punk version of *The Hobbit*' – *USA Today*

A young photographer, Mikael, finds a small, man-like creature in his courtyard: a troll, known from Scandinavian mythology as a demonic wild beast, a hybrid like the werewolf, and supposedly extinct. Mikael takes him home but soon discovers that trolls exude pheromones that smell like Calvin Klein aftershave and have a profound aphrodisiac effect on all those around him. But what Mikael and others who come into contact with the troll fail to learn, with tragic consequences, is that the troll is the interpreter of man's darkest, most forbidden desires.

A bestseller in Finland and translated into ten languages *Not Before Sundown* (*Troll: A Love Story* in the USA) is a multi-award-winning novel of sparkling originality and a wry, peculiar and beguiling story of nature and man's relationship with wild things and of the dark power of the wildness within us.

Peter Owen books can be purchased from:
Central Books, 99 Wallis Road, London E9 5LN, UK
Tel: +44 (0) 845 458 9911 Fax: + 44 (0) 845 458 9912
e-mail: orders@centralbooks.com

**www.peterowen.com**

## SOME AUTHORS WE HAVE PUBLISHED

James Agee • Bella Akhmadulina • Tariq Ali • Kenneth Allsop
Alfred Andersch • Guillaume Apollinaire • Machado de Assis • Miguel Angel Asturias
Duke of Bedford • Oliver Bernard • Thomas Blackburn • Jane Bowles • Paul Bowles
Richard Bradford • Ilse, Countess von Bredow • Lenny Bruce • Finn Carling
Blaise Cendrars • Marc Chagall • Giorgio de Chirico • Uno Chiyo • Hugo Claus
Jean Cocteau • Albert Cohen • Colette • Ithell Colquhoun • Richard Corson
Benedetto Croce • Margaret Crosland • e.e. cummings • Stig Dalager • Salvador Dali
Osamu Dazai • Anita Desai • Charles Dickens • Fabián Dobles • William Donaldson
Autran Dourado • Yuri Druzhnikov • Lawrence Durrell • Isabelle Eberhardt
Sergei Eisenstein • Shusaku Endo • Erté • Knut Faldbakken • Ida Fink
Wolfgang George Fischer • Nicholas Freeling • Philip Freund • Carlo Emilia Gadda
Rhea Galanaki • Salvador Garmendia • Michel Gauquelin • André Gide
Natalia Ginzburg • Jean Giono • Geoffrey Gorer • William Goyen • Julien Gracq
Sue Grafton • Robert Graves • Angela Green • Julien Green • George Grosz
Barbara Hardy • H.D. • Rayner Heppenstall • David Herbert • Gustaw Herling
Hermann Hesse • Shere Hite • Stewart Home • Abdullah Hussein
King Hussein of Jordan • Ruth Inglis • Grace Ingoldby • Yasushi Inoue
Hans Henny Jahnn • Karl Jaspers • Takeshi Kaiko • Jaan Kaplinski • Anna Kavan
Yasunuri Kawabata • Nikos Kazantzakis • Orhan Kemal • Christer Kihlman
James Kirkup • Paul Klee • James Laughlin • Patricia Laurent • Violette Leduc
Vernon Lee • József Lengyel • Robert Liddell • Francisco García Lorca
Moura Lympany • Dacia Maraini • Marcel Marceau • André Maurois • Henri Michaux
Henry Miller • Miranda Miller • Marga Minco • Yukio Mishima • Quim Monzó
Margaret Morris • Angus Wolfe Murray • Atle Næss • Gérard de Nerval • Anaïs Nin
Yoko Ono • Uri Orlev • Wendy Owen • Arto Paasilinna • Marco Pallis • Oscar Parland
Boris Pasternak • Cesare Pavese • Milorad Pavic • Octavio Paz • Mervyn Peake
Carlos Pedretti • Dame Margery Perham • Graciliano Ramos • Jeremy Reed
Rodrigo Rey Rosa • Joseph Roth • Ken Russell • Marquis de Sade • Cora Sandel
George Santayana • May Sarton • Jean-Paul Sartre • Ferdinand de Saussure
Gerald Scarfe • Albert Schweitzer • George Bernard Shaw • Isaac Bashevis Singer
Patwant Singh • Edith Sitwell • Suzanne St Albans • Stevie Smith • C.P. Snow
Bengt Söderbergh • Vladimir Soloukhin • Natsume Soseki • Muriel Spark
Gertrude Stein • Bram Stoker • August Strindberg • Lee Seung-U
Rabindranath Tagore • Tambimuttu • Elisabeth Russell Taylor • Anne Tibble
Roland Topor • Miloš Urban • Anne Valery • Peter Vansittart • José J. Veiga
Tarjei Vesaas • Noel Virtue • Max Weber • Edith Wharton • William Carlos Williams
Phyllis Willmott • G. Peter Winnington • Monique Wittig • A.B. Yehoshua
Marguerite Young • Fakhar Zaman • Alexander Zinoviev • Emile Zola